Death in a Far Country

Death in a Far Country

PATRICIA HALL

First published in Great Britain in 2007 by
Allison & Busby Limited
13 Charlotte Mews
London W1T 4EJ
www.allisonandbusby.com

A CIP catalogue record for this book is available from
the British Library.

10 9 8 7 6 5 4 3 2 1

ISBN 0 7490 8179 1
978-0-7490-8179-9

Typeset in 11/16 pt Sabon by
Terry Shannon

Printed and bound in Wales by
Creative Print and Design, Ebbw Vale

PATRICIA HALL is the pen-name of journalist Maureen O'Connor. She was born and brought up in West Yorkshire, which is where she chose to set her acclaimed series of novels featuring reporter Laura Ackroyd and DCI Michael Thackeray. She is married, with two grown-up sons, and now lives in Oxford.

PREFACE

She lay for a long time with her arms wrapped around her knees, to try to ease the pain, her teeth clamped tightly over her lips to prevent the slightest groan escaping. The darkness was not quite absolute. There was no moon but she could faintly see reflections shimmering on water and occasionally the sky lightened as a vehicle's headlights flickered for a moment some distance away and then vanished. She knew she needed help, but did not dare call out for it in case her attackers were still looking for her. They had not been far behind when the two of them had stumbled onto this dark pathway and she had slumped to her knees, feeling the skin tear on the sharp gritty surface, unable to run any further. She had urged her friend to make her own escape. For a long time she had refused and they had huddled together against the cold, arms around each other, but at last she had persuaded her to go, to save herself, her friend's voice strangled by sobs as she promised to return with help. But she knew she would not come back. She would not dare, in case they were waiting for her. She knew she was utterly alone.

She clutched herself more tightly, the pain in her chest more intense, impossible to assuage, and she gazed into the chilly darkness in despair. At home, she thought, the night was

warm and soft, a relief after the searing heat of the day, and
full of the smell of cooking and the noise of cicadas and dogs,
the rhythm of music and occasional shouts of anger and
laughter as people relaxed on their verandahs and children
played in the dust. At home, she had liked the night. Here it
seemed always hostile, cold and angry and full of the
threatening shadows of the men who had made her life hell.

She let out her breath in a faint hiss of agony as the pain
ratcheted up one more intolerable notch and convulsed her
body. She was not sure what they had done to her in the mêlée
of fists and boots when they had caught up with the two of
them, but she knew it was serious, and that she was sodden
with blood. Her friend, she thought, had got off more lightly,
slipping out of their grasp somehow at the height of the attack
and then coming back and pulling her upright and dragging
her away when the men were frightened off by the lights of
passing cars, leaving the two of them briefly alone in the
gutter, just long enough for them to run. But she had not been
able to keep it up. She had soon stumbled and fallen to her
knees, trying to stifle her groans, and her friend had been
unable to pull her to her feet again.

'Go quickly. Run,' she had said. 'Save yourself.'

And then she was finally alone, facing the icy darkness and
the surging waves of pain, knowing they would find her, and
when they did, that would be the end.

She never knew how long she lay there. Once or twice she
tried to drag her protesting body into a patch of deeper
shadows, but the agony of movement was too great. For what
seemed like hours, she drifted between the reality of pain and
bleak darkness and the soothing half-conscious dreams of

another life where there had been safety and warmth and hope and the promise of happiness. Then, increasingly, the present nightmare became jumbled in her mind with previous nightmares, seemingly endless brutalities that she could never have even imagined in her earlier life, and as her strength ebbed away she began to sob, the hot tears coursing through the caked layers of dirt and blood she could feel on her face. And she knew they would find her soon.

They came quietly in the end, a single pencil beam of torch light focusing on her face, dazzling her. There was no strength left in her, and she did no more than moan as they picked her up roughly, carried her a little way and then let her slip into the icy waters of the canal, where the water closed over her unresisting body with scarcely a ripple.

CHAPTER ONE

Detective Chief Inspector Michael Thackeray sat uncomfortably across a desk from Superintendent Jack Longley, drumming his fingers on the polished surface in frustration. If Longley himself felt any tension, he was concealing it well, his rubicund face bland and his balding head gleaming slightly in the artificial light. But he was watching the younger man intently for all that, as if someone had deposited an unattended package in his office that had to be checked out for explosive possibilities.

'I'm not saying that's what I expect, Michael,' he said. 'I'm just saying it's something maybe you should consider. You may feel OK but I'm buggered if you look it. You were on the critical list for a week, for God's sake. Maybe it's time to think about a quieter life.' The senior officer's eyes ran quickly over his junior's untidy hair and a dark suit that looked in need of pressing, before fixing on the blue eyes which seemed weary even at the beginning of a working day. Thackeray glanced away before squaring his broad rugby-player's shoulders and meeting Longley's sharp eyes again.

'And do what?' he asked. 'Run some crummy security firm? Go fishing? Take up golf?' Thackeray was offering deliberate provocation to the golf-addicted superintendent but he refused to rise directly, though sufficiently provoked to step onto forbidden territory himself.

'You could marry that long-suffering lass of yours, for a start,' he said. 'That might make you feel better.' Thackeray, thinner faced than he had been, the creases around mouth and eyes deeper and his unruly dark hair a touch greyer at the temples, froze for a moment and then shook his head angrily.

'You really think she'd be willing to have me when I'm on the way to the knacker's yard?'

'That's a "no" to early retirement then, is it?'

Thackeray looked at his boss consideringly for a moment.

'Are they pushing for me to go, the brass?' he asked quietly. Longley shrugged and suddenly looked almost as tired as Thackeray himself, as if deflated by the thought of the official hierarchy looming threateningly above them both, looking for scapegoats for their own incompetence.

'I don't think they'd shed many tears if either of us went,' he said. 'Don't kid yourself. We didn't cover ourselves with glory in Staveley, did we? Two dead who needn't have been? And you as good as. A right cock-up, as I'm sure this inquiry they've launched will conclude. And whatever connivance they got at the top, we were the ones in charge of the case. I took over as senior investigating officer while you were away, remember.'

'I took a risk I shouldn't have taken by not waiting for back-up in a hostage situation,' Thackeray conceded cautiously. 'I felt I had no choice – in the circumstances.'

'And damn near got yourself killed. They don't like that, the brass. It looks bad when the Home Office inspectors come sniffing around.'

'We'd have done better if we'd had proper cooperation

from our so-called friends in London,' Thackeray said, anger in his voice now. 'I complained at the time and I'll tell them again when they ask me for my opinion, don't worry.'

'Aye, well, we'll both put the best case we can,' Longley said. 'But I blame myself for the little girl. We should have looked after her better. They can't lay that at your door, any road. You weren't even here.'

Thackeray nodded, his eyes sombre. The case that now seemed to threaten Bradfield CID with unforeseeable retribution had been a harrowing one, and Longley was not the only one to blame himself for an unsatisfactory and blood-soaked outcome. But Longley suddenly squared his shoulders.

'Right then, let's not fret about what we can't alter,' he said. 'I'd rather you stayed than went, Michael, you should know that. So fill me in on where you are now you're back. Are you up to speed?'

'Just about,' Thackeray said cautiously, though feeling relieved at that unexpected vote of confidence. He was aware that for a long time Longley had regarded him with extreme caution, knowing of his near terminal career difficulties elsewhere, but he had thought he had earned his trust. 'I'm ploughing through the reports. The crime figures look reasonably encouraging. Maybe I should take a couple of months off more often. They seem to have been doing pretty well without me.'

'I kept a close eye,' Longley said.

'I was sorry Val Ridley fell by the wayside,' Thackeray said, thinking of the cool, blonde young woman detective who had resigned in the aftermath of the series of murders that had left him in intensive care himself.

'Kevin Mower was bending my ear, trying to get her to change her mind,' Longley said. 'I had a chat with her, but she was adamant she wanted to go. Planning to train as a social worker, she said.'

'So Kevin told me. She got too involved with the child who died. She got burnt out, as you do if you lose your objectivity. It's a great pity. She was a good officer.'

Longley looked at the DCI, knowing how bitterly difficult he had found the same case, and wondered, not for the first time, at Thackeray's dogged capacity for survival.

'You coped,' he said.

Thackeray smiled grimly, thinking that it was a very good thing that Longley did not know how close he had come to giving up himself as he had lain in his hospital bed going over the mistakes that had put him there. Only his growing sense that he could not leave a job half done had persuaded him to come back.

'Only just,' he admitted. 'It gets no easier.'

They were interrupted by Sergeant Kevin Mower himself, who tapped on the door and put his head round when Longley called for him to enter. Mower nodded briefly at the Superintendent, his face grim, but addressed himself to the DCI.

'Uniform have found a body in the canal, guv,' he said quietly. 'Suspicious death – looks like murder.'

Thackeray pulled his heavy six-foot frame out of his chair and sighed, feeling the cogs of the police machine slipping relentlessly into place again and threatening, as never before, to grind him to a pulp.

'We'd best have a look,' he said.

'Keep me in touch, Michael,' Longley said as the two detectives departed, shoulder to shoulder. And, as the door closed behind them, he muttered to himself: 'Please God, we don't bugger this one up.'

Laura Ackroyd was sitting in the morning editorial meeting at the *Bradfield Gazette* feeling more than usually bored. She twisted a long strand of her copper hair around her fingers as she listened to the sports editor, Tony Holloway, a small chubby man in his early thirties, already balding, who had an inexplicably fathomless enthusiasm for the local football team. Bradfield United's normally dire performance, in Laura's view, earned nothing like the uncritical loyalty it got on the back pages of the local newspaper. But just for once, she had to admit, Tony had something to crow about and it was obvious that the paper's editor, Ted Grant, who was sitting inscrutably at the end of the table like a basking bullfrog, was ready to allow him full rein.

'So how much cash will they make out of playing Chelsea, then?' Ted asked. 'Thousands? Tens of thousands?'

'Well, the stadium'll be full on Saturday for the match, not much doubt about that. Tickets are like gold dust, so certainly tens of thousands,' Tony said. 'But you get into the big money when you get a share of the take at a big stadium like Chelsea's. If they could only draw next week and go back to Stamford Bridge for the replay, they'd be quids in. They've already done pretty well out of this Cup run, because they've played away from home so often. A share of the take on a crowd of thirty thousand is a damn sight better than a share on the ten thousand United can cram in at Beck Lane when they're on this sort of roll and fill all the seats.'

'And can they draw against Chelsea?' Ted asked, doubt written all over his heavy features. A deep and abiding scepticism was his stock-in-trade, hallmark, he believed, of a serious player who had done his stint on a London tabloid.

'Stranger things have happened,' Tony said cheerfully. 'No one gave them a chance in either of the last two games, so you never know. The Nigerian lad Okigbo is a real star. The two goals against Sunderland were gems by any standard. Chelsea'll come looking to buy him if we're not careful.'

'And what about this lass they've got running the club now?' Grant asked. 'Is she going to make a go of it?'

Laura's interest in the discussion flared momentarily at that. Even she, with her minimal interest in football, had been intrigued to see a woman apparently jump at the chance of taking over the chairmanship of the struggling local club when her father, Sam Heywood, the major shareholder, had unexpectedly died. But her interest had turned to dismay as she realised that Jenna Heywood's succession had aroused real hostility in and around the club, a hostility that Tony Holloway seemed only too happy to encourage in his weekly column of United news and gossip.

'Why shouldn't she make a go of it?' Laura asked, mildly. 'She's an experienced businesswoman, from what I've heard. Chances are she'll do a much better job than her father.'

Tony flushed slightly at the unexpected interruption from the only woman amongst the senior staff at the table and glanced at Ted for support.

'From what I've heard, she knows absolutely zilch about football,' he said. 'The way things are these days for these small clubs you need a tough chairman if you're going to survive. Someone with a bit of financial nous and the guts to stand up to the players' agents and the rest of the sharks out there.'

'And running your own PR firm in London doesn't need all that?' Laura asked with her sweetest smile. 'I reckon there's as many sharks down there as there are in the Football League. What you football nuts really don't like is the fact that she's a woman.'

'Some of the old guard directors, maybe,' Tony admitted, looking flustered at this unprecedented attack from the least likely direction. 'There's no doubt they're upset. And as I hear it, she's not exactly built up a rapport with the coach, Minelli. And he's easy enough to get on with, for God's sake. A really good bloke – for an Italian.'

'With the accent on bloke?' Laura came back sharply. 'And the regulation Italian as well? How trendy is that?'

'Give us a break, Miz Ackroyd,' Ted Grant broke into the spat heavily. 'I tell you what, though. With the town buzzing like it is over the Chelsea match, we could do worse than run a profile of the lovely Jenna Heywood. How about that?'

Tony Holloway looked doubtful but obviously hesitated to contradict the notoriously irascible editor of the *Gazette* directly.

'I've a hell of a lot to go on my pages,' he prevaricated. 'Interviews with both managers, a profile of Okigbo...'

'I'll do it,' Laura broke in quickly. 'You don't even have to give up an inch of your precious sports space if you don't want to. It can go on my features page on Friday before the match. You've made it pretty clear you don't think it's a suitable job for a woman, and you obviously all expect her to make a hash of it. Let's see what she's got to say for herself. What do you think, Ted? Good idea?'

'Not bad,' Ted conceded. 'Not bad at all. Fix it up, then, Laura. I'm told quite a few women watch football these days so let's give them summat to think about, shall we? A bloody good idea, as it goes.'

And as the meeting broke up, Laura met Tony Holloway's accusing eyes across the table and smiled sweetly.

'OK, Tony?' she asked. 'Perhaps you can give me a few cuttings as background?'

'Fine,' Holloway came back, but the expression on his face told her it was not so fine at all, and she spun on her heel to hide her satisfied grin.

It was years now since Laura had begun to feel that the *Gazette* had taught her all it could about journalism. Colleagues who had joined the paper at the same time as she had, straight out of the local university, had long ago moved onwards and upwards to jobs elsewhere, and she herself still harboured the embers of a once fierce ambition to work in London. In fact she had tried more than once to break into a wider professional world, but again and again she had been dragged back to her home town by the only force in her life that had outweighed her ambition and would, perhaps, she thought sadly, end up stifling it completely.

She had hoped to have married Michael Thackeray by now, but she was beginning to wonder if she ever would. She still found it hard to escape the memory of the moment she had thought he was dead. In fact, his heart had stopped, she had been told later, and only the attentions of a particularly determined paramedic had got it beating again in the ambulance. But since she had sat by his bedside watching him struggle back to a semblance of normality after being shot, she had felt nothing but coolness on his side, as if his brush with death had taken something away from his capacity to feel as well as some of the physical vigour he had always put into life. But he seemed to have pulled himself out of his initial apathy and in the end he had insisted on going back to work as soon as he could persuade his doctor to sanction it but long before Laura thought he was fully mended. He had dismissed her objections impatiently.

'I need to work,' he had said. 'Just like you do. You once told me the job is what I am, and you were right.'

But Laura still doubted that the fevered intensity with which Thackeray seemed to have launched himself back into running Bradfield CID was what he or the job really needed. Thackeray seemed to be treading a thin line between commitment and hysteria, and nothing she said seemed to convince him that there was any danger in that. In fact, she thought, nothing she said these days seemed to reach him at all. And if that was where they were, perhaps it was only prudent to give some tentative thought to her own ambitions in case she had to face the future without him.

Anyway, it would be interesting, she thought, to tease out Jenna Heywood's reactions to exchanging her high-powered job in the south for such an unorthodox job close to her roots in Yorkshire. Laura could remember Sam Heywood in his early days, one of her own father's business cronies who occasionally came to the house for drinks and long discussions in Jack Ackroyd's smoke-filled study. He had taken over

Bradfield United during one of its periodic financial crises and allegedly pumped millions of his own money into supporting the club, which yo-yoed alarmingly from one year to the next between the lower divisions of the Football League, permanently hovering on the brink of some disaster or other.

'Our Sam', as he was affectionately and sometimes contemptuously known to the fans, had ricocheted from hero to villain and back again in the pages of the *Gazette* more or less in line with the club's fortunes, until his sudden death a couple of months ago while on holiday in the West Indies. And then suddenly Jenna Heywood had materialised, a young woman few people in Bradfield seemed ever to have heard of, but now the sole inheritor of her father's majority stake in the club. And as if her arrival in Bradfield had not created enough of a shock, her announcement that she intended to take her father's place as club chairman created a local earthquake.

Interviewing Jenna just as United, defying the odds and their own indifferent record, faced one of the best teams in the country in the FA Cup would be an interesting assignment, Laura thought, and that was something she desperately needed. And if it also helped her clarify her own mind about whether to stay in Bradfield or whether, at last, to go, that might be for the best. She did not think that continuing her life on its present track was tenable much longer, although how she was going to tell Michael Thackeray that she simply did not know.

The canal in Bradfield's narrow town centre had never led anywhere. Built in the nineteenth century as a spur to the busy Leeds to Liverpool waterway, it had always come to an abrupt halt at the back of the textile mills and warehouses that had transformed the village of Bradfield at breakneck speed into a smoky but booming manufacturing town. A couple of wharves had made space for barges filled with coal or bales of raw wool to unload, and a broad basin allowed them to turn and make the return journey through a lock and down the narrow valley to rejoin the main artery.

There had been talk over the best part of two centuries about filling the canal in when its usefulness was overtaken by the railways as a means of transporting heavy goods, but in spite of complaints about noxious dumping, stagnant water and threats to health, nothing had ever been done to close it down. Eventually the new interest in leisure pursuits on the waterways had seen the basin dredged, the cut cleared of shopping trolleys and other rubbish and its leaks sealed, the wharves restored and the towpath resurfaced to allow pleasure boats access to the town and a few houseboats to moor just a stone's throw from the shopping centre. In Bradfield's latest stuttering regeneration, some of the mills and warehouses nearby were being converted into studios and flats, and the first signs of a modest waterside night life were springing up around the basin itself.

DCI Thackeray stood for a moment close to the last stone hump-backed bridge before the narrow waterway opened out into its new incarnation. This was a quiet, isolated spot, where the towpath was overshadowed by a still disused and derelict textile warehouse and sight-lines from the more open water beyond were effectively blocked by the bridge over the cut and the towpath. Behind him was a high stone wall, breached only by a narrow alleyway giving access from a quiet street of offices and commercial premises behind. At night, he thought, out of reach of streetlighting and probably out of earshot of the small community of houseboat owners, it would be cut-off and secluded, the perfect place for an assignation or a murder – or both.

Behind him he was aware of the bustle of the crime team clustered around the body, which had now been lifted from the dark water of the cut. But he knew that at night this place would be totally empty, in spite of being only a couple of hundred yards from well-lit shopping streets and passing traffic. Even now, on a wintry day of pale sunshine, beyond the police tape that had closed off the towpath in both directions, the unusual activity appeared to have attracted no curious sightseers at all.

Reluctantly he turned back towards the well-organised team behind him. Kevin Mower looked up as Thackeray approached, turning away from the overweight figure of the pathologist, Amos Atherton, who was crouched in a protective suit close to the sodden form of a young woman.

'Seriously hurt, possibly dead, before she went into the water,' Mower said, his face grim. 'Heavy bruising, and what looks like a stab wound just below the ribs.'

Thackeray focused reluctantly on the limp form that had been dragged from the dark, still water and made his own mental evaluation of the victim: a tall, thin black girl, dressed in the skimpy skirt and cut-off top of the typical youngster on a night out, and without any sort of coat or sweater although the year had so far held out no hint of spring warmth. Her feet and legs were bare and although someone had pulled her mini-skirt down to afford some sort of decency to the body, she looked as sexually vulnerable in death as she had probably been in life.

'Any ID?' he asked.

Mower shook his head. 'No pockets in that gear,' he said. 'And no sign of a bag. We'll have to get the divers down to have a look for anything else, including a weapon.'

'Shoes,' Thackeray said. 'She must have been wearing shoes.'

Atherton struggled to his feet, indicating to the waiting assistants standing by with a stretcher and body bag that he had finished his initial examination, and pushed through the crowd to Thackeray.

'I can't tell yet whether she was dead when she went into the water,' he said. 'But the stab wound to the upper abdomen is deep. She must have bled a lot.'

Thackeray glanced at the compacted gravel of the pathway in irritation.

'There's been rain,' he said. 'But I'll get the SOCOs to see if they can find traces of blood.'

'They'll have their work cut out with the body, an' all,' Atherton said. 'The water will have washed her clean. We'll have to see what the post-mortem gives us.'

'Has she been in there long?' Thackeray asked, glancing again at the iridescent black water for inspiration and finding none.

'Doubt it,' Atherton said, beginning to peel off his plastic suit. 'No sign of decomposition that I can see. At a guess, she went in last night.'

'She was spotted about eight o'clock this morning by a bloke from one of the houseboats walking his dog,' Mower broke in. 'It was barely light, he said. And he'd had the dog out here last night too, about nine o'clock. He's not sure he could have seen her in the dark, but he didn't notice anything unusual. And the dog behaved quite normally. For what that's worth.'

Thackeray smiled faintly. 'You know we should always take dogs that don't bark seriously,' he said. 'We'd better talk to everyone in the houseboats. They're the only likely witnesses around, I should think. No one else is likely to be on the towpath in the dark.'

'Except the victim and the killer,' Mower said.

CHAPTER TWO

Laura Ackroyd turned over in bed in the dark, focused with some difficulty on the radio-alarm on the bedside table, and groaned. It was six a.m., and she was aware of Michael Thackeray lying on his back beside her, rigid and obviously awake. She turned back towards him and slipped an arm round his chest.

'Can't you sleep?' she whispered. Thackeray half-turned towards her and put a hand on her arm, although Laura could not be sure whether it was intended to encourage her embrace or fend her off.

'Just a bit of pain,' he said. 'Go back to sleep. I'll get up in a bit and take a painkiller. It won't hurt if I get in early this morning. I've got a post-mortem to go to at eight-thirty.'

Laura ran a finger across his back gently and located the surprisingly small scar left by the ricocheting bullet from a rifle that had come close to killing him, lodging so close to his heart that it presented the surgeons with an operation of nightmare delicacy to remove it. The pain was proving surprisingly intractable, she thought, but probably not as intractable as the sense of failure he obviously still felt at having failed to protect so many innocent victims of the psychopath and his hangers-on who had come so close to killing him too.

'Another murder?' she said and listened soberly, wide awake now, to the bare details he offered about the body of the black girl found submerged in the canal the previous day.

'Don't you know who she is?'

'There's no ID,' Thackeray said. 'She was wearing surprisingly little for a cold winter's day. Looked as though she'd been clubbing or to a party.'

'A lover's quarrel, maybe,' she said softly.

'I don't think so,' Thackeray said. 'She wasn't just beaten up. She was stabbed.'

'Ah,' Laura said. The Bradfield canal was not an area of the town she was at all familiar with. She was aware that it was the latest part of the town to be redeveloped and was no doubt changing fast, but as a teenager spending her boarding school holidays in one of the town's more leafy suburbs, she knew it only as a place that most parents routinely warned their children against: a noisome dumping ground for rubbish, both animate and inanimate; a haunt of prostitutes and drug-addicts who valued its seclusion so close to the town centre. Laura realised that this was not a path she, or probably Thackeray, should travel down at this hour. He would have enough of it when he got to work.

'Would you like me to make you breakfast?' she asked. He kissed her gently on the cheek, a peck that was more brotherly than loverly, and rolled himself off the edge of the bed with a grimace of pain.

'Go back to sleep,' he said. But when he had moved slowly to the bathroom and she heard the shower switch on, she found his suggestion impossible to follow. Her mind was racing now, as she guessed his had been, but almost certainly not in the same direction. Sleep looked like a remote possibility as she watched the digits of the clock creep towards six-thirty and agonised over whether the passion that had brought the two of them together had disappeared for good.

Eventually she got up, pulled on her dressing gown against the chilly air, and went into the kitchen to brew a large pot of coffee. By the time Thackeray emerged, dressed for the day, she was sitting at the table with her hands round a steaming mug, gazing out of the window at the first streaks of grey in the morning sky.

'Can I get you something to eat?' she asked.

'Not before a post-mortem,' he said. Laura looked at him closely as he poured himself coffee, absorbing just how much older he seemed to have become in the three short months since the shooting. But maybe, she thought, he had been changing even then. The process had started when Aileen finally died and brought back all the memories that he had been so intent on burying for more than ten years. It seemed an impossible irony, she thought, but she was beginning to feel that they had been better off before Aileen's death, before the shadow she had always cast over their relationship had been so suddenly removed. With Aileen gone, they were free to look at each other in the clear light of day and, as far as Laura could tell, the light left her somehow wanting in Thackeray's eyes, diminished in some way from what she thought she had been before. She sighed.

'I thought maybe we could go out for a meal tonight,' she said. 'We haven't done that for a long time.'

'I'll give you a call later,' he said. 'You know what it's like at the start of a murder investigation. I may be late finishing.'

She nodded as he pulled on his coat without meeting her eyes.

'Take care,' she said, her voice dull as he moved towards the door, but he did not respond as he pulled it shut behind him.

Of course it was partly her own fault, she thought, as she stood under the shower herself a few minutes later, hoping the hot water would galvanise her from her depression. She had told Thackeray, on one of the long evenings when she had sat at his hospital bedside as he slowly recovered from his own trauma, how her former boyfriend had helped himself to information she had been entrusted to pass on to Thackeray himself. She had been a fool to get drunk in Vince Newsom's company, she had admitted, and he had taken advantage of her, as she should have known he would. What she had never passed on was Vince's suggestion that he had not only put her to bed that night, but had joined her there. It was a claim that Laura had never accepted, and which she found more unbelievable as time went by. Unbelievable and unbearable, and never, she had decided, to be revealed.

Thackeray drove straight to the infirmary without calling in at his office. He made first for the hospital cafeteria, where he gulped another scalding hot cup of coffee before making his way down to the basement to be met by a bleary-eyed Amos Atherton, still in his outdoor clothes.

'You're bloody early,' Atherton said, without enthusiasm. 'Couldn't you sleep?'

'I don't like taking too many painkillers,' Thackeray said brusquely. 'I need to keep a clear head.'

'Aye, we all need to do that,' Atherton agreed, as he hung up his coat in the small cloakroom alongside the mortuary and pulled clean scrubs from the cupboard where they were kept. 'You can go in if you like,' he said, as he pulled a green smock over his head. 'The Technician's already in there prepping up.'

'I'll wait,' Thackeray said. 'I'll just have a cigarette before we start.' Atherton raised an eyebrow at that but said nothing as Thackeray pulled a packet from his pocket and opened a side door, which led outside into a narrow courtyard where it was permitted to smoke. The infirmary was a place he hated more than any other, never able to banish the memory of the day he had paced these aseptic corridors while Atherton had performed the autopsy on his own son. He should not have been there then, although no one in the department, most of whom already knew him as a copper although it was long before he had come to Bradfield to work as DCI, had found the courage to turn him away. So what, he wondered, bitterly, had driven him here, of all places, too early for the routine duty he disliked so much to have even got close to starting. He ground out his half-smoked cigarette under his heel after a few minutes and went back inside, to find Atherton fully dressed in scrubs and apron and ready to start his own routine under the glaring lights of the morgue. He put on a gown himself and joined him.

The dead girl lay naked and statuesque on the stainless steel table, long-legged, broad-hipped, firm-breasted and strangely beautiful in death. There was no massive disfigurement. The bruises she had suffered showed up less against her smooth dark skin than they would have done on a fairer victim, and the stab wound on the left side of her body revealed itself only as a small pink nick washed clean by the water of the canal. Atherton spoke quietly and monotonously into his tape recorder as he made his external examination, only raising his voice and glancing at Thackeray to emphasise some point that he regarded as significant. Taking swabs from her mouth and other orifices with a surprisingly gentle touch he glanced at the stony-faced policeman.

'Sexually experienced,' he said, closing the girl's legs again. 'But we'll be lucky to find any traces of recent activity after she's been in the water.'

'Any sign of rape?' Thackeray asked, dry-mouthed.

Atherton shrugged. 'She's extensively bruised, so I couldn't exclude it. I'll look for internal evidence.'

As usual in this situation, Thackeray tried to turn his mind away from what was happening on the table as Atherton reached for his scalpel and proceeded to conduct his internal examination of the body. But these days he found that his escape mechanisms did not work as effectively as they used to. As he got older, the tragedies he had to deal with as part of his daily routine seemed to become harder rather than easier to bear. He had never joined in the culture of black humour with which many police officers and medics tried to shield themselves from the worst of the horrors they witnessed, preferring to withdraw into himself behind what he had thought was an impregnable armour of dispassion. But the last case he had handled, which had nearly cost him his life, had only shown him how fragile that armour had become. The death of children had eaten away at his defences, reduced them to no more than egg-shell after all these years, he realised now, as he stood so close to yet another death of such youth and beauty that it screamed out for retribution. The last case had left him feeling terrifyingly vulnerable.

A faint exclamation from Atherton claimed his attention and he focused again on the now mutilated cadaver from which the pathologist was carefully extracting internal organs.

'She was pregnant,' Atherton said. 'Only just. Six, eight weeks maybe. She might not even have known.'

Thackeray nodded, not trusting himself to speak. Two deaths, not one, he thought.

'And there's vaginal bruising and scars. Was she a prostitute?'

'I've no idea,' Thackeray said. 'She was carrying no ID and we've not found a handbag. We're going to search the canal today in case there's something down in the mud. Can you give any estimate of how old she was?'

Atherton stepped back from the table and studied the body as his technician began to tidy it up before the major incision was closed up again.

'I'd say about eighteen,' he said. 'But I could be out by two years either way. She's obviously of African or Caribbean origin. If I had to guess I'd say West African. And the knife wound didn't kill her. It came close to the heart, with an upward trajectory, but hadn't touched it. Her lungs are full of canal water. She undoubtedly drowned.'

'So she either fell or was pushed into the canal after she was attacked?'

'Looks like it,' Atherton said, his face as impassive as Thackeray's as he began to stitch his subject together again as delicately as if she had been alive. 'I'll let you have the toxicology and other test results as soon as I have them. But at least you've got a definite cause of death. I'll let you have it in writing by the end of the day.'

'I'd like an artist's drawing of her,' Thackeray said. 'If we don't find any more information on who she is, and no one's reported her missing, we'll need it for the Press.'

'Tell your artist to get in touch. We'll arrange for access.'

Thackeray nodded and turned away, only to find Atherton close behind him as the doors swung shut.

'Michael,' Atherton said, his voice unusually uncertain. Thackeray faced his old colleague for a moment without speaking. Atherton swallowed and seemed to make up his mind.

'Are you sure you should be back at work?' he asked. 'You look terrible.'

Thackeray smiled thinly. 'Thanks for that,' he said. 'I seem to be getting votes of no-confidence from every direction just now. Just for the record, my doctor says I'm fine.'

'Physically, maybe,' Atherton said, his face flushed. 'But that's not everything, is it? I'm only talking as a friend...'

'I'm OK,' Thackeray said angrily. 'Sitting on my backside brooding isn't going to do me or anyone else any good. I need to work.' He stopped abruptly, knowing he had said much more than he intended. He held out his hand to Atherton, who shook it briefly.

'I'm sorry, Amos, but I'm fine.' The pathologist nodded and turned on his heel to go back to his mortuary, but Thackeray knew he was no more convinced than anyone else that he could cope. That was something he was going to have to prove the hard way.

Laura Ackroyd drove through the gates of the West Royd Golf and Country Club with a faint sense of disbelief. It was an area on the edge of Bradfield that she recalled as one of scruffy allotments and small-holdings against a backdrop of hill farms, which grazed their sheep on the lower reaches of the fells to the west of the town. She had not been up here, she thought, for several years and the transformation had been startling. She recalled the outcry when the allotments and some of the farms had been bought up by a developer, but the transformation was more complete than she had ever imagined. The flat area where local gardeners had once grown their runner beans and rhubarb now housed an extensive club-house, and beyond that the farmland had been transformed into a pristine golf course where she could see several groups of bright-shirted players making their way across the rolling, well-manicured terrain.

She parked her modest Golf alongside ranks of Beamers and an occasional Jag, and wondered, as she made her way up the shallow stone steps to the main entrance, whether her working outfit of dark trouser suit, cream shirt and low heels was classy enough for this assignment. Inside, a low key but elegant lounge, almost deserted, stretched out in all directions and she hesitated for a moment to take stock. It was, she thought, more like the entrance to a five-star hotel than a sports club, the directions to the gym, the squash courts, the pool and the changing rooms so discreet as to be almost invisible. But she was not alone for more than a couple of seconds before a young man in an understated uniform of light trousers and blue club blazer approached with a welcoming smile.

'Can I help you?' he asked.

'I'm meeting Jenna Heywood,' Laura said.

'Ah, yes, Ms Heywood said she was expecting a guest for lunch. She's in the bar already, I think. Would you like to come through?'

Laura followed her guide through a door to one side of the lounge into an extensive bar with picture windows overlooking the rolling golf course on one side and offering a view of an indoor swimming pool on the other, where a number of young men were powering through the water with splashy aggression. Jenna Heywood apparently spotted her guest before she spotted her, and Laura became aware of a tall woman of about her own age breaking away from a convivial group at the bar and approaching across the thick pile carpet in a black skirt not much longer than a mini teamed with breathtaking heels and a plunging neckline in embroidered scarlet silk.

'Laura?' she said enthusiastically. 'I'm so glad you could make it. I thought it would be good to have a quiet chat up here before I take you to United. This is so much more comfortable. It's a real asset to the old town, don't you think?'

Reluctant to admit she had never been to the club before, Laura just nodded and allowed herself to be steered towards a table by the window with two comfortable armchairs arranged to face the windows and the view of the golf course. A waiter was hovering almost immediately.

'Just a tonic with ice and lemon,' Laura said. 'I'm driving.'

Jenna looked disappointed. 'You'll have a glass of wine with lunch?'

'Yes, that would be fine,' Laura said, and sank back into her chair while Jenna dealt with the waiter, thankful for a moment to observe this phenomenon who appeared to have shaken Bradfield's sporting community to its foundations simply by being young, elegant and female, an effect that Laura had hoped, maybe naïvely, had passed into history.

Jenna was tall and fashionably slim, her blonde hair worn loose, long legs crossed to display her Jimmy Choos, and her clothes evidently straight from the sort of designer shops that Laura could only gaze at in a state of financial shock when she occasionally passed them by. But when Jenna turned back to her guest Laura could see that she was not some ditzy clothes-horse. There was humour in the perfectly made-up face and a sharp intelligence in the blue eyes. Jenna Heywood was no fool, Laura thought, any more than her father had been, and she guessed that the middle-aged and complacent directors at Bradfield United, who seemed intent on derailing her plans, might find that they had bitten off more than they could chew.

'So,' Jenna said consideringly. 'You're the features editor for the *Gazette*? You don't do sport then?'

Laura shook her head.

'That's Tony Holloway's baby,' she said. 'I expect you've met him.'

'Yes,' Jenna said noncommittally, with a faint smile. 'My father had a run-in or two with Tony, I think, as the team lurched from the bad to the appalling over the years.'

'I think Tony's mother put him in United colours from the moment he was born,' Laura said with a grin. 'I'm not sure why sports reporters think they're exempt from trying to be objective, but a lot of them do.'

'Well, maybe it's no bad thing on a local paper,' Jenna said easily. 'The public expect their paper to be partisan for the local team. But you? If you don't do sport, what's all this about? Why have I attracted your particular attention? I like to know where I stand.'

Jenna's stock-in-trade was attention, Laura thought wryly, and how it could be manipulated to the best advantage, and she knew that she was playing in the big league here.

'I'm intrigued by a woman taking over a football club,' Laura said. 'Or rather, taking over this particular football club. I know it's not unheard of these days, but United is such a basket case. Why bother?' She knew she was being provocative, but was interested to see how Jenna would react to such a frontal assault. But Jenna Heywood just threw back her head and laughed.

'A bloody good question,' she said. 'It's one I ask myself in the small watches of the night when I wake up from a nightmare about the balance sheets I've seen. I reckon my father was barmy to keep pumping money into the club, and I must be even more barmy to follow suit.'

'But like Tony, you're a fan?'

'Oh, I was always that,' Jenna admitted. 'If your sports editor wore blue and gold Babygros in his pram, I think I got the bug even earlier. My mother always said she went into labour in the directors' box at one particularly fraught game when United scored a winning goal in the ninety-first minute. She leapt out of her seat to cheer and the next thing she knew they were sending for the ambulance. There's no logic in my trying to rescue United, any more than there was for my poor old dad. It's an emotional thing. We'll have to see how it goes. Just at the moment, with the Cup run, things are looking up. But I expect Chelsea will thrash them eight-nil on Saturday and it'll be back to our normal gloom and doom on Monday – and that's not for quoting by the way. We don't want the players suspecting me of lack of confidence before a game like that.'

She glanced over her shoulder. 'There are a couple of them in here, as it goes, certain to be taking a close interest in what I'm up to.' She gestured at a group of young men in the latest smart-casual gear by the bar, accompanied by a couple of young women in short skirts and abbreviated tops, and strappy sandals with heels so high they looked in imminent danger of toppling off them.

'The black lad is our star, "OK" Okigbo. I hope he's not spending too much time in here with the big game coming up. I'm surprised the coach hasn't got them out training today. I'll have to have a word with him about that.'

'You're going to be a hands on boss, then?' Laura asked.

Jenna grinned. 'I've been running my own business for ten years,' she said. 'I'm not likely to take a back seat in this one. They haven't seen anything yet.'

'But some of the directors don't like it?'

'There's still a lot of men who don't like working for a woman,' Jenna said. 'I don't know what it's like in newspapers.'

Laura smiled faintly at the idea of Ted Grant knuckling under to a female boss.

'Some editors don't even like women on their staff let alone giving the orders.'

'Yes, well, I've come across plenty like that, not so much in my own profession, but amongst the clients. Companies that hire a PR firm and are then taken aback when a woman turns up with a critical report on how they do things. I don't imagine Bradfield United will be any different.'

'Not different, but quite possibly worse,' Laura said, with a smile. 'Your unreconstructed Yorkshireman can be an intransigent fellow. They don't take happily to change, especially in their hallowed sanctums like football and cricket clubs. I think you may be in for an interesting time.'

'I control the club,' Jenna said, her mood darkening slightly. 'She who pays the piper, and all that. There are two things United needs – good results and a new stadium. And both depend on hard cash, firstly for better players, and OK is a start. And then to build a bigger venue so we can increase our revenue. It's the same with all these small clubs. They can't survive by standing still.'

'Can you get the finance?' Laura asked. 'Won't being a woman make even that harder? And with some of the directors against you?'

'I have contacts,' Jenna said. 'I think it can be done.'

'You didn't stay in Bradfield though. Why was that, if you're so wedded to the team?'

'Are you born and bred in Bradfield?' Jenna came back quickly.

'I am, as it happens, though I was sent away to boarding school.'

'Ackroyd? Are you Jack Ackroyd's daughter?'

'That's right,' Laura said. 'Did you know him?'

'Not really,' Jenna said. 'But he and my father were close financially at one time, weren't they? They had some sort of business deals going?'

'They could well have,' Laura said. 'I'll ask my dad next time I talk to him. He and my mother live in Portugal now. He retired out there when his heart started playing up some years ago.'

'He was lucky, then,' Jenna said soberly. 'My father's heart only played up the once and that was it.' She drained her glass. 'Shall we eat?'

Jenna led the way, nodding slightly to the group at the bar who returned her attention, Laura thought, with slightly uncertain smiles, and took their place at a table for two, again in a prime position by the window. Jenna flicked a menu in Laura's direction.

'It's not three star Michelin,' she said. 'But it could be worse. I usually have the smoked salmon and then a steak. Difficult to spoil.'

Laura nodded and agreed to have the same and then pulled her tape recorder out of her bag.

'You don't mind?' she said, and Jenna smiled.

'Harder for you to distort what I say,' she said. 'Record away.'

'So tell me how you got from youthful supporter to owner, by way of a career in London. From what I read in the business cuttings about your company, you need to come back to Bradfield about as much as you need to go to Baghdad. What's it all about?'

Jenna nibbled at her smoked salmon and shrugged.

'Maybe I need a new challenge,' she said. 'I haven't lived up here since I was at school, and I'm not really intending to live here now. I'll come up as often as I need to during the season but my apartment in London is still going to be home. All my friends are down there, and the business, of course, although that runs itself to a large extent these days. The sign of a good boss, in my book, is the ability to appoint good people and then delegate. I can do that.'

From most people the statement would have sounded like overconfidence, Laura thought, but this was a woman who did not over-estimate her capabilities, she just understood them.

'PR?' she said. 'A dirty word to us reporters. If you want the truth about a story you don't go to PR looking for it. You call it spin, we call it lies.'

'That's out of date,' Jenna said, without apparently taking offence. 'Companies that know what they're doing are willing to pay a lot of money to present their best face to the public. But if there are problems they know it makes no sense to lie. You always get found out in the end. PR should be part of corporate strategy, not crisis management. That's what we do for a number of blue chip companies. And we do it very well.'

'And make a lot of money out of it?'

'Oh, yes,' Jenna said. 'I never apologise for that. My dad only sat up and took notice of what I was doing when he saw a healthy profit on the balance sheets.' They paused for a moment as the waiter brought their steaks, rare and medium, exactly as ordered, and fussed with the bottle of Burgundy Jenna had ordered to go with them.

'You'll have that glass of wine?' she asked after she had

tasted the vintage and nodded her acceptance of it.

'Thank you,' Laura said. She could easily get used to lunching here every day, she thought.

'So did you meet prejudice setting up your company in London?' Laura asked.

'Not really,' she said. 'But it's a different planet down there. Or at least it was ten, fifteen years ago. The north's beginning to catch up now, I think. Harvey Nicks in Leeds can't be bad.'

'There's a lot of money sloshing around up here now,' Laura said. 'But still a lot of problems, too. Leeds is Leeds but Bradfield's something else. You should have a look at Aysgarth Lane. It's still a bit third-world around there. There's some real poverty. And on some of the estates.'

'Yes, I've noticed. The place needs a good kick up the backside in some respects,' Jenna said. 'Not least at United.'

'So you could say you're on something like a crusade?' Laura said.

'I suppose you could. And I hope the *Gazette*'s going to be right behind it, as well.'

CHAPTER THREE

Michael Thackeray's face tightened as he read Amos Atherton's preliminary report on the body of the young woman who had been found in the canal. Somehow seeing facts like these in black and white always seemed worse to him than hearing the pathologist's conclusions tossed over his shoulder almost casually from the operating table while he watched. The spare, scientific prose reduced the victim to a specimen in a way that did not quite happen when the body was actually present in the all-too oppressive flesh. Even the bare list of injuries sickened him. There were twenty-five separate fresh bruises and contusions on the girl's face and body; three broken ribs; one smashed finger; one stab wound, three inches deep and a quarter of an inch wide caused by a pointed blade with no serrations; there was internal bruising and scarring; her lungs were filled with water and she was carrying a foetus of approximately six weeks gestation. And there was evidence that she had suffered similar brutality over a period of time. Before she died, she had been beaten, stabbed, quite possibly raped and finally drowned, as she had fallen or been pushed into the canal in no fit state to even attempt to save herself. He hoped that by then she had been unconscious.

He called Superintendent Longley on the internal phone.

'It's definitely murder,' he said quietly.

'Was she on the game?'

'Possibly,' Thackeray said, wondering why he hoped quite so fervently that she was not. There were some police officers who might take prostitution as a signal not to put too much effort or resources into a murder investigation, regarding violence as a professional hazard for 'working girls', something they 'asked for', and which occasionally went too far and killed them. He did not count himself amongst them.

'On drugs?' Longley asked.

'No external signs of that,' Thackeray said. 'But we won't get toxicology results for a few days.'

'Best keep speculation about her lifestyle under wraps for a while till we see if anyone claims her,' Longley said. 'A "respectable family" won't be too thrilled if we cast aspersions.'

'There's been no missing person report that fits,' Thackeray said. 'But at that age, she could be a student. No one may notice that she's not around until she fails to turn up for something important.'

'Or a refugee,' Longley said. 'Legal, illegal, she may be difficult to pin down.'

'I'm setting inquiries in motion,' Thackeray said.

'Talking about inquiries,' Longley said. 'I've just heard that they've appointed an assistant chief constable from West Midlands to look into our recent problems. No one I've ever heard of. Man called Brian Richards, started off with the Met, made commander and moved up there about six years ago. I've got feelers out to find out a bit more.'

'Right,' Thackeray said. 'When's he coming up to Yorkshire?'

'They're sending him all the reports and he anticipates starting preliminary interviews next week. Obviously they want to get on with it now you're fit and back on duty.'

Thackeray took a deep breath. Fit, he thought, was a relative concept. 'Right,' he said again as Longley hung up without further comment.

They would waste no time now, and he wondered whether he or Longley would still have careers by the summer. There was no doubt in his own mind that if the Chief Constable and the senior officers at County Headquarters wanted either of them out of the force they would be able to justify it to this outside investigator: Longley seemed to have inexplicably left a vulnerable child unprotected; he himself had thrown away a life-time's training in an attempt to protect Laura. He had never regretted that decision, made in the heart-stopping heat of the moment, but he knew that if he had gone by the book the resulting shoot-out might have been avoided and the life of a man might have been saved. He shifted uneasily in his chair, jarred by the now familiar stab of pain from the wound in his back. He and Laura could also very easily have died that day, he thought, and maybe ACC Richards from Birmingham would find that a mitigating factor. Or maybe not.

He got up with Amos Atherton's report in his hand and walked slowly through to the main CID room, feeling old. Most of the desks were empty, the detectives already deployed on inquiries around the canal area, but Sergeant Kevin Mower glanced up from his computer screen, with questions in his eyes.

'You need to read this,' Thackeray said, dropping the report onto Mower's desk. 'She was beaten, stabbed and then drowned. I'm organising a briefing for two o'clock. We need to get a murder inquiry on the road, even if we don't know who she is.'

'There've been no missing person reports that fit in the whole of the county. I just checked again, guv,' Mower said.

'Identification is the first priority,' Thackeray said. 'But we mustn't let potential witnesses by the canal off the hook. We need to check if anyone saw or heard anything that night. Door-to-door, though that's a relative concept down there. Most of those buildings are empty, and those that aren't are offices closed at night. But there's the houseboats.'

'Uniform are on to all that,' Mower said.

'What about the underwater search?'

'Zilch,' Mower said. 'Used condoms and needles, which is more or less what you'd expect round there. It's a quiet spot. But no sign of a handbag or a weapon.'

'According to Amos we're looking for a knife with a three- or four-inch blade, less than half an inch across, pointed, smooth edged. If they've had no joy in the water you'd better intensify the search along the bank. And I can't believe a girl wouldn't be carrying some sort of bag or purse. You may not carry ID as a matter of course, but everyone needs money.'

'Maybe the motive was simply robbery,' Mower said.

Thackeray shook his head slowly. 'She'd been hit and kicked in a sustained attack,' he said. 'Read the report on her injuries. You don't do that just in the course of snatching a purse.'

'Race then?' Mower said, his face darkening. 'There's

enough nutters out there these days who don't like anyone a shade darker than they are.'

'There are, but do they hang around a lonely towpath on the off-chance someone they don't like will turn up? But you're right, that's another line of inquiry. We'll have to see what we can pick up amongst the right-wing racist groups. But ID is the first priority. Until we know who she is we can't even begin to work out what she was doing down there in the first place. It's not somewhere you'd choose for a stroll on a dark winter night with no coat on. Remind the search teams that she was distinctly under-dressed for the conditions, will you? As under-dressed as that, she must have been noticeable. Or there may be a coat or jacket somewhere. If she was down there for sex, paid for or not, she may have taken a coat off in the heat of the moment.'

'Odd things people do,' Mower said. He glanced away, as if thinking of something else. Thackeray hesitated for a second himself, before ploughing on.

'The other thing you need to know is that the inquiry team looking into the Christie deaths is expected up here next week for preliminary interviews. I expect they'll want to talk to you.'

'I'm sure they will,' Mower said. He leant back in his chair and took in Thackeray's sunken cheeks and pale complexion.

'I saw Val Ridley the other night,' he said quietly, making sure none of their colleagues could hear what they were saying. 'She's all geared up to give evidence and I don't think the Super's going to like what she has to say. She's still furious that someone got to the little girl.'

Thackeray nodded. Val Ridley had resigned while he had been fighting for his life in hospital after a child she had become attached to had been killed. It was not something she would either forget or forgive, and he was not sure how far and wide she would apportion blame when she was asked. The very fact that she had resigned probably meant that she wanted to escape the pressure she would be under to close ranks in the face of an inquiry. The canteen culture of officers covering each other's backs still ran deep and although he did not condone it, he understood it. Val was a wild card, he thought, who certainly threatened the Superintendent, and possibly himself as well.

'They won't confine themselves to serving officers,' he said. 'I fully expect they'll want to talk to Laura. And then there'll be the inquests. A lot of things will be said there that we could do without. I guess the Chief Constable wants this inquiry finished before the trial and then the Coroner opening full hearings. That way he'll reckon he can put the best gloss possible on what happened – and maybe say he's sacked the people responsible for any mistakes as well. I wouldn't be surprised.'

'It's a bloody shame we lost Val,' Mower said explosively. 'I did try to get her to change her mind while you were in hospital, you know.'

'I know,' Thackeray said. 'But it's water under the bridge now. Is she still planning to be a social worker?'

'So she says.'

'She'll be good at it,' Thackeray said.

'She was a good copper.' Mower was not bothering to hide his anger.

'Yes,' Thackeray agreed. 'But in the end she couldn't hack it. She got too involved. And I'm sure that when she's asked she won't hesitate to tell the inquiry who she thinks is to blame.'

'It could be a year or more before the case comes to trial,' Mower said. 'This thing will run and run.'

'And mud sticks,' Thackeray said, tiredly. 'Anyway, put all that on the back burner for now. We've more urgent things to think about, like a dead pregnant girl. I'll see everyone at two, and we'll see where we're at. Two lives were lost in the canal, the girl and her baby, and they both deserve our attention. Don't let's get distracted.'

Across town at the *Gazette*, Laura Ackroyd stared contemplatively at her computer screen as she tried to compose a final paragraph for her profile of Jenna Heywood for the next day's paper. She could see an anxious-looking Tony Holloway watching her from the other side of the newsroom, where his and the other sports reporters' desks were clustered together in a defensive hollow square. Ever since she had returned to the office from her long lunch with Jenna, Tony had been eagerly offering snippets of information and advice and, in return, she knew that he was hoping for first view of what she had written. First view, she thought, and quite probably a pre-emptive input to her article if it in any way impinged on his entrenched opinions about United, its new chairman and members of the old guard to whom he felt that he owed favours.

She had enjoyed her lunch with Jenna, and had begun to think that she understood why she had taken up part-time residence with her mother in Broadley while they both took time to come to terms with the loss of Sam and Jenna took stock of her newly inherited position as chief shareholder of the club. The latter was not a job any of her co-directors hoped she would keep for long, Jenna had admitted with a faintly satisfied smile. She reckoned she knew of at least two groups – one of existing directors and one of people with no apparent connection to Bradfield at all – who seemed determined to buy her out if they possibly could. But if Laura was reading Jenna Heywood correctly, she guessed that sort of challenge would only make her the more determined to do her own thing, as soon as she had taken time to reflect on exactly what that might be.

'What my dad was really worried about was that some outsider would buy the club and then just asset strip it,' Jenna had said quietly, after a few glasses of wine had evidently made her more forthcoming than she had been at first. 'The stadium site, so close to the town centre, is worth a fortune, and if you didn't want to build a replacement you could just flog it off for redevelopment and pocket the profit. I really don't want the bastards to do that. United was part of my life when I was a kid. Going to the match on a Saturday afternoon was the highlight of my week until I went away to uni. And I still kept it up whenever I was at home. It was one of the few things that my dad and I had in common. And I know it's part of the lives of the fans in just the same way. It's still a family thing here, isn't it? Passed on from generation to generation. I know the big clubs have moved into a different financial dimension, but it's not like that at United. So it's struggling? I think I can fix that. And I'm certainly going to give it a try.'

'But it's not just a question of money is it?' Laura had asked. 'You have to keep the club in the League to survive as well, don't you? Isn't that a much harder nut to crack?'

'You mean do I know enough about the game to make it a success?' Jenna had come back quickly. Laura shrugged.

'My father had a lot of faith in the new manager, and he signed the Nigerian player, Okigbo, who's certainly turned out to be very good. So we'll have to see, won't we? Why don't you come to the Chelsea game on Saturday and see how we get on? Be my guest. You never know, we may give the commentators a surprise. Stranger things have happened in the Cup.'

'Why not? Thanks,' Laura had said, carried along by Jenna's obvious enthusiasm and well aware that Bradfield was in a state of hysterical excitement over the forthcoming David and Goliath clash, with gold and blue favours and pictures of the so-far unexpectedly victorious local team appearing in every shop window.

Still considering her final paragraph, she was suddenly aware of a presence behind her shoulder and turned to find Tony Holloway unashamedly reading what she had written on her screen.

'Tony, I'm not after your job, you know. This is just a profile of a woman taking on an unusual role.'

'It'll be very unusual if she runs the club into the ground,' Holloway grumbled, still reading. 'She rates Minelli, does she? I'm not sure I do. I think old Sam made a mistake with him.'

'Well, she's hardly going to announce that she thinks he's a waste of space in a piece like this, is she?' Laura countered. 'This is pretty innocuous stuff. I've no doubt you'll be the first to know when she runs into difficulties, as I'm sure she may do. She says herself it's going to be a tough call, and from what you say it doesn't look as if anyone's going to give her an easy ride at the club, or in the *Gazette*, for that matter. But I don't see why we shouldn't give her the benefit of the doubt. She's a breath of fresh air and she's nobody's fool. She's a successful businesswoman in a cut-throat profession, so I don't see why we should pander to the whingers and whiners just yet. Give her a chance, for God's sake.'

'It's not just me. The fans are grumbling too,' Holloway said defensively. 'They don't like it. They've not got much time for political correctness on the terraces. They liked old Sam Heywood. He was one of them, in spite of his brass. But a public relations woman from London? Who's not been to a match in years? They just think she's having a laugh.'

'Well, I daresay the Chelsea game will fill me in,' Laura said. 'Jenna's invited me into the directors' box to see the game. I've never been to a football match before. It'll be a new experience.'

Holloway looked at her for a moment in apparent disbelief, his lips a perfect O of surprise in his rounded face.

'She's invited you to the Chelsea game? A lot of people would sell their grandmothers for a ticket for Saturday.'

Laura smiled sweetly.

'Why not?' she asked. 'I don't think I'm taking any fan's ticket as a guest of Jenna's. And who else would I support?' She was surprised to recognise just how much she and Jenna Heywood had in common in their unfashionable tendency to stick to Bradfield in spite of the temptations to play on a bigger stage.

'If these clubs are going to survive at all, she reckons that you need to attract women and families to become fans. And some of the ethnic minorities. You can't rely on elderly white men in cloth caps any more. There aren't enough of them left, are there?' Laura knew that such sentiments were often regarded as sacrilegious in the context of United, although she was equally sure that Tony Holloway, who was not stupid, recognised the truth of them. If something dramatic was not done at the club, it would continue its long slow decline into oblivion, in spite of the current season's unexpected Cup success. And that, too, would in all likelihood dribble away into the sand this coming Saturday afternoon when the poor bloody infantry of Bradfield faced the stratospherically expensive guided missiles from Stamford Bridge. As Jenna had admitted – not for quoting, of course – it would probably be a massacre.

'What's all this about some millionaire property developer being interested in buying the club, anyway? You haven't written about that, have you?' Laura asked.

Holloway shrugged and looked uncomfortable.

'She knows about that, does she?'

'No, I don't think she's heard more than the odd rumour,' Laura said. 'She was asking me about it, thinking that I would know. What's it about, another Russian billionaire like the one who bought Chelsea or what?'

'We should be so lucky. But it is just a rumour,' Holloway said. 'I've not been able to make it stand up as a story, though stranger things have happened. Football clubs are getting a bit like trophy wives – something every self-respecting millionaire wants to spend his money on. Worse things could happen to United.'

'Just as long as it's the football club he's interested in and not just the property for redevelopment. That's what Jenna says she's afraid of.'

'You're not putting anything about that in your piece, are you? Ted Grant'll think I'm falling down on my job if you do.'

'No, I wasn't planning to. I was concentrating on the personal in this piece. I'll leave the financial skulduggery to you.'

'You obviously got on well with our Jenna, then?'

'Yes, I did actually,' Laura said with a smile. 'I liked her. She seems to know what she wants and she's not going to be put off by unreconstructed Yorkshiremen who still think women should only speak when they're spoken to. I don't know much about football but I do recognise a breath of fresh air when it hits me. I think you're going to be in for an interesting few months on the sports pages, Tony. I really do.'

When she had finally finished her feature and received Ted Grant's grudging grunt of approval, Laura took a detour to see her grandmother on her way home. Joyce Ackroyd still lived in one of the old people's bungalows on the edge of The Heights, always known locally as Wuthering, one of Bradfield's most notorious estates where the tower blocks were at last in the process of redevelopment. Apparently unfazed by the noise and dust as she watched the blocks of flats she had helped to plan as a young town councillor come down, Joyce Ackroyd was proving very reluctant to move away to any quieter corner of the town that Laura suggested.

She came to the door slowly, reliant on a walking frame now for her arthritic hips and knees, but delighted as always to see the granddaughter who had inherited her once red hair and more than a little of her fiery temperament.

'You look tired, love,' Joyce said sharply when Laura had made them both tea and settled in her tiny living room. 'How's that man of yours? Is he better now?'

'More or less,' Laura said cautiously. She knew Joyce had always harboured reservations about her relationship with what she called 'her policeman'. 'He's back at work, though I'm not sure he should be.'

'You both work too hard,' Joyce said. 'How are you ever going to...' Joyce hesitated, with unusual tact though Laura knew well enough how she had intended to end the sentence.

'Don't go there, Nan,' Laura said. 'It's all a bit fragile. Anyway, I didn't come up to talk about my love life, such as it is. I came to ask you about Dad.'

'Ha,' Joyce said. She had recently returned from a holiday with her only son, Laura's father, and had been succinct in her criticisms of an ex-pat lifestyle in Portugal, which she regarded as self-indulgent and futile. 'Next thing you know he'll be back in England,' she said. 'He's in a panic over this drought and the forest fires they've been having in Portugal, reckons the place won't be worth living in if he can't fill his swimming pool and play on a nicely watered golf course.'

'I wouldn't bank on it being any better here in a few years' time, the way things are going,' Laura said. 'Anyway, that's not what I wanted to ask you. What I'm interested in is Dad and Sam Heywood. Weren't they big mates at one time? I seem to remember meeting Sam at home once or twice, a long time ago, when he first took over United and they did quite well for a bit. I don't remember Dad having any interest in football, but Sam was one of the local wheelers and dealers and Dad never let one of them pass him by.'

'I think he had some shares in the club at one time,' Joyce said slowly. 'I've no idea if he still has. He wouldn't tell me owt like that. But if he thought he could make a bob or two he'd be in there like a flash. And that time United got into the second division and won that Cup – what was it? The Milk Cup? I think that's when he was making up to Sam Heywood, jumping on his bandwagon, was even a director of the club for a while. As he would be if it looked like yielding a profit.' Joyce's incomprehension of her successful businessman son's money-making activities masked one of the major disappointments of her life. She had put her only son, whom she had brought up as a widow, down to become the socialist prime minister she would have liked to have been herself but, as sons do, Jack had gone his own way and made a fortune in business and broken his mother's heart. Joyce looked forlorn for a second.

'I don't remember all the details, love,' she said. 'You'll have to ask him yourself.'

'I might do that,' Laura said. 'As I hear it, there's a few predators circling United, aiming to buy Jenna Heywood out.'

'Oh, well, your dad'll be interested in that,' Joyce said. 'If he's still got any shares and there's money to be made out of them, he'll be in there like Jack Flash.'

CHAPTER FOUR

Michael Thackeray parked his car outside the Victorian stone house where he shared the ground-floor flat with Laura Ackroyd and sat for a moment after he had switched off the engine, going over an exhausting and unsatisfactory day in his mind. As he had supervised that afternoon's briefing of his detectives he had felt somehow detached, as the well-oiled wheels of a murder investigation had rolled into motion once more. Evidence, such as it was, had been reviewed, lines of inquiry delineated and tasks allocated, but while the rest of the team had seemed well-focused, he had found his mind only half on the matter in hand, and it was only partly because the supposedly healed wound close to his spine had begun to throb with an intensity he was becoming all too familiar with.

The months he had been off work had distanced him from the day-to-day routine of CID and he was not finding it nearly as easy as he had expected to take up where he had left off. He was desperately tired tonight, as he often was these days, but he knew that the malaise which afflicted him was not simply, or even mainly, physical. The surgeons at the infirmary, he thought, had saved his life three months ago, for which he could only be grateful. But they had left him facing this intermittent fierce pain, a confusion of emotions that he had hardly begun to come to terms with and, worst of all perhaps, a sense of futility rooted in the knowledge that so often his best efforts could not stave off disaster of the most brutal kind.

It had not been the first time Laura had put herself in danger, but it was the first time he had felt impelled to throw away years of professional training and his own natural caution to put himself so comprehensively in the way of harm on her behalf. He knew that the formal inquiry into the mayhem that day would probe that impulsive moment remorselessly and, when it came to it, he would be very reluctant indeed to admit that he had done the wrong thing, that he had taken an unacceptable risk, that he should have left Laura as a helpless hostage until back-up arrived. Would the outcome have been any different if he had acted in some other way, he had asked himself relentlessly ever since that night. He would probably have escaped injury himself, but the rest of the night's events would probably still have played out with the terrifying logic of a Greek tragedy. He did not think that any life that was lost could, with any certainty, have been saved if he had taken another track. He just hoped he could convince the inquiry of that. And that eventually he could convince himself.

But what filled him with anxiety even more than his own situation was the knowledge that Laura would be interrogated too. Information which should not have reached the newspapers had leaked out from the police inquiry, with tragic consequences, and she had played a part in that disaster. Thackeray believed her role had been innocent, but he was not so sure his senior colleagues would come to that conclusion. He did not think that Laura really understood how culpable she might seem to the members of the inquiry, nor how unpleasant their conclusions might be for her.

Thackeray shook himself irritably and slammed the car door behind him with some force before making his way to the flat. He found Laura in the kitchen stirring something in a large pan. He took off his coat and came up behind her quietly, put his arms round her waist and kissed her on the neck.

'That smells good,' he said.

'A bit exotic, maybe?' Laura said. 'Risotto? Can you bear that?' Thackeray's stolid preference for traditional British food had become a joke between them.

'Foreign muck again? What's wrong with meat and two veg?' he mocked her gently.

'Boring, is what's wrong with that,' Laura said firmly. 'This is mainly for you, as it goes. I'm not very hungry. I had a very nice lunch at that country club up at West Royd with the new football impresario, Jenna Heywood. She's invited me to go and see the big match on Saturday afternoon. You don't mind, do you?'

'I dare say I'll be busy. I have this unidentified black girl lying in the morgue.'

'Ah, yes,' Laura said quietly. 'I'd forgotten about her.' She turned to Thackeray, putting down her wooden spoon and looking into his blue eyes. They had discussed this moment interminably while Thackeray had been off work, but never reached any conclusion. He had been determined to get back to work as quickly as he could, and nothing she had said about less stressful alternatives had moved him in any way.

'Another murder,' she said. 'This is the crunch, isn't it? Can you cope with another murder?'

Thackeray did not answer immediately. He turned back into the living room and slumped into an armchair, his expression unreadable. Laura followed him and sat on the arm of his chair, one hand touching his shoulder gently.

'Well?' she said. 'Can you? Are you sure?'

'They say you should get back on a horse immediately after you've fallen off,' Thackeray said slowly. 'I didn't have the chance to do that, did I? Perhaps I won't be able to manage it now. We'll have to wait and see.' He could barely admit to himself, and certainly never to Laura, how close he sometimes felt these days to disintegration. The pain in his back jabbed viciously and he turned his face away so that she could not see him wince.

'Who is she, this girl?' Laura asked.

'We still don't know. She was very young. She was pregnant. And she was black. That's it, so far. There'll be a picture for the *Gazette* tomorrow morning, an artist's impression, so we're hoping someone will identify her from that.'

'Nobody's reported her missing?'

'Nobody.'

Laura shivered.

'How awful,' she said. 'Where's the boyfriend? The baby must have a father somewhere.'

'She may not have known herself that she was pregnant, Amos Atherton says. So the boyfriend, husband, whoever, certainly may not have been aware.' He shook his head irritably. 'Come on, Laura. Let's leave all that and taste this

Italian concoction you've cooked up. I'm sure it'll be delicious. And you can tell me all about your football woman. How's she going to survive among all those testosterone-fuelled blokes? It'll be even harder than in the police force, won't it? All those highly paid lads in love with themselves. Will she love it, or will they gobble her up and spit out the pips?'

Laura laughed, although she could see from the strain around Thackeray's eyes that this attempt at cheerful normality was forced. 'I don't think anyone's going to gobble Jenna Heywood up. She's as tough as her father, I reckon, and that's as tough as old boots – and a damn sight more attractive. Which reminds me. I saw Joyce on the way home and she thinks my father still has an interest in United. I'll call him later and find out what he thinks. He's far enough away not to be involved in any in-fighting that's going on at Beck Lane.'

'I wouldn't bank on that,' Thackeray said. 'If I know Jack he'll be in there scrapping with the best of them, particularly if there's a hint of a profit involved.'

'Jenna Heywood reckons that the only way to make a profit out of United would be to close the club down and sell off the land for redevelopment. She's desperately trying to avoid that, and I'm not sure that even my dad would go along with such a drastic solution. I think he's still got a bit of affection for poor old Bradfield United.'

Thackeray raised an eyebrow at that but said no more. A fiercely competitive rugby player as a boy and young man, he knew little of soccer and cared less, but was quite sure that if there were vultures gathering around the club, Jack Ackroyd could well be one of them. He had liked Jack on the couple of occasions he had met him briefly on his rare visits to the UK, but he did not underestimate his businessman's edge, still keen even after all these years in the sun. He did not think Jack had mellowed, and if he still had any financial stake in the club he would want it maximised.

'I'll call him after the match tomorrow, and tell him the result,' Laura said. 'He'll be interested in that at least. Now let's eat, shall we?' She looked at Thackeray, slumped in his chair, and her heart tightened.

'You look tired out,' she said.

But he just shrugged as he got up to join her at the table. 'I'm fine,' he said. But they both knew that was a lie and when they went to bed later, Laura could see just how exhausted he was as his eyes closed almost as soon as his head hit the pillow. She put an arm round him, curling her body round his and aching for something more than the companionable hug he offered in return before he fell asleep, and she wondered where the downward slide that their relationship seemed to have entered would end.

Sergeant Kevin Mower walked up the hill to Bradfield University the next morning in a sour mood. He had the typical Londoner's aversion to ever walking more than an urban block if he could avoid it, but the parking problems around the town's academic quarter meant that even he had to accept that taking his car the half mile from police HQ to the university made no sense. He glanced up at the utilitarian modern blocks that towered over the Victorian technical college, from which the university had directly descended and grunted in recognition. It reminded him of the former polytechnic he had attended himself, and he knew it attracted the same degree of contempt from those who had attended more prestigious institutions. But he knew the strength of these places, willing to offer those, like himself, from troubled or poverty-stricken backgrounds, the chance to succeed at something for the first time and, as he pushed his way through a polyglot and multiracial crowd of students milling about the entrances, he smiled faintly. He felt at home here.

But his inquiries were frustrating. Without a name to attach to the artist's impression of the dead girl, the registry officials could do no more than promise to circulate copies of the picture to all their departments, which kept photographs of their own students. They would let him know, they promised, if any members of staff recognised the girl as one of theirs. And the students' union was little more help. The young black woman in charge of the union office readily agreed to put copies of the sketch on the noticeboards and ask people to get in touch with the police if they thought they knew her. But she gazed at the picture for a long moment, her expression troubled.

'If she was a student here, I'd probably know her,' she said. 'There are not so many black students here. More Asians, obviously, in this part of the world.'

'Do you reckon she's African or Caribbean?' Mower asked. 'Can you tell?'

'I'd say African, though I wouldn't be sure. She looks very like a friend of mine from Sierra Leone. But younger. In fact, she looks too young to be here at all, really. Most overseas students are a bit older, you know? Especially the Africans.

They take extra time to learn English or retake their A Levels. Quite often they have children of their own. This looks more like a schoolgirl, don't you think? She can't be more than seventeen. Are you sure she's a student?'

'We're not sure of anything,' Mower said. 'Her picture will be in the evening paper this afternoon but we know students don't often see that, so we need a more direct approach here.'

'You could try the further education college. Some overseas students take English exams there before they apply to university.'

'We're circulating the drawing there too,' Mower said shortly.

'How was she killed?' the girl asked.

'She was attacked and pushed, or maybe fell, into the canal,' Mower said.

'Because she was black?' the girl asked.

Mower hesitated for a moment before replying as the girl twisted her hands into a knot, the knuckles showing white.

'We don't know,' he said at last. 'We've no reason to think that, but we simply don't know at this stage. Until we know who she is…' He shrugged. 'Is there much racism on the campus?' he asked.

'Since the London bombings we have all felt at risk if we're not white,' the girl said flatly. 'We advise students – Asian and black students as well, some people don't seem to make any distinction – not to go around the town on their own. We've got a leaflet we give them when they arrive. You should know what it's like. We're all under siege if our skin's the wrong colour.'

'I can imagine,' Mower said. 'The registry didn't tell me any of this, though.'

'They wouldn't, would they? Their priority is protecting their precious image. This place relies heavily on overseas students. If they stop coming, it might have to close down.'

'You'll put as many copies of the picture and the police phone number up as you can, then?'

'Of course,' the girl said. 'I hope you catch the bastards that did it.'

'We will,' Mower said. 'Believe me, we will.'

The young woman hesitated for a moment as Mower turned away.

'You could try the churches and mosques,' she said. 'Most Africans are more religious than the white population. So are West Indians, come to that. But remember, if she comes from West Africa she could be a Christian or a Muslim.'

'Good idea,' Mower said. 'Thanks for that.'

The Sergeant made his way back onto the street feeling more depressed than when he had come in and with none of the confidence with which he had tried to reassure the young woman he had just left. The hilly street outside was buzzing with young people of all races, chattering excitedly in the pale sunshine, but he knew that this was not typical of Bradfield as a whole. Londoners might talk complacently about their harmonious multiracial society but in some of these northern towns different groups kept themselves more clannishly to themselves, and since the bloody arrival of Al Qaeda-inspired terrorism in Britain, suspicion had burgeoned and racist incidents had spiralled almost out of control. There were hundreds of thousands of second- and third-generation immigrants in this part of the world, he thought, and it took only a handful of fanatics from Leeds to jeopardise years of patient work towards racial harmony. He hoped that the girl whose picture he was distributing did not turn out to be the victim of a racially motivated crime, but he knew it couldn't be ruled out, and the thought made him angry. He was dark-complexioned enough himself, the son of a Cypriot father he had never known, to have felt the lash of racist abuse more than once in his career. It was not pleasant, and as far as he could see it was as far from being rooted out as ever.

He turned up the steep hill, making his way a little further from the town centre, and pushed open the door of a shop-front with opaque windows and no indication of its business. The room inside was divided by a wooden counter and a couple of people sat on chairs, as if in a waiting room. There was a bell on the counter, which Mower rang, and a pale, fair-haired young woman in a brightly patterned peasant blouse over her worn jeans came out from the back of the shop and offered a slightly nervous smile.

'This is Refugee Aid?' Mower asked, flipping open his warrant card in the young woman's direction, at which she looked slightly reassured. She nodded.

'Can I help you?' she asked. 'I'm Rosemary Bennet. I'm a volunteer here. There's no one official in at the moment.'

Mower offered her the artist's impression of the dead girl.

'Do you know this girl?' he asked.

Rosemary hesitated. 'Why do you want to know?' she asked, suspicion suddenly closing her face tight.

'I'm trying to identify her,' Mower said, keeping his voice level. 'She's been found dead.' Rosemary's face crumpled slightly and she turned even paler as she shook her head.

'Oh, I'm sorry,' she said, with a catch in her voice. 'I

thought...it's just that we meet so many people here who don't want anything to do with the police.'

'And you cover for them, do you?' Mower snapped.

'No, no, I didn't mean that. But you have to be so careful. We need people to trust us if we're to help them. So many of them are so very frightened...'

'This girl isn't frightened. Not any more, anyway. She's been murdered, drowned in the canal,' Mower said more quietly. 'She's not going to need your help, if she ever did. But we owe her ours. And first, we need to know who she is.'

Rosemary took the artist's impression and studied it carefully for a moment, then handed it back to Mower, who took hold of it irritably and slammed it down on the counter with the flat of his hand.

'That's for you – to keep, to help trace her,' he said. 'Have you ever seen her before?'

'No,' she said. 'I don't know her. Do you want me to ask my colleagues when they come back?'

'I want you to ask everyone who comes in here,' Mower said. 'Colleagues, clients, legal, illegal, everyone. This is a murder inquiry and so far we don't even know who the victim is. Do you understand what I'm saying?'

'Yes, of course,' Rosemary said, flinching slightly from the Sergeant's vehemence.

'Do you deal with many African clients?'

'Some, from Somalia and Eritrea, asylum seekers who've been dumped – I mean moved – here from London,' Rosemary said. 'But this girl looks more like a West African. We don't get so many West Africans.'

'Sierra Leone, someone suggested.'

'Maybe, or Nigeria. I'll make sure we show the picture to all our black clients. Someone may know her.'

'*All* your clients,' Mower said again. 'Including illegals we may not know about?'

'Yes, all our clients,' Rosemary agreed quickly. 'But if they're here illegally they don't necessarily come near us. Or anyone else for that matter.'

'You've got the phone number,' Mower said. 'Get in touch if you hear anything. Anything at all. Right?'

'Right,' the girl said, and watched, pale-faced, as Mower spun on his heel and left the shop before picking up the phone on the desk to make a call.

The girl ate the loaf she had stolen ravenously. She had not eaten for two days and had drunk only the rainwater she had been able to scoop up from the puddles on the roof of the condemned block of flats where she had taken shelter. She had slept on the floor in one of the empty flats where she had found an abandoned mattress, but she preferred it up here on the roof, in spite of the biting wind. Most of the flats stank of urine or worse, and she knew that there were rats. She had heard them scuttling in the night, waking every half hour or so and listening until her ears rang for any sound that might tell her that her pursuers had tracked her down or that the rodents were close enough to threaten her. But there had been nothing but distant rustling, and as grey daylight woke her for the final time, she had crept down the filthy stairway and slipped outside briefly, long enough to find the single shop which served the estate, still shuttered and closed but with a couple of trays of that day's bread delivery left outside the back entrance. She had grabbed a loaf and run back to the safety of the fenced off block, slipping through the gap she had found between the wooden boards and pushing open the heavy glass doors that no longer locked, picking her way up the littered and evil-smelling concrete stairs again to her eyrie to eat something at last.

Pale sunlight began to warm her slightly as the morning wore on and, with food inside her, her mind began to distinguish between the reality of her position and the garbled images that had tormented her fitful sleep. Occasionally she crouched against the parapet and glanced down the dizzying side of the block to see what was happening below. Soon after daylight men had begun to arrive to continue work on the neighbouring block, which had been reduced to little more than a mound of rubble that was being gradually loaded onto huge trucks and taken away. She guessed that the block she was hiding in was due for the same fate. The flats below her had been trashed and vandalised, whether by their last residents or by others who had moved in later, she did not know. The entrances and ground floor windows had been ineffectually boarded up, the stairwells left open to rain and wildlife and whatever human flotsam chose to take refuge there, the lifts vandalised and the shafts gaping open. She did not think she was always alone in Priestley House but had so far avoided any contact with other people who were undoubtedly there as illicitly as she was herself.

She gazed across the busy building site below to take in a view of the whole of the town whose name she did not even know and the blue-grey hills beyond. They were gentle hills here, she thought, not like the craggy mountainsides at home where the village she had left what seemed like a lifetime ago had crouched underneath the peaks as if trying to conceal itself, as more than once in its history it had needed to. Here she could see roads climbing up the hillsides, and cars, like ants, crawling up and over the rounded summits to whatever lay beyond.

Closer at hand, there were busy urban streets with red buses and people moving about their business in ever-changing groups, cars swirling round circular intersections, an occasional small train trundling down rails that shone in the damp air and slid into what she recognised as a station even from this distance. There were the spires of churches and, to her surprise, the minarets of a couple of mosques, and an occasional tall chimney whose purpose she could only guess at. And then rows and rows of houses, snaking up the hills and down the valleys, until they gave way to the green fields and woods of open countryside. There was normality down there, she thought, hundreds, even thousands of people living safe lives without the fear that paralysed her and kept her chained to her cold and windy vantage point, choking with panic if she saw anyone approach the doors to the flats.

When she had crept back to the canal-side path two nights earlier she had found no trace of her friend. At first she had hidden for more than an hour in some bushes in a tiny area of open land not far away, hardly daring to breathe in case their pursuers heard her. She had listened for footsteps, but heard nothing she could identify, no sounds of struggle, no car, no audible hint that the dark water had been disturbed, only her own heart thudding behind her ribs and her teeth chattering eventually as the cold air threatened to freeze her blood. Then, when she had summoned up the tattered remnants of her courage and crept back to where she had left her friend there was nothing at all, the black water was still and silent, the towpath deserted, the houseboats moored a little farther up the cut in total darkness. The only movement in the bleak silent landscape came from a few bright stars in the black sky, which were twinkling a million, million miles away as if to mock her bitter isolation.

She did not know how long she had sat beside the water, crying silently, before faint streaks of grey in the sky to the east told her that she had to move before the town woke to a new dawn. She had pulled her thin cardigan around her then and slipped away, keeping to sidestreets and back alleys as she climbed the long hill to the west of the town where, in the faint light of dawn, she had seen the skeletal remains of the flats on The Heights, and realised that these abandoned relics might offer her temporary shelter at least. Finding a way through the fencing had not been hard. Others had been there before her. The doors of the one remaining block that looked relatively intact had been half open. The early morning light was sufficient to show her the way up the staircase to the top level, where she collapsed on the floor of what had evidently once been someone's home, the plumbing ripped out now, the electricity wires dangling uselessly from the ceilings, the windows smashed and mouldering wallpaper hanging in strips like tattered bunting from the walls.

And there she had stayed. She was no longer very sure how long she had been there, days and nights merging in the half light of the abandoned flat and the winter daylight when she emerged occasionally on the rooftop. The men below would move into this last block soon, she thought, as she watched them from above. Then she would have to decide where she could go next. Or not, she thought. Because of one thing she was quite sure. If her pursuers found her here, or if anyone else threatened her, she would not run any more. She could not. And there was another solution, obvious in its desperate simplicity. As she gazed down she could already see her own body, smashed and bloody, on the concrete far below.

CHAPTER FIVE

Saturday dawned heavy and dismal, with the threat of rain carried over the hills by a biting wind, but nothing could dampen the excitement of the thousands of football fans who thronged the narrow streets around United's stadium in Beck Lane, a narrow thoroughfare in the valley surrounded by retail outlets and motor showrooms and new housing, which had mushroomed where old stone textile warehouses had once stood. There was a heavy police presence on foot and on horseback, shepherding the gold and blue bedecked crowds towards the stadium as Laura Ackroyd approached the main entrance to the looming and slightly dilapidated stands where the local team had played for almost a century. She thought briefly of Thackeray, who had gone into CID headquarters that morning with an unconvincing explanation that the murder inquiry demanded his attention for the whole weekend. Laura had not believed him and she wondered how long it was going to take him to confront the demons that were coming between them. And how long she could wait.

She shook her head sharply at the memory, tossing her red hair back and letting the wind take it behind her in a cloud.

'Hi, copperknob,' a young man in a gold and blue flat cap yelled as he passed her in the jostling throng, and she felt unaccountably cheered up. When men stopped noticing her, she thought with a grin, was when she should start to worry. And she determined to enjoy the new experience of a big FA Cup match in Bradfield with more cheerful anticipation than she had felt all day.

She had not felt threatened in the jostling, excited crowd, but she remembered that Tony Holloway – when he had recovered from his chagrin after learning of Laura's coveted invitation to the directors' box – had warned her to take care. There were enough wild local lads still around, he thought, to take the arrival of a major London club, especially one with its own reputation for supporter violence, as a challenge. In other words, he said, there could be trouble, more likely these days outside the ground than in, and it was clear to Laura, as she pushed her way to the main entrance, that he might well be right. Amongst the press of mainly men and boys garlanded in the club colours, there were a few pockets of cold-eyed young men who looked as if they might have more than raucous and foul-mouthed support for their team on their mind.

Avoiding the queues for the turnstile entrances, she made her way to one side where glass doors gave access to the offices and other facilities of Bradfield United's administration. Security guards looked at the invitation Jenna Heywood had sent to the office and one of them guided her inside the building to the boardroom, where another club official studied her credentials again before opening the imposing panelled doors for her and ushering her in.

'Miss Heywood's over there by t'window,' the man said, gesturing vaguely across a throng of burly men in suits to the far side of the room, where picture windows gave onto the main stand and the so far empty green pitch beyond. Everyone was clutching a glass, and to judge by the heat and the noise, everyone had had their glass filled more than once already, although there was still more than an hour to go before kick-off. Laura dodged her way through the crush and joined the group around Jenna, who noticed her arrival with an unexpectedly warm smile.

'Laura,' she said. 'I'm glad you could come.'

'I wouldn't have missed it for the world,' Laura said. 'A chance of glory like this?'

Jenna's eyes lost their warmth for a second as she glanced out onto the pitch, which was being lashed by a sudden squall.

'We hope so,' she said quickly, glancing at a well-tanned, dark-haired man at her side wearing what Laura guessed was a casually elegant Armani suit and a slightly strained smile. 'Right, Paolo?' she said.

'We can 'ope,' he said, and Laura realised, even before Jenna introduced them, that this must be Paolo Minelli, the Italian coach who had been unexpectedly lured to the club by Jenna's father. Minelli nodded in Laura's direction and just for a second his expression switched from anxious to interested as the melancholy brown eyes in a crumpled face flickered over Laura's trim figure. She had chosen her black trouser suit and emerald shirt carefully to set off her copper hair and was inevitably flattered by their effect.

'And this is Angelica Stone, Paolo's girlfriend,' Jenna had continued smoothly. 'And her brother Stephen, who runs the new nightclub in Northgate. I haven't made it there yet, but I hear it's very good.' The Stones nodded briefly in Laura's direction with little interest until Jenna added that Laura was features editor of the *Gazette*.

'Are you here to write something?' Angelica asked. She was thin enough to verge on the anorexic and wore a revealingly low-cut silk top that did not meet her designer jeans and exposed a tanned midriff and a pierced navel. Her expression, Laura realised, was somewhat less than friendly.

'No, I've already written about Jenna taking over the club,' she said. 'If you saw the *Gazette* yesterday you might have read it. The sports editor will do the rest of the coverage. Football's not something I know much about, to be honest. This is a new experience for me.'

'Ah, you wrote that article, did you?' Minelli asked, also looking at Laura with even greater interest and practised eyes that travelled again from her cloud of loosely swept back hair to her new high-heeled red boots in seconds. 'I thought that was very good, very nice. *Simpatico, si.* So much writing about football is fantastic – is that the right word in English? I mean not true, made up?'

'Sorry, I should have called to thank you for the article,' Jenna said quickly. 'It was quite a pleasure to read something that wasn't having a go at me for being female, which is what's happened on most of the sports pages. You wouldn't think this was the twenty-first century, the way some of the tabloids go on. But that was a good piece. I liked it.'

'Thank you,' Laura said.

'Now, will you excuse me for a minute,' Jenna went on quickly. 'Paolo and I need a word before he goes downstairs to join the team. Perhaps Steve will get you a drink and introduce you to some more people. I won't be long. You're sitting next to me in the box when the time comes.'

With that Jenna spun on her elegantly shod heel, followed by Paolo Minelli, who gave Laura a last appraising glance as he turned away, a glance, Laura realised, that was not lost on Angelica who watched her boyfriend depart with a face like thunder.

'Vodka and tonic, please,' Laura said in answer to Stephen Stone's enquiry and he too moved away, leaving the two women to survey the now rain-lashed pitch outside, and the sight of the fans beginning to fill up the stands, in a prickly silence.

'What do you do, Angelica?' Laura asked, trying to break the ice.

'Modelling, mainly,' the other woman said, without enthusiasm.

'What, here or in London?' Laura asked, thinking that there could not be a great deal of modelling work on offer in Bradfield.

'Oh, in London mainly,' Angelica said airily. 'Leeds, Manchester, you know. Around.' She reached in her bag and took out a pack of cigarettes and lit one, without offering them in Laura's direction. She drew the smoke into her lungs hungrily and Laura wondered if the addiction was how she maintained her stick-thin figure.

'It must be an interesting life,' she said, trying again to break the palpable tension between them. 'What's the ultimate in modelling? Doing the shows in Paris and New York?'

'If you look like a twelve-year-old druggie,' Angelica said with unexpected venom. 'I know I'm not in that league and never will be.' Before Laura could answer, she found herself uncomfortably close to Stephen, who had come up behind them and thrust a glass in her direction.

'V and T,' he said. The brother and sister duo were uncannily alike, Laura thought as she took a sip of her drink and found herself the focus of another sharp-eyed gaze, almost as chilly as Angelica's. They were both tall and fair, although Angelica's hair was highlighted with gold, and their high cheekbones hinted at an ancestry that was not totally rooted in Yorkshire. Angelica would photograph well with that bone structure, she thought.

'Thanks,' Laura said to Stephen. 'So how's the new club going? I heard about it when it opened, but I haven't got there yet.'

'I'll put you on the guest list if there's a gig you'd especially like to see,' Stone said, but without much warmth.

'Thanks,' Laura said again.

'Ackroyd,' Stone said. 'Weren't you the reporter who was involved in some shooting a few months back? What was it? A siege of some sort and someone was killed. Did you get shot?'

Laura swallowed another mouthful of her drink to cover the inevitable pang of distress that clenched her stomach before she could bring herself to answer.

'No, I didn't get shot. It was a man the police wanted to talk to who was killed and my boyfriend who was hurt.'

'Do reporters often get involved in that sort of thing?' Stone asked.

'Not if they have any sense,' Laura said lightly, and felt relieved when Jenna Heywood rejoined them and the subject dropped.

'Would you like some lunch?' she asked Laura. 'There's a buffet through here.' She waved to a door that was now crammed with burly men heading like hungry bears towards the aroma of food.

'What does Paolo Minelli think of your chances this afternoon?' Laura asked quietly as they moved in the same direction. Jenna laughed.

'That's the question you mustn't ask,' she said. 'We're going to win, of course. Aren't we, Les?' She directed her attention with practised ease to a florid, heavily built man in a tweed suit with what was left of his hair combed over his largely bald pate.

'This is Les Hardcastle, my father's best mate. Laura Ackroyd, from the *Gazette*.' Hardcastle stopped dead, a plate piled high with food in his hand, and fixed his eyes on Laura's.

'Jack Ackroyd's daughter?' he asked without preamble.

'That's right,' Laura said. 'Did you know him?'

'Aye, of course I did. I knew him when he were a director here,' Hardcastle said. 'It were a right shame he had to retire like that. We could do with him here now. He knew a thing or two, did your dad.'

'Still does,' Laura said with a grin. 'But he's enjoying his life in the sun. I'll tell him I saw you next time I speak to him. He'll be keen to know how this match goes.'

'He will that,' Hardcastle said. 'Give him my best, will you, Laura, love. It's nice to meet you. I remember him talking about you years ago when you were away at school. You were the apple of his eye.'

Hardcastle disappeared as abruptly as he had appeared into the now enthusiastically chomping mêlée, everyone with piled plates and drinks balanced precariously in hand. For self-protection, Jenna and Laura retired to a corner by the window again, where they rested their plates on the windowsill and picked at refreshments lighter than most people's, Laura thought, by several thousand calories.

'You don't realise quite how macho this set-up is until you see them all assembled like this,' Laura said quietly. 'You can almost smell the testosterone.'

'Some of this lot are from Chelsea,' Jenna said. 'I should be chatting them up really, but they're so bloody smug that I can't bear it. They could buy this club and not even notice a blip on their balance-sheet. I just hope our boy Okigbo can get one past their goalie and take the condescending smiles off their faces. I'd really enjoy that.' She gave her guest a wicked smile and Laura realised that United was just as close to Jenna's heart as it had apparently been to her father's, which explained a lot.

Laura glanced at her watch. 'Nearly time to go and cheer them on, isn't it? What a baptism for a football novice.'

'You'll enjoy it,' Jenna said. 'It's a tribal thing, and you're obviously one of the Bradfield tribe.'

The girl woke with a start and sat up. She had been dozing again on the damp, lumpy mattress, as she did most of the time now. She was bitterly cold – her thin cardigan little or no protection from the wind that whistled through the broken windows of the flats and the damp that permeated everything – and she had begun to cough, and knew that she was becoming sick. But she did not think that was what had disturbed her shallow sleep. She had been conscious of a noise, and noise meant a threat, though whether human or merely animal she could not be sure. She struggled upright and crept silently across the littered floor of the small room that had become her refuge to the window, standing away from the cracked glass and looking obliquely down to the ground below. The builders were not working today and she guessed it must be a weekend or a holiday. She had only the vaguest idea what day, or even what month it was. She seemed to have spent so long in darkness, most of it in pain and disgust or utter despair, that time seemed to have lost its meaning. She had no watch, but she knew from the failing light outside that this was dusk and it would soon be night.

Below she could see the main entrance to the flats, which led to the disused lifts and the foot of the stinking staircase. She could just glimpse three or four boys or young men standing close to the doors, wearing jackets with hoods that were pulled up to conceal their heads. They seemed to be talking and making animated gestures and then, to her horror, they glanced around cautiously before pushing the doors open and disappearing from sight into the hallway below her.

She caught her breath and thought that her heart would stop. She had thought before that other people were using the building but had never had definite proof. Now she knew she was not alone, and that she would have to move. But she could barely control the shivering that had overtaken her and her mind, once agile, had become so sluggish that she could barely think at all. She stood close to the window, hugging herself for a long time to try to overcome the cold, before moving very slowly towards the door. Cautiously she made her way to the front door of the flat, hanging askew on smashed hinges, and glanced out onto the walkway that gave access to a dozen flats on this level with a staircase at each end. She knew that if the men were coming up the main stairs she might still escape them by using the ancillary stairs, which gave access to each of the walkways below her and eventually to what must have been an emergency exit on the ground floor.

But what her near paralysed brain was telling her to do was to go the other way, to the main stairwell, where another door gave access to the short flight of narrow steps that led to the roof. There, she knew that the parapet was low enough for her to climb, even in her weakened state, and the long drop to the ground would end the months of torment she had suffered once and for all. But as she leant wearily against the wall just inside the flat she knew that she did not have the courage to risk going that way in case she met the men who had come into the block. Men, she thought, any men, were the greatest threat of all. She could not, would not, suffer like that again. But here, on the walkway outside, a high parapet and a wire grille that must have been erected to prevent just what she had in mind, made it impossible for her to achieve her end. She would have to work her way downwards, she thought, and wondered if her weary body could even attempt her task, much less make an escape into the town outside in the twilight without being seen and reported to the authorities.

Eventually she gathered all her dwindling strength and, ducking low below the parapet, ran to the stairs furthest from the flat that had been her refuge. At each landing she stood listening carefully before inching down the next flight, but the raucous laughter she heard was a long way away and eventually she had dropped down all eight flights and stood behind the emergency door, which was hanging on weakened hinges like most of the rest of the doors in the block. She inched it open and glanced outside anxiously. But she found that this end of the block was almost completely shielded from view by the protective fence that the builders had erected in their vain effort to keep intruders out.

She glanced down at herself before she dared move, and knew that she could not go far, partly because she had not the strength and partly because her appearance would arouse instant suspicion. Her short skirt and thin cardigan were filthy, her bare legs were stained with dirt and several smears of blood, and as she ran a hand across her dark hair she realised that it was filthy and matted. She guessed, too, that the time she had spent in the flats without access to running water had left her smelly. She would need to find another refuge and quickly, she thought, as above her she heard shouts and more laughter, closer this time, filling her with dread.

It was darker now, and she could see that above the fence the first street lights were beginning to come on. Very cautiously she worked her way around the fence to the first gap she could find, where she could see, beyond the rubble of the building site, a deserted road and a row of small, low houses, with tiny gardens in front and narrow pathways leading to the back. Some of the houses had lights on behind drawn curtains but as she scuttled across the road, looking fearfully behind her to make sure that she had not been spotted, she headed for one that was in darkness, opened the gate, and still glancing over her shoulder nervously, made her way down the path to the back of the building. In the dim light she could just make out the back door to the house, a dustbin beside it, and a small outhouse with its door ajar. There was not much room inside, but by this time she was gasping for breath and her heart was thumping painfully and she slumped to the floor inside, pulling the door closed behind her. The darkness was almost total but she hardly noticed as her mind went blank and an even greater darkness overwhelmed her.

Thackeray was already home when Laura got back from the match, her face flushed and eyes sparkling in a way that set his heart beating faster in spite of the nagging pain in his back.

'Did you hear the result?' Laura said, peeling off her coat and flinging it on a chair. 'A one-one draw. The new boy Okigbo got the equaliser right at the end. The crowd went completely mad. I've never seen anything like it. Grown men were hugging each other and dancing around. And the singing. You could have heard it in Leeds.'

'You had a good time, then?' Thackeray said drily. Laura glanced at him and grinned.

'Oh, come on,' she said. 'It's quite an achievement. Everyone thought Chelsea would win eight- or nine-nil. But the Bradfield lads played their socks off. The goalie made six or seven brilliant saves. I don't know anything about the game, really, but I have to admit it was exciting. The whole town's going to go bananas until the replay.'

'And when's that likely to be?'

'Week after next,' Laura said. 'Not that I expect an invitation to go to London, but I expect we can watch on the box.'

'I expect we can,' Thackeray said, and as Laura calmed down she could see that her enthusiasm was washing over him without any discernible impact.

'OK, I can see United aren't going to touch your rugby soul, but I enjoyed it,' she said, more calmly. 'Even Tony Holloway gave me a hug on the way out, though he's furious that Jenna Heywood invited me into her precious directors' box. I know he thinks it should have been him.'

She dropped onto the sofa beside him and put a hand tentatively on his.

'How was your day?' she said. 'Did you make any progress?'

'Not really,' Thackeray said. 'We had a couple of lines of inquiry to follow up, but most of the people we wanted to talk to seemed to be at the match. The African player seems to have built up quite a following in the black community.'

'Well, I suppose he would do,' Laura said. 'He's very good. Jenna's sure he won't stay in Bradfield. Some team like Chelsea will snap him up.'

'What nationality is he?'

'Nigerian,' Laura said.

'Someone suggested the dead girl might be Nigerian, but we've no evidence on where she came from yet. But that explains why when Kevin Mower went to the African social club today there was no one there.'

'Well you can meet OK Okigbo tomorrow if you like. Jenna's invited us to the United celebration party at West Royd, if you feel like going. I think you deserve a bit of time off for good behaviour, don't you?'

Thackeray sighed. 'I need to go into the office again,' he said.

'The party's at six. You can do both,' Laura said. 'Come on, Michael. You're not going to get through this inquiry business if you don't relax occasionally. Go in to work, do what you have to do, and then come to West Royd with me. Please?'

Thackeray shrugged slightly. 'All right. If it'll make you happy.'

'Good,' Laura said. 'Now, I'm going to call my father and tell him about the game. And then I'll cook us something good for supper. OK.'

Before she could move, Thackeray pulled her towards him with unexpected force and kissed her hungrily, and just for a second it seemed to Laura that all the old magic of their affair was about to be rekindled. But just as suddenly he pulled away again.

'An early night?' Laura whispered.

'Maybe,' he said, flinging himself back against the cushions, looking drained. 'I'm shattered.' Trying to hide her disappointment, she went into the kitchen with the portable phone and dialled her parents' number in Portugal. It was answered almost immediately by her father's typically peremptory tone.

'Ackroyd.'

'Dad, it's me, did you hear the result? I was actually there.'

'I caught it on BBC World,' Jack Ackroyd said. 'Something of a turn-up, that. And what were you doing at a United match, young lady? I've never known you to show any interest in football.'

Laura laughed, and described how she had come by her invitation to the match.

'I met someone who was asking after you,' she said. 'Les Hardcastle? You must remember him.'

'Aye, I remember Les,' Jack said. 'A canny lad, Les. He's still a director then, is he?'

'He's leading the opposition to Jenna Heywood taking over as chairman,' Laura said.

'Aye, he'd not want to see a lass in that job. Especially if she's that keen to turn the club around.'

'Why do you say that?' Laura said, puzzled. 'Surely all the directors want to turn the club around.'

'Oh, I wouldn't bank on that, love,' Jack said loftily. 'That's a bit too simplistic. I don't know what's going on there now. I don't keep my finger on that particular pulse. But I do know from my broker that someone's trying to buy up any stray shares in Bradfield United they can get their hands on, like the few I've got myself.'

'Have you sold them?' Laura asked.

'Not yet,' Jack said. 'I just told my lad to wait to see how high the offer price went.'

'Could it be Jenna Heywood, trying to consolidate her position?'

'I doubt it,' Jack said. 'More likely someone trying to take over and boot her out.'

'Oh, dear. Just when they've had this fantastic Cup run and built up their following again,' Laura said softly.

'Aye well, I doubt this has got much to do with football,' Jack said. 'But don't quote me on that, love, will you? I'm staying well out of this one. Well out.'

CHAPTER SIX

Sergeant Kevin Mower had no doubt that the African Social Club, based in a church hall on the busy main road out of town towards the M62 motorway, was open and jumping when, just before lunchtime on Sunday morning, he opened the door and stepped into a decibel level he could not even begin to estimate. The conversation inside was loud enough to make it almost impossible to hear the music, although as his ears became attuned to the clamour, he recognised the rap artist JJC's inimitable mixture of English and Yoruba lyrics, music he had heard and liked when he watched *Dirty Pretty Things*, a film about an illegal Nigerian immigrant in London a few years back. He glanced around the entirely black crowd inside the hall and wondered how many of them might not like their papers to be inspected too closely.

DCI Thackeray was a couple of steps behind him, having decided at the last moment that some hands-on investigation was preferable to sitting in his office on a Sunday morning reviewing the slow progress of a murder inquiry that already threatened to run into the sand. Mower had driven him across the town centre, where Sunday shoppers thronged the pavements, in almost total silence, and up the hill past many of the surviving relics of Bradfield's industrial past: several churches and chapels converted to new uses, one or two still derelict mills and some council housing that had replaced the old stone terraces in the Sixties and was already looking seriously dilapidated.

Thackeray, never the most outgoing of men, Mower thought, seemed to have retreated almost totally into himself since he had come back from sick leave, only an occasional wince of pain giving the lie to his assurances that he was completely recovered from his injury. Mower had never believed that, and believed it less and less as the days went by, though he was at a complete loss to know what, if anything, he should do about it. Now, as they stood in the doorway of the church hall, Thackeray seemed to hesitate, as if intimidated, before stepping into the heaving throng inside.

Mower allowed himself a grim smile as he surveyed the room, alive with men, women and children of all ages, and waited until the presence of their white faces attracted attention. It came eventually in the form of a buxom black woman in a fiercely patterned long skirt and tunic, who threaded her way through the animated crowd and looked both men up and down with dark eyes and a serene smile.

'How can I help you?' she asked. Thackeray nodded for Mower to continue, evidently reluctant to get involved himself. Mower showed the woman his warrant card and her expression became more solemn as she studied it.

'I am Hope Kuti and I am the secretary of the club here for my sins. The rest of the time I am at the university, studying for a PhD. Are you here about the young black girl who was found dead? I read about that in the local paper. Most of us did, I think. It's a terrible thing.'

'Exactly that,' Mower said, realising that he was being offered more information by Hope Kuti than he really needed, and how defensive that made her seem. 'Could we talk somewhere a bit quieter?'

Hope smiled again and led the two men back outside and into the small graveyard between the hall and the soot-blackened Victorian church next door and then to a wooden seat where she sat down, apparently oblivious to the chilly wind that whistled through the narrow space between the two buildings. Mower glanced dubiously at the stained wooden seat for a second before sitting down beside her, while Thackeray remained standing, clearly determined to maintain only a watching brief.

'Sunday lunchtime is a favourite time for a *faji* – a party,' Hope said. 'It's the only time most people are free. The church lets us open the hall after the morning service is finished next door at midday. They don't mind us being here but they don't want the *faji* to drown out the hymns, you know? There's few enough people in there to sing them these days. Anyway, a lot of people here go to other churches first. I do myself. And then we come on here.'

Mower pulled out a copy of the drawing of the unknown girl and passed it to Hope.

'It's been suggested she might be African,' he said. 'Although personally I think Caribbean's more likely. You don't know her, by any chance, do you? We've had almost no response to the appeal in the *Gazette*.'

That was not strictly true. The only bright spot in a Saturday of dead ends had been a phone call from a young woman who had been near the canal the night the girl was found and reckoned she had not only seen her, but had seen her in the company of another girl, small, white and mini-skirted, hurrying in the general direction of the towpath. But their informant was away for the weekend in Scarborough and would not be available to make a statement until Monday.

Hope Kuti shook her head sadly as she gazed for a long time at the artist's sketch of the dead girl.

'No, I don't recognise her,' she said. 'But you're right. She would look quite at home on the streets of Lagos. That's where I'm from, incidentally. Though I haven't been home for about five years. I'm hoping when I get my doctorate I may get a university job back home, but nothing's certain. Back there, who you know counts as much as what qualifications you've got. It's improving a bit, but not that much, I think.'

'Best known here for prising cash out of gullible Internet users,' Mower said.

'Ah, the 419 scam?'

'419?'

'It's the number of the legislation that is supposed to be stopping it,' Hope said, with a shrug. 'It wasn't doing the country's reputation much good. The rapper the kids are all dancing to in there calls his group the 419 Squad. Joke.'

'Right,' Mower said, slightly bemused by the torrents of information Hope offered. 'So how do you suggest I circulate this picture to your friends in there? Are many of them West Africans?'

'Not many,' Hope said. 'Most West Africans head to London and stay there. I know a couple of Nigerian nurses in Bradfield, and a family who came as asylum seekers and have been given leave to remain.'

'How many members do you have altogether then?'

'About a hundred, though that includes the children, and most of them must be here today, as you see. The place is packed. But there are more members from the other side of Africa – Somalis, Eritreans, and a few Zimbabweans, of course. A lot of them are asylum seekers who've been shunted up here into empty properties, and some don't have good English, or any English. We arrange free classes for them if they want to learn. They can't afford to go to college classes if they're not working.' She shrugged. 'And they're not allowed to work, of course. One of the more stupid rules you impose.'

'So talking to the adults will be quite difficult, then?' Thackeray broke in suddenly. 'We may need translators?'

'Some of them will have difficulty understanding English, yes,' Hope said. She glanced at her watch. 'But we have a lot of informal translators. Very often the children have learnt some English at school and help their parents. When we serve the food in about fifteen minutes, I'll make an announcement to tell them all who you are and what you want. You can show them the picture of this poor girl. And then anyone who has anything to tell you can do so. Does that make sense?'

'Perfect sense,' Mower said. 'Thanks.' He hesitated, knowing that Hope would not like his next question, but that he had no choice but to ask it.

'Do you have any contact with illegal immigrants?' he asked. 'We have to consider the possibility that she's not being identified because that's what she is and her friends or family are to frightened to come forward.'

'I don't know anyone here illegally myself, but I wouldn't

bank on there not being any in Bradfield,' Hope said slowly. 'And I doubt very much that anyone here would tell you about illegals if they knew. That would almost certainly be pushing it a step too far.'

Mower glanced down again at the artist's impression of the dead girl and then at Thackeray.

'Someone somewhere has lost a daughter,' the DCI said fiercely to Hope. 'And quite a young daughter, at that. Our chances of finding her killer are very slim if we don't even know who she is or what she was doing in Bradfield.'

'I know all that,' Hope Kuti said, glancing away from Thackeray's angry eyes. 'But you know as well as I do that there's an underworld out there, an underworld of desperate people with no money and no hope who'll work for next to nothing because the alternative is to starve. You can't blame people for doing the best they can to survive and avoid being sent back to whatever particular hell they've escaped from. And believe me, there are some hells in Africa. I sometimes think God has turned his back on that continent.'

'Let's do your appeal, then,' Mower said, recognising the impasse. He would not argue with her analysis but he knew many people who would. 'You never know. It might come up with something.'

But when he and Thackeray walked back to the car half an hour later they had to accept that they had drawn a blank again. With the music turned off and food being hungrily wolfed down, the crowd of Africans had listened politely enough to what Mower had to say, and various bits of informal translation appeared to have explained his message to everyone there as they had passed the artist's impression of the dead girl amongst themselves, but most shook their heads and shrugged their shoulders and although both Mower and Thackeray watched closely, there did not appear to be any hint of recognition from anyone in the crowd. As the groups of young men and families switched their attention back to their Sunday lunch, a multi-ethnic buffet with several dishes Mower did not even recognise, Hope Kuti made her way back towards them with a plateful of food in her hand.

'Who's that?' Mower said to her when he had guided her out of earshot of any of the other party-goers. He nodded at a solidly built man, broad-faced and very dark, in whose eyes he had detected just the faintest flicker of some emotion as he had stood at the front of the crowd listening to the appeal for information. As their eyes met for the second time, the man cleared his plate of its last mouthful of food and made his way purposefully towards the door, shouldering slighter people out of his way.

'Emanuel,' Hope said. 'I can't remember his other name. I could look it up for you. I've never spoken to him. He doesn't often turn up.'

'Is he Nigerian?'

'Yes, I think he is.'

Mower watched as the tall, broad figure in a brightly patterned orange shirt stretching against his belly, pushed through the swing doors, but made no comment.

'Would you like some lunch?' Hope asked. Mower was tempted for a moment but he could see the frozen expression in his boss's eyes and knew that this was not the moment, if there ever was one, to persuade Thackeray to try Africa's varied cuisine.

'Thanks, but no thanks,' he had said with a faint grin in Thackeray's direction. 'My boss wants to get back. Some other time, maybe. And if you hear anything, you'll get in touch?' He gave Hope his card.

'Of course,' she said. 'Of course I will.'

'I reckon if she was African someone there would have recognised her, guv,' Mower said as he drove back towards police HQ.

'So she's an illegal, or she's not African at all,' Thackeray said.

'If she was West Indian and local, someone would have identified her by now,' Mower said. 'We'll have the picture on TV tomorrow, local and national, so maybe that'll come up trumps.'

'Why did you ask about the man who left? What was his name? Emanuel?'

'I just thought he looked a bit anxious when someone passed him the picture, that's all. But maybe he doesn't like the police for some other reason.'

'Didn't want his papers looked at, maybe,' Thackeray said.

'Or maybe he's importing bush-meat. Some of those dishes on the table didn't look like chicken or beef to me.'

'Bush-meat?'

'I don't think you want to know, guv,' Mower said.

'I want to know,' Thackeray insisted grimly.

'Chimpanzee, all sorts of wild animals, smuggled in. There's a flourishing trade in London apparently,' Mower said, grinning at Thackeray's appalled expression.

'Dear God,' the DCI said.

Mower swerved suddenly as they passed a pub where a

group of youths in Bradfield United colours suddenly spilt into the road, with silly smiles on their faces.

'Still celebrating, I see,' Mower said. Thackeray gave a half-smile.

'Laura actually went to the match,' he said, still sounding faintly astonished at the idea. 'Seems to have enjoyed it.'

'I'd have been rooting for Chelsea,' Mower said. 'They were just up the road when I was a kid. Not that I could often afford to go, even then, and now you have to take out a mortgage to get a season ticket.'

'We've been invited to a club celebration at West Royd this evening, but I don't think I'll bother.'

'Oh, you should go,' Mower said, wishing he could just tell his boss to lighten up for once. But he knew that would be taking a liberty too far. 'You could combine business with pleasure and ask their Nigerian star whether he knows our victim.' Mower was joking but to his surprise Thackeray seemed to take him seriously.

'Okigbo? I might just do that,' he said.

The bar and reception area at the West Royd club was heaving at six o'clock that evening when Thackeray and Laura arrived for the celebration party. Laura was wearing a short low-cut black dress, which she knew did her a lot of favours, and had brushed her hair into a froth of copper curls under Thackeray's watchful, and she hoped lustful, gaze.

'Who are you trying to impress?' he asked, as she picked up a wrap and inspected his dark suit and the silk tie she had bought him the previous Christmas with equal attention.

'Just you,' she said, brushing his cheek with a kiss. 'Come

on, cheer up. I think we both deserve an evening out.'

Thackeray had driven slowly up the hill out of town to the country club where the car park was already almost full. He wished that he was as confident as Laura that they would enjoy the evening, but he had his doubts. Football was not his game, parties were not his scene, but he knew that if he did not make an effort Laura was quite prepared to go on her own, and of the two options, he had decided that was the worse.

As soon as they had left their coats, Laura was hailed by Tony Holloway, snaking through the crush towards them with a glass in his hand and a glazed look in his eyes that indicated that it was by no means the first drink of the day.

'Laura,' he said, giving her an unexpected kiss on both cheeks that she was too slow to evade. 'Our lovely Laura,' he went on, and Laura could feel Thackeray bristling beside her. 'You know,' the sports editor ploughed on, addressing himself to Thackeray now. 'You know, your lovely Laura has suddenly become a football expert? Amazing, isn't it? I'd no idea she understood the off-side rule, had you?'

He put an arm round Laura's shoulder and glanced around the room, swaying slightly.

'Jenna invited you, did she? Wonderful lady, Jenna Heywood, but not long for this job. You wait. The old guard'll have her out, one way or another. You'll see.'

'You sound as if you've been celebrating since the final whistle,' Laura said tartly. 'Have you written your report for tomorrow? I reckon Ted will want it on the front page.'

'All taken care of, sweetie, all wrapped up and ready to go, the front page splash, of course,' Tony said blithely. 'Ted's here somewhere, by the way.' He glanced across the room in the direction of a group of heavy men with dark suits and flushed faces amongst whom Laura could see their editor chomping on a cigar and waving a whiskey glass in the air, evidently haranguing his listeners in a way that was all too familiar to his staff.

'I didn't know he was a footie fan,' Laura said.

'Oh, it's not that game with Ted, is it, darling? It's another sort of game entirely.' And with that Holloway wove off into the crowd again with what she guessed he hoped was an enigmatic smile. Laura turned back to Thackeray with a shrug.

'Sorry about that. You know, I think my foray into sport may be strictly a one-off,' she said. 'It's not the game, it's the company you have to keep. But let's make the most of it while we're here, shall we? The drinks seem to be over there.'

After a couple of glasses of champagne, Laura's party turned into a dizzy whirl of introductions and brief conversations as alcohol-fuelled young men in designer gear, almost invariably accompanied by fiercely tanned young women, tottering on high heels and wearing very little, grouped and regrouped around her. She lost sight of Thackeray after a short time and suddenly found herself face to face with Paolo Minelli, who looked rather too enthusiastically pleased to see her. His girlfriend Angelica did not seem to be in sight.

'*Ciao, Laura, cara,*' he said, pronouncing her name as Dante would have done and kissing her on both cheeks. 'You look ravishing tonight.'

'Paolo,' Laura said, dodging what appeared to be an

attempt at an even closer embrace. 'You must be delighted by the result yesterday.'

'I am delighted, Jenna is delighted, OK is delighted.' For a second his face clouded as he seemed to catch the eye of someone in the crowd behind him. 'I just hope we can keep OK for the rest of the season,' he said quietly, although there was little chance of being overheard amongst the frantic chatter and laughter all around them.

'He wouldn't go so soon, would he?' Laura asked, surprised. 'I thought he'd only just arrived.'

'He was Sam Heywood's last purchase,' Minelli said. 'No one rated him very highly so he came cheap and his contract is short. But there's always pressure at clubs like this to sell the best players on. There's never enough money.' Suddenly his crumpled face took on an expression of tragic intensity. 'If you're talking to Jenna, tell her how crucial you think OK is to the team. She likes you. She'll listen to you.'

'Surely she wouldn't sell him,' Laura said.

'There are people who would,' Minelli said. 'And he's ambitious. What young man with his talent isn't? I'm doing my best to keep him happy here, but you never know what others will offer. We pay him as much as we can afford, I helped him get a good car, a top-of-the-range Beamer, he has a nice flat, girls, whatever he wants. But I know that look in his agent's eye. I see the pound signs there.'

Minelli took another pull at his drink and then smiled suddenly.

'But I shouldn't bore you with my troubles. And that's all off the record, by the way. I almost forgot that a beautiful woman like you earns her living as a reporter.' He put his arm around her waist and she could feel his hot hand move very close to her breast and she pulled away abruptly.

'I must find my partner,' she said, although she could see no sign of Thackeray in the milling and increasingly raucous crowd. But with a feeling of relief she did see Jenna Haywood moving towards her with a welcoming smile on her face. Minelli spotted her too, and with an ingratiating nod headed immediately in the opposite direction.

'Hi,' Jenna said. 'I'm glad you could come. The egregious Paolo wasn't bothering you, was he? Don't give him any encouragement is my advice.'

'Thanks,' Laura said. 'I'm certainly not going to do that. How's it going? Has yesterday's result made you a few more friends?'

'Well, among the fans, maybe,' Jenna said, with a wry smile. 'Though they're only as reliable as last Saturday's result.' She glanced around the room and fixed her gaze on the same group of middle-aged men to whom Ted Grant had been talking earlier.

'I think Les Hardcastle's still conniving to get me out,' she said. 'It's not really results that interest him. He's much more interested in selling United's ground and – he says – moving out of the town centre. The plan is to buy a bigger tranche of land and build a new stadium with some sort of lucrative leisure complex attached. It's not a bad idea, as it goes, but I reckon some of the directors wouldn't be too upset if they didn't have to bother with a stadium at all. I can't prove that, of course, but football at this level is not a very cost-effective business. Everyone knows that. The shareholders would prefer a few other fish to fry. But for God's sake, don't say I said that.'

'My father's still got some shares, apparently,' Laura said. 'And he reckons someone's trying to buy them up.'

Jenna looked at Laura in silence for a moment.

'That doesn't surprise me,' she said. 'You know I reckon all this stuff about not liking a woman running the club is a load of cobblers. The real reason they want to get rid of me is because I'm determined to keep the club alive for the fans. That's what gets up their noses.'

'You wouldn't be thinking of selling OK Okigbo then?' Laura asked. 'Paolo Minelli seems to think you might.'

'Do I look that stupid?' Jenna said. 'Managers at this level are always the same: they can't decide whether they want to keep a brilliant player or sell him on and buy two or three cheaper ones. And I'm convinced some of them still line their own pockets during these transactions. Of course OK'll go in the end. He's bound to. He'll want to move up to a bigger club and we'll benefit from buying cheap and selling at a profit. Someone will make us an offer we can't refuse. But I hope it won't be soon. Anyway, I've got the majority of the shares safely locked up in my name, so they're going to have a fight on their hands if they try any dirty tricks.'

'Keep me in touch,' Laura said lightly.

Jenna looked at her with a more serious expression than Laura had expected.

'I will,' she said. 'I don't trust your sports editor colleague. I reckon he's in the pocket of Les Hardcastle and his mates. And I'm not at all sure where your editor stands. This is a small town and he wields a lot of power.'

'Ted Grant will stand wherever he reckons will do him a bit of good,' Laura said candidly. 'But he will listen if there's a good story going. In the end he's a newspaperman first and won't let an exclusive pass him by. So let me know if you have trouble with Tony Holloway and there's anything you think's worth printing.'

Laura felt a hand on her arm and spun round, thinking Minelli had returned and ready to take him on, only to find Thackeray behind her, still holding the glass of tonic water with which he had started the evening. She introduced him briefly to Jenna, who nodded and half-turned away.

'Good to meet you, but I have to circulate,' she said. 'Keep the troops motivated, and all that.'

Laura glanced at Thackeray, who seemed restless and unaccountably annoyed.

'Is your back hurting?' she asked quietly. But he shook his head.

'I'm fine,' he said. 'I just wondered who that dark-haired chap was who was pawing you.'

'That's the coach, Paolo Minelli,' she said. 'I can deal with him. He's got a girlfriend here somewhere who'll keep him in line anyway.'

'How long do you want to stay?' Thackeray asked.

Laura shook her head.

'Let's have something to eat and then we can go,' she said, suddenly dispirited. 'You go and look at the food. I just want to say hello to Les Hardcastle. He's a friend of my father's.'

She slipped away through the crowd but Thackeray did not take her advice. Instead he spotted the Nigerian striker Okigbo, less tall and more rounded than he expected the star player to be. He was on the other side of the room with another older, heavier black man beside him, whom he recognised as the man who had left the African Social Club that morning. The press of party-goers moved out of the way as he shouldered his way across the crowded room and he interrupted the two men's conversation with a curt introduction.

'I wasn't at the match but I hear congratulations are in order, Mr Okigbo,' he said to the younger man, who grinned with obvious delight at the compliment.

'I was so lucky,' he said. 'The goal just opened up for me. The eighty-ninth minute, you know? Unbelievable.'

'And are you connected with the club too?' he said to the man he knew as Emanuel.

'Oh, just a fan really, but I knew OK's family in Lagos before he came to this country. We are both Nigerians, and there's not so many of us in Bradfield, so we made contact again. He kindly invited me to the party.'

'But you didn't recognise the girl whose picture we were showing this morning at your Social Club? We thought she might be Nigerian.'

'No, I didn't know her.' Emanuel was clearly not intending to offer any further information about himself and Thackeray wondered why. OK Okigbo looked puzzled.

'What girl is this?' he asked.

'I'm a police officer, Mr Okigbo,' Thackeray said, watching the footballer closely for any sign of alarm, which he knew was not unusual and far from incriminating when the word 'police' was introduced into casual conversation, but the young man's cheerfulness did not dissipate. 'I'm investigating the death of a black girl we can't identify and I went to the African Social Club this morning to see whether anyone could place her. Nobody did. You haven't come across a young African girl recently, have you?'

'Afraid not,' OK said easily. If he was lying he was good at it, Thackeray thought.

'If she was Nigerian we would know her,' Emanuel said flatly.

'You know all the Nigerians in Bradfield, do you, Mr – erm – I don't think I caught your name?'

'Emanuel Asida,' the man said. 'And yes, I think I probably do.'

But before Thackeray could pursue his questions two more men joined the group.

'All right, OK?' a heavily built ginger-haired man in an electric blue suit asked aggressively. He turned his gaze on Thackeray when the young footballer nodded slightly uncertainly. 'Jenkins,' he said. 'Dennis Jenkins. I'm OK's agent. I keep an eye on his interests, and all that malarky.' The eyes Jenkins kept on the world were blue and very sharp.

'Steve Stone,' the other man said. 'We've met before, Mr Thackeray. I didn't expect to see you here. United is your secret vice, then, is it?' He held out a hand, which Thackeray ignored as his mind flashed back to the last occasion he had seen Stone: across an interview-room table at the beginning of an ultimately abortive investigation into the man's connection with several different vices in Bradfield a couple of years before. In spite of what the police reckoned was sufficient evidence for Stone's financial involvement in a brothel masquerading as a club, the Crown Prosecution Service had not been impressed and Stone had walked away laughing, an episode, Thackeray thought, that seemed to have done nothing to dent his cocky self-confidence. He nodded.

'You're another football fan?' he asked.

'In the family,' Stone said with an easy smile. 'My sister Angelica's Paolo Minelli's partner.'

'Ah, yes,' Thackeray said. 'I've seen Mr Minelli at work.' Stone scowled at that and seemed about to demand an explanation when Jenkins cut in.

'I'll have to drag OK away now,' he said, taking the young footballer's arm firmly. 'A photo-call for a snapper from London, and we can't ignore them, can we? Not with OK's prospects. It was quite a result we had yesterday and OK's a star now.'

He and Stone virtually escorted the footballer out of the room, reminding Thackeray of a pair of coppers with their prisoner, but when he glanced at Emanuel Asida quizzically the older Nigerian's smile was bland.

'He'll go far, that boy,' he said.

'I'm sure,' Thackeray agreed. 'He looks as if he's being well advised.' And he turned away to seek out Laura again. But his search was interrupted by a sudden shriek from the far side of the room. Peering over the heads of the crowd as it turned in the direction of the continuing noise, he could see two young women, in the regulation stilettos and revealing dresses of the players' wives and girlfriends, being pulled away from a red-faced young man in a smart Italian suit who appeared to have had a drink thrown over him and was cursing volubly. And slipping through the crowd from their direction, with a broad smile on her face, was Laura herself.

'What's all that about?' he asked.

'Some spat between one of the players and his girlfriend

about who else he's been seeing, as far as I can work out. She threw the drink and he slapped her face.'

'Nothing new there, then,' Thackeray said, still watching as the two women who had attacked the player pushed and shoved their unsteady way towards the door. One was in tears and the other attempting to comfort her, with an arm around her bony shoulders.

'There's nothing in it, Katrina,' the comforter said, as they passed Laura and Thackeray. 'They're just effing tarts, those girls, always hanging around to see what they can get their minging hands on, nothing serious, believe me.'

'But I thought Lee and me *were* serious,' the other woman said, wiping her eyes and smearing mascara across her cheeks. 'What's he doing playing away when we're supposed to be getting wed next year. What the hell's he think he's doing? It's not as if it's the first time.' She waved a hand decorated with a couple of large diamonds in the air wildly.

When they had gone, Thackeray glanced at Laura, who had watched their departure with a faint smile.

'Enough?' he asked.

'Enough,' she said. 'I'm not sure I've got the stamina for all this drama. They should put it on TV.'

'I think they already have,' Thackeray said, lightly, but catching his eye she realised how exhausted he suddenly looked.

'Come on then, drive me home,' she said.

CHAPTER SEVEN

'They were running,' Karen Wilson said flatly. She was sitting, looking slightly nervous, across an interview room table from Kevin Mower, a slim young woman with nicotine-stained fingers huddled into a black puffa jacket over her lacy blouse and skin-tight jeans. She glanced at her watch, her pale eyes anxious.

'I'll be late for work,' she said. 'I'm on at nine.'

Karen had finally turned up at the police station at about half past eight that Monday morning to make a formal statement about what she had seen on her way home from one of Bradfield's clubs very early the previous Wednesday morning.

'I won't keep you long, but it's very important,' Mower said. 'You seem to be the only person who saw the dead girl. Can I ask why you took so long to contact us. Her picture was in the *Gazette* on Friday.'

'I don't read the *Gazette*, do I?' Karen said irritably. 'Any road, me and my boyfriend went away for t'weekend on Friday, to Scarborough. What I saw were a picture of the girl on the telly in our hotel on Saturday. I thought I recognised her but for a while I couldn't think where I'd seen her.'

'So you were in Metcalfe Street at one-thirty on Tuesday night – Wednesday morning, in fact?'

'Me and Craig were at the Moonlight Club, weren't we, and we had a row. So I said I were going home. I left him outside t'Club and I were taking a shortcut down Metcalfe Street towards the taxis at the end on t'corner of Kirkgate. You can usually get one there without a great long queue. But I were walking quite fast because it's right dark down there.'

'It's not an area I'd want a girlfriend of mine walking down alone,' Mower agreed. 'It must have been quite a row you had.'

'He gets a bit above himself, does Craig, when he's had a few,' Karen said easily. 'We made it up next day.'

'Was there anyone else around when you got into Metcalfe Street?'

'No, it were right quiet. But then these two young lasses came running past.'

'Two girls, not just one?'

'Two. A black lass and a white lass. They passed me under a lamp post so I could see them clear enough. Nearly knocked me over, they did, as they ran past. I shouted at them, as it goes, but they took no notice. And then one of them went over on her ankle, the dark 'un, looked as if her shoe heel had broke or summat. They stopped for a minute and I caught up with them again. That's what made me remember them so well. She took her shoes off and chucked them into that bit o'waste land at t'side o't'road, and bloody ran off in her bare feet, didn't she? They were white underneath, her feet. I never knew that. Like straight out o't'jungle, she were. I were laughing, it were so funny.'

'And where did they go next?' Mower asked, struggling not to respond irritably.

'Down that little alley that takes you to the canal, just a snicket, like. I thought that were peculiar an'all. It's really pitch dark down there at night. I'd not risk it.'

'And did you see anyone else?' Mower asked.

'Oh yeah, there were a couple of blokes come along just after. They were in a hurry an'all, and I didn't like the look of 'em. I got a bit scared then and ran to t'corner myself, where t'taxis are, and there were one waiting so I got straight in. I thought there were summat funny going on but I'd no idea anyone would get killed. I can't believe it, even now – that she were killed.'

Karen's pale face crumpled for a moment and then she squared her shoulders and gave Mower a faint smile.

'Funny old world, innit?'

'Tell me what the two girls looked like,' Mower said more gently. 'Start with the white girl. Did you get a good look at her?'

'She were only tiny,' Karen said, screwing up her eyes as if to try to visualise that late night scene more clearly. 'Shorter than me, any road, and thin. She weren't much more than a kid really. She had dark hair, but she looked pale, not like a Paki or anything. She were white.'

'What was she wearing? Could you see that clearly?'

'Not the colours so much. She were only under t'street light for a minute. A dark mini-skirt, it looked like, black or dark blue maybe, and some sort of a pale jacket, or cardigan. She were in and out o't'light so fast it were hard to tell. And the black lass, she were bigger altogether, big hips and bum, but she were wearing a short skirt an'all and a little top, a bit shiny, and short, showing her midriff, you know?'

'I know,' Mower said softly, recognising the description of what the dead girl had been wearing when she had been pulled out of the canal. That and the fact that she was barefoot clinched the identification as far as he could see. Karen had undoubtedly seen the dead girl alive and running and quite probably afraid for her life. And all she had done was laugh.

'If you had to estimate how old they were, what do you reckon?'

Karen thought for a moment and then shrugged.

'They were just teenagers, weren't they? That's what I thought, any road. I thought they were teenagers just larking about.'

'And the men you saw? Could you describe them?'

'Not really,' Karen said. 'I only glanced over my shoulder when I heard them coming up behind me. I didn't like the look of them so I didn't hang about.'

'Could you see if they were black or white?' Mower persisted.

'Could have been either,' Karen said. 'I really couldn't see owt, just two dark shapes.'

'And did you think they were following the girls, chasing them?'

'They were in a hurry, that's for sure, so I suppose they must have been. But I were thinking more of myself than the two lasses by then. I didn't like the look of the blokes, so I got out of there as fast as I could.'

'You did the right thing,' Mower reassured her. 'So, going back to the girls, could you see if either of them was carrying a handbag?'

Karen screwed up her face again and thought for a moment.

'I didn't notice,' she said. 'They could have been, but there again they might not. The shoes I noticed, because they stopped, and I were so surprised when she chucked them away, but I didn't notice bags or owt else. I'm sorry.'

'Right,' Mower said. 'I'm going to have what you've told me typed up.' Karen looked at her watch.

'I've got to get to work,' she said.

'Can you come back at lunchtime to sign your statement? I don't want to get you into trouble at work.'

'It were the dead girl I saw, weren't it?' Karen asked as she got to her feet and pulled on her coat.

'I think so,' Mower said, his tone cautious.

'Bloody hell,' Karen said, picking up her own bag and tugging her coat collar up. 'They only looked like kids. And where's t'other one? Is she in t'canal and all?'

'I really don't know,' Mower said, with a feeling of almost painful foreboding. 'We'll be looking for her as a top priority, don't worry about that.'

He saw Karen out and went back upstairs to the CID office, tapped on DCI Thackeray's office door and told him what little their first and only eyewitness had reported.

'Find the shoes,' Thackeray said. 'And when she comes back at lunchtime ask her to try to describe the other girl in more detail. We might get a photo-fit picture out of it, though I doubt if it'll be very accurate if it was so dark.'

'She got a good enough look to identify the dead girl pretty definitively,' Mower said. 'And she was quite certain what she was wearing.'

'She'd be going partly on the location and partly on the girl's race,' Thackeray said dismissively. 'Describing someone less distinctive she saw for a couple of seconds will be harder. But see what you can get out of her. And in the meantime, start another search of the canal banks – in both directions from where the body was found. It could well be that we're looking for another body.'

'Right, guv,' Mower said. He hesitated for a moment. 'This disciplinary inquiry, do we know when it's starting?'

'Later this week,' Thackeray said shortly. 'They'll be based at County HQ, not here, so we'll be summoned down there as and when. As I understand it, they'll be talking to the Super first.'

'Not what we need with another murder inquiry on the go,' Mower said. He hesitated for a moment before he went on. 'Is there anything you or the Super don't want me to say, guv? Anything you want me to play down?'

Thackeray looked at the Sergeant for a long moment and then shook his head.

'You shouldn't have asked me that, Kevin, and I'll pretend you didn't. You shouldn't be threatened personally in any way by this investigation. Just tell them what they want to know.'

Mower nodded bleakly and closed Thackeray's door behind him. What he told the inquiry, he thought, would be a whole lot less than he knew in one respect at least and even if the DCI never knew anything about it, he knew he would be grateful. Back at his desk he called the *Gazette* and asked to speak to Laura Ackroyd.

'Hi,' he said when she answered her phone. 'Can I buy you a drink at lunchtime? There's something we need to talk about.'

*   *   *

Laura put the receiver down slightly uncertainly after agreeing to meet Kevin Mower in a quiet pub called the Angel, which was not normally a haunt of either the journalists from the *Gazette* or the detectives from CID. She was not at all sure that she wanted to talk to Mower at all, especially as she guessed precisely what it was he wanted to discuss. Her own involvement in the traumatic case that had almost led to Thackeray's death, and which was now being investigated by the police themselves for disciplinary reasons, was something she had tried to bury at the back of her mind. She knew it was going to be dragged into the spotlight, and probably very soon, and that would not be a pleasant process. Maybe, she thought with a sigh, she could no longer avoid it. She and Thackeray had always feared that their professional lives and their personal relationship might one day clash and damage them both. Now, it seemed, that had happened and she just hoped that the fallout would be survivable.

She turned back to her computer screen and carefully read what she had written. That morning's news conference had brought her into conflict again with Tony Holloway when the sports editor had been over-ruled by Ted Grant, and she did not want to add to the insult by making any stupid mistakes in an article she had not envisaged writing when she came into work that morning.

'Did you enjoy the match on Saturday, Laura?' Ted had asked when the editorial meeting had turned quickly and enthusiastically to Bradfield United's unexpected draw against Chelsea.

'I did,' Laura had said with a smile. 'Though I still don't know my offside from my four-two-four. But it was a great afternoon.'

'Why don't you do us a novice's eye view to go with the rest of Tony's stuff?' Grant asked expansively. 'We could run it on the front with the main report. Five hundred words or so on your first impressions of the beautiful game? What do you think, Tony?'

What Tony thought was written in the horrified expression on his face, but he swallowed hard and gave a minimal nod. Anything less might have provoked one of Ted's cataclysmic rages.

'I'm a bit tight for space,' he said faintly.

'Bollocks,' the Editor said, moving into tabloid editor mode as he always did if he encountered opposition to his slightest whim. 'We need a female angle,' he said loudly. 'They'll be accusing us of being all for the blokes if we run six pages of football coverage. We can put a mug-shot of Laura at the top of the column and encourage the lasses to celebrate along with the lads. It's a bloody good idea that. Right, Laura?'

'Right,' Laura said, not displeased with the idea but careful not to let Holloway see the gleam in her eye. 'That sounds like fun.' And she had gone back to her desk to hammer out her five hundred words of lighthearted description of her initiation into the mysteries of football quickly enough to make the deadline for the front page of the first edition of the day. But she knew Tony Holloway was not best pleased and she was not surprised when he came to read her copy over her shoulder before she had quite finished.

'I hope you're not going to make a habit of muscling in on my territory,' he said sourly.

Laura glanced over her shoulder at him with her sweetest smile.

'It wasn't my idea,' she said, as she concluded her final sentence. 'It would never have crossed my mind, actually.' She saved her work and sent it to the sub-editors who were waiting to slot it onto the front page right-hand column on their computer screens.

'One thing did surprise me,' she said turning back to Holloway. 'Paolo Minelli seemed really worried that he might lose Okigbo, that the club might sell him. That would be pretty crazy in the circumstances, wouldn't it?'

'Not necessarily for United, and certainly not for Okigbo, or his agent. It's all about money these days, Laura. Sam Heywood bought Okigbo, and probably paid his agent over the odds to get him here. The odd bung still goes on in spite of what people would like to believe. But now Sam's gone to football heaven and if the club prefers the cash that's what they'll go for. Minelli will have to do as he's told, although if he cuts up rough it wouldn't be unusual for him to be paid off as well. And of course, the agent takes a cut every time he moves on, so he won't be averse to offers. If OK scores against Chelsea again in the replay he'll be an even better bet for a lucrative transfer. Minelli maybe hasn't been offered enough to let him go willingly yet.'

'What a dodgy business it is,' Laura said. 'Does Jenna Heywood stand any chance of keeping the club alive?'

'Not her,' Holloway said dismissively. 'She knows damn all about it. But some of the directors might. But first they need to get her out. And they'll not do that until this Cup run fizzles out, as it will in the end. Probably next week at Stamford Bridge, as it goes. Then we'll see.'

'Cut throat?' Laura said.

'Oh, yes.'

By lunchtime Laura was ready for a change of scene and met Kevin in the Angel, where she found him with a lager and a V and T already on the table in waiting.

'Thanks,' she said, raising her glass to the Sergeant with a smile. She and Mower had always got on well and he was the only other person she knew in the police force who had Michael Thackeray's interests at heart.

'So what can I do for you?' she asked.

'This inquiry,' he said, looking suddenly deadly serious. 'They're bound to want to talk to you.'

'Yes, Michael told me that. I was there when he was shot, after all.'

'That won't be the only thing they'll be interested in,' he said quietly. 'They'll want to know how the *Globe* got hold of the information they printed about the little girl. Val Ridley will be giving evidence and she won't pull her punches. She's furious about the whole business and she's not a serving officer any more so there'll be no way of putting any pressure on her. She'll tell them she gave information to you to pass on to the guv'nor because he wasn't in the office at the time, and that was the information that the *Globe* printed. They'll want Vince Newsom to tell them how he got the information as well. And you're well and truly in the middle of that line of questioning.'

'Ah,' Laura said softly. 'You've no idea how dreadful I feel about all that. I lie awake at night thinking about it.'

'Will Vince tell them how he got his scoop, do you think?'

'I've no idea,' Laura said. 'He should protect his sources but he may not be at all bothered to protect me. On the other hand, he won't much want to admit that he nicked that piece of paper out of my handbag. All I'll tell your inquiry is that Val's note got lost, which is true. I won't go any further than that unless they already know more than that. Then I won't have much choice, will I?'

'Did you tell Michael everything that happened that night?'

Laura glanced away, avoiding Mower's eyes.

'No,' she said. 'There are things that I don't want him to know. Things that I still don't know are true or not.'

'Do you think Newsom will open that can of worms?' Mower persisted.

'And lay himself open to an accusation like that?' Laura whispered. 'I shouldn't think so, because if he raises the issue he knows exactly what I'll say.'

'If I were you…' Mower said hesitantly. 'If I were you, I'd have a chat with Vince Newsom and get clear just what you are both going to tell the inquiry. It could be in both your interests. And Michael's.'

Laura sipped her drink and looked away.

'I wish I'd never had to have anything to do with Vince Newsom again,' she said. 'How the hell did he come back to haunt me like this?'

'The inquiry's not out to get you – or Vince Newsom, for that matter,' Mower said uncomfortably. 'It's disciplinary and it's us they've got in their sights – Val Ridley, though she's clear of disciplinary action now she's resigned, and the chief investigating officers. Your newspaper friends haven't been slow to point the finger at a mishandled case, and that's what they'll be looking at: what, if anything, the DCI and the Super got wrong while they were in charge of the case.'

'And the security services? They hardly covered themselves in glory.'

'Maybe,' Mower said. 'But they have an uncanny habit of ducking out of sight and avoiding blame. Get it totally wrong and get promoted is more like it for them, on past experience. Justify a war on the basis of a load of half-truths and queue up here for your knighthood.'

Laura smiled faintly, though she felt sick inside.

'Without the job Michael would fall apart,' she whispered.

'I'm sure it won't come to that,' Mower said, putting his hand briefly on hers. 'But all you can do is get your own story straight. Talk to Newsom. I would. He must be bricking it as well. That was a dirty trick he pulled and he won't want it out in the light of day if he can avoid it. In the meantime, I'll talk to Val Ridley about what she's going to say to the inquiry. Her main gripe is with what the Super failed to do while the boss was on holiday. If I can persuade her that she might damage the DCI as well as Superintendent Longley she may think more carefully about what she says. But now she's out of the force she's got nothing to lose personally.' He shrugged. 'It could all go pear-shaped.'

Laura walked slowly back to the office feeling deeply depressed. Her own professional reputation wouldn't be much damaged by anything the police inquiry chose to dig up and perhaps publish, but Vince Newsom still represented an unexploded bomb that, if detonated, could destroy her relationship with Thackeray. And there was no doubt that the events that had led to his near-fatal shooting could seriously damage his career. It was no wonder that he was as tense and miserable as he was, she thought, and she felt in little better shape herself. She should have asked Kevin Mower just how long the inquiry process was likely to take, just how far away an end to the tension might be. If this thing dragged on, she thought, someone was only too likely to snap.

Back in the office she began to sort out her feature pages, which she had neglected that morning in favour of her new-found, and she reckoned, very short-lived enthusiasm for football. The work had piled up and she buried her own uncertainties in that, until at around four her phone rang and she was surprised to hear her grandmother's voice, filled with her usual cheerful resolution.

'Can you come up when you've finished work?' Joyce asked. 'I need to talk to you.'

'Yes, of course,' Laura said. 'Is there anything you want me to get you on the way?'

'Can you pick up some bread and some cans of soup? And some antiseptic cream and plasters?'

'Have you hurt yourself?' Laura jumped in, feeling a sudden anxiety. At her grandmother's age even minor injuries were a concern.

'They're not for me, love,' Joyce said and, to Laura's surprise, hung up.

Laura did her grandmother's shopping as soon as she left work and drove quickly through the thickening rush-hour traffic to The Heights, where the derelict block of flats that was still standing loomed darkly through the evening's mist and drizzle like an abandoned medieval castle surrounded by a wasteland of ruins. The lights were on in her grandmother's tiny house and the curtains were drawn tightly, but Joyce opened the door quickly when Laura tapped on the glass panel.

'Come in, love,' she said, and closed the door behind Laura so sharply that her anxiety immediately returned.

'Whatever's wrong?' she asked as she followed Joyce's bent and hobbling arthritic figure into the living room.

'I've got a visitor,' Joyce said, waving a hand towards her faded settee, where a small pale girl, little more than a child, lay stretched out, apparently asleep. Laura took in the thin figure in a skirt and a thick blue cardigan that she recognised as belonging to Joyce herself, the tangled dark hair against the cushion and the fragile blue skin that flickered slightly beneath her closed eyes. She looked at her grandmother in astonishment.

'Who is she?' she asked. 'Where on earth did she come from?'

Joyce drew Laura by the elbow into the kitchen, took the shopping from her and put the kettle on.

'I found her,' she said. 'Out the back in my outhouse. I thought for a moment she was dead but when I touched her she opened her eyes and I realised she was freezing cold and half starved. When I got her into the house she came round a bit and I gave her some sweet tea and some bread. She was ravenous. She's got a few scratches and bruises but apart from that she doesn't seem to be hurt so I didn't get an ambulance or anything. She says her name's Elena, but I don't know if she's telling the truth. What I do know is that she's terrified of something, but when I mention the police she was even more terrified. She tried to get out of the door, but she's not strong enough to get away, even from me, with my gammy knees. I managed to get her back inside and persuade her to stay for a bit. Then she fell asleep. I thought maybe you could get her to talk. I'm not right sure I can. You never know, there might be a story in it for you.'

'Phew,' Laura said, sipping the tea Joyce had handed her automatically. 'That's a tall order. Do you think she's English?'

'She's not said much but I don't think so. She seems to understand what I say but she's got an accent of some sort.'

'You'll have to tell the police, Nan,' Laura said. 'Whoever she is, she doesn't look as if she's even sixteen. She's a child. Someone somewhere will be looking for her.'

'Whoever it is who's looking for her, she's scared rigid of them,' Joyce said fiercely. 'We've got to find out a bit more about her before we make any decisions about what to do.' For many years Joyce Ackroyd had been a popular and effective town councillor in Bradfield, and this crisis, Laura thought wryly, had put the iron back into her soul.

A slight noise behind them made the two women turn and they found themselves facing the girl herself, standing behind them unsteadily, clutching the blue cardigan around her thin body and gazing at them with dark, frightened eyes. Laura took the girl's arm gently, appalled at how stick-like it felt inside the thick knitted sleeve.

'Come and sit down,' she said gently. 'No one is going to hurt you.'

The girl allowed herself to be steered back to her seat and collapsed into it with a low moan.

'Elena?' Laura said, perching on the edge of the sofa beside her. 'Is that your name?' The girl nodded silently, her eyes full of unshed tears, gazing at the world with a curiously dead expression as though she was surrounded by sights she could not bear to remember.

'You can speak English?' The girl nodded again.

'A little,' she said. 'I learn in school.'

'Where are you from, Elena?' Laura asked. 'Where is home? Where is school?'

The girl looked at her and shook her head, glancing towards the door as if wondering if she had the strength to run.

'We can help you,' Laura said. 'But you must tell us who you are.' The girl gazed at Laura and Joyce for a long time and then gave a sharp little nod, as if accepting that she could trust them, at least a little.

'One morning,' she said. 'I go school, like every day, like all days, yes?'

Laura nodded.

'Man...men...come when I walk on road. Men in car. I go in car with men.'

'Did you want to go with them?' Laura asked sharply. The girl looked at her blankly for a moment and then nodded again in understanding.

'No want,' she said, her voice rising. 'I no want. They take me.' She reached out both hands to Laura's arm and took hold of it, dragging her a little and then pushing her hard. 'They take me,' she said. Laura's mouth felt dry and she could hear her grandmother's sharp intake of breath behind her.

'And they took you to England?' she asked quietly. The girl nodded, a single tear creeping down her pale cheek now.

'To England, yes.'

'How long ago?' Laura asked. She glanced around her for

Joyce's calendar and showed it to Elena. 'One week,' she said, counting out seven days. 'One month? One year? How long?'

The girl studied the calendar for a moment and then turned the pages back, looking carefully at the name of each month.

'I think then,' she said, pointing to the picture of a spring scene which illustrated the entries for the month of May. 'Then, when snow go, flowers come.'

'Spring?' Laura said softly. 'Last spring.' It must have been eight or nine months ago since Elena had been dragged into a car on her way to school.

'What happened in England?' she asked. 'Why did they bring you here?'

'Men,' Elena whispered. 'Many, many men. Many, many, many men.'

'Oh God,' Laura said, understanding only too clearly what the girl meant and with that understanding a dam seemed to break within the girl's emaciated frame and she was suddenly wracked with sobs. Laura reached out and took her in her arms and felt her tears soak through her shirt.

'Oh God,' she said again. 'I'm so sorry, so sorry, Elena. I really am.'

CHAPTER EIGHT

Laura found the official letter in the postbox at the flat when she returned home from her grandmother's that evening. It invited her to present herself at County Police HQ the following week to give evidence in the inquiry into the events three months previously surrounding the deaths of members of the family of Gordon Christie. She put the letter down carefully on the table, as if it would explode if handled roughly, took off her coat and sat down heavily in a chair, which was where Michael Thackeray found her some fifteen minutes later, gazing at the silk flowers in the fireplace with a dazed look in her eyes.

'What is it?' he asked, and picked up the letter when she gestured in the direction of the sheet of paper lying on the table. He glanced at her pale face after he had read it and put a hand on her shoulder.

'You really don't need to worry about it,' he said quietly. 'You did nothing wrong. Just tell them exactly what happened.'

'I don't want to make it any worse for you than it already is,' she said. 'If they're going to hang you I don't want to be the one kicking away the chair.'

'Look, I know what I did,' Thackeray said. 'They know what

I did. It was impulsive, and officers of my rank aren't supposed to do impulsive things, let alone put themselves at risk of being shot. I chucked twenty years' training and experience out of the window in a crisis. As far as I'm concerned, it's just a case of dotting the Is and crossing the Ts, and taking whatever they throw at me afterwards. Nothing you say is going to make any difference, believe me.' He put as much confidence into his voice as he could, which was far more than he felt.

'You only did it because I was there,' Laura said. 'I feel responsible, and now you could lose your job.'

'I doubt it,' Thackeray came back quickly. 'What I did may have been stupid but it wasn't criminal or even particularly negligent. I didn't put anyone else at risk. Jack Longley's in far more trouble. I chanced my own life, he risked a child's. He came back from County this afternoon looking like death warmed up and shut himself in his office without saying anything to anyone. They want to talk to him again tomorrow. And I guess that once they hear what Val Ridley's got to say he could be for the high jump. But I wasn't involved in any of that. I wasn't even in the country.'

'What a mess, though,' Laura said.

'Have you thought any more about what you'll tell them about the story in the *Globe*?' Thackeray asked. 'I'm sure they'll ask you about that as well, given the chance. Vince Newsom's story didn't help.'

'I won't tell them any more than I have to,' Laura said. 'But I guess they'll work out exactly what happened from what Val and Vince tell them anyway. It wasn't my fault he got hold of that document but Val undoubtedly blames me. But like you, I did nothing wrong.' Her plea of innocence was more heartfelt than Thackeray could realise, and he merely nodded.

'You're right, it was a mess,' he said. 'And we'll have to live with the consequences.'

'Do you know when they want to talk to you?'

'Not yet. I think they'll be dealing with Longley and the much more serious failures first. They'll get round to my misdemeanours later.'

'I hate all this,' Laura said.

'It'll soon be over,' Thackeray said. 'So forget about it for now. I saw your football story on the front page of the *Gazette* this afternoon. How did that come about? I didn't think your sports editor was encouraging your new found interest.'

Laura smiled faintly.

'He's very definitely not, but Ted thought it was a good idea, and I need brownie points with him more than I do with Tony Holloway. But I think that's the end of me and Bradfield United. No one's thinking of sending me to London to cover the replay next week. That would definitely be a match too far.'

'Good,' Thackeray said. 'I'm not sure I fancy you being turned into a sports commentator. I wasn't much taken with the people we met at that party on Sunday. Young men and women with more money than sense, as far as I could see, and a gang of cynical vultures feeding off their talent.'

'That sounds a bit harsh,' Laura said. 'But maybe not a lot.' She recalled the weeping girlfriend tottering away from the celebration and wondered if she had forgiven her errant fiancé by now. 'How about you?' she asked. 'Have you identified your murder victim yet?'

Thackeray shook his head.

'No. No one admits to knowing who she is. The only new development is that we've found her shoes. Someone saw her chuck them away and run off barefoot. We thought they were at the bottom of the canal, unfortunately, and have wasted a lot of time looking for them there. That will have dented the budget.'

'Who was she running from?' Laura asked, intrigued.

'That we don't know.'

Laura thought of another girl who seemed to be running as well, but quickly pushed the recollection out of her mind. She had promised Joyce, against her better judgement, that she would tell no one about Elena's existence until the girl had regained some strength and explained more clearly what had happened to her.

'Do you think she might have been an illegal immigrant, this black girl?' she asked.

'It's possible,' Thackeray said. 'It has crossed our minds. In which case people might be reluctant to identify her in case they expose themselves.'

'They'd be deported?'

'In theory. Unless they could persuade the immigration authorities it was too dangerous for them to go home. We're going to have to get a bit tougher questioning the African community in Bradfield, I think. I feel sure this girl is African, even though no one admits to recognising her. Even your football hero, Okigbo, is worth a look. I get the distinct feeling that someone's covering something up.'

'If I didn't know you better I'd say you were being a tad racist,' Laura said.

'I didn't take to Okigbo's friend Emanuel Asida, but that's nothing to do with the colour of his skin.'

'There's a lot of people trafficking, isn't there? What happens to girls who are smuggled in for the sex trade?'

'They're here just as illegally as someone who came here of their own free will,' Thackeray said. 'They may be allowed to stay while they give evidence in a criminal prosecution, but after that they'll usually be sent back to wherever they came from. Why do you ask?'

'Oh, I was just reading something about a charity that helps girls like that,' Laura said. 'I thought I might write something about it.'

Thackeray seemed to lose interest and Laura saw him wince.

'Have you taken your painkillers?' she asked. He shook his head, his expression grim, and they both knew that it was more than paracetamol he needed to dull the pain he was feeling.

'It'll be all right,' Laura said with more confidence than she really felt, and he managed a faint smile.

'Maybe,' he said.

Laura went into the editorial meeting next morning with a thumping headache, fit only to go through the motions of planning the day's paper. She and Thackeray had spent a desultory evening watching television and she knew that his depression was unlikely to lift while the disciplinary inquiry hung over his head. She had called her grandmother on the way into work to be told that Joyce's unexpected visitor was still sleeping soundly.

'I gave her my bed and slept on the sofa,' Joyce said,

sounding as weary as Laura felt herself after a restless night.

'You can't go on doing that for long,' Laura said sharply. Joyce's arthritic knees would not be improved by such *ad hoc* sleeping arrangements. 'I'll come up at lunchtime and see if we can't find somewhere safe for her to go.'

'She's fine here for a while,' Joyce said. 'Let her be.' But Laura knew that the arrangement was not fine and determined to find some other refuge for Elena as soon as she could. Once she was in a place of safety, she thought, the legal implications of her situation could be safely explored.

In spite of her abstraction, her attention was suddenly grabbed by angry voices at the other end of the editorial table. She looked up to see Ted Grant's face flushed with rage and a determined scowl on the face of Tony Holloway, who appeared for once to be in a mood to defy the editor.

'If you thought there was funny business going on when they bought Okigbo, why the hell didn't we report it at the time?' Grant demanded.

'I couldn't prove it,' Tony said. 'And you'd be the first to complain if they'd slapped a libel writ on us. It was just a rumour. You know what sport's like these days. It's more about money than the lads on the field. It's one thing to be told that brown paper bags of cash are being passed around, something else to prove it. Although I reckon it's a bit more sophisticated than brown paper bags these days. Deposits in off-shore bank account's more like it.'

'It's your bloody job to prove it, any road,' Grant said. 'My God, in my day on the *Globe* you wouldn't have lasted five minutes. Use your imagination man, get off your backside and do a bit of investigating. If it was old Sam Heywood shelling out to get the Nigerian lad here, we can't libel him, can we? The beggar's dead and buried. Find out what he was up to.'

'It might not have been Sam,' Tony said, his face sulky now.

'So find out who it was, why don't you? And find out who's going to benefit if they sell Okigbo on. Follow the money, that's what they say, isn't it?'

'Are they really looking to sell OK?' Laura asked mildly. 'It seems very odd when they've suddenly started attracting crowds again. What sort of investment is that?'

Grant flicked a sharp glance at Laura before turning back to Tony.

'That's what you should be asking Jenna Heywood,' Ted snapped. 'There's a good story buried in the woodwork at that club and you seem to be doing bugger all to winkle it out. On your bike, lad. Dig a bit of dirt for a change.'

Laura watched Tony Holloway simmer in his seat for the rest of the meeting, which turned at that point to more routine matters, and she was not surprised when she felt him hovering over her when she got back to his desk.

'Well, thanks for that bit of solidarity in there,' Holloway said sarcastically. 'I'd be really grateful, you know, if you'd keep your nose out of my patch.'

'Fine,' Laura said. 'But it does all seem a bit odd, even to someone like me with a minimal interest in your beautiful game. If it was worth Sam Heywood shelling out illicit cash to get OK here, to help save the club presumably, why is someone now trying to sell him, which can only damage the club? It can't be the same person, can it? This time it must be someone trying to undermine Jenna.'

'Any fool can work that out,' Tony said sourly. 'The problem is finding out who's done what and why. Investigate, Ted says, but when the hell can I find the time to do any investigation. I work a ten-hour day as it is, six days a week in the football season. The trouble with Ted is that he still thinks he's got all the resources of a London tabloid to run this one-horse operation. It's bloody stupid.'

'Oh well, I'm sure someone else will annoy him before the day's out and take the heat off you. You'll have a big story anyway, won't you, if OK goes? The fans will be furious.'

'As if anyone cares about the fans,' Tony said, turning away with a scowl.

Laura logged off her computer at lunchtime, collected some sandwiches in the town centre, where she was surprised to see how quickly some of the local shops had decked their window displays with blue and gold United colours and supportive slogans for 'the Lads', and drove thoughtfully up the hill to The Heights to visit her grandmother again. Joyce opened the door to her looking anxious and Laura followed her into the living room where Elena was sitting on the sofa watching television with dull eyes that Laura guessed were seeing very little on the screen. She busied herself organising lunch for the three of them and then sat beside Elena, who began to sip listlessly at a mug of soup.

'Are you feeling better?' she asked the girl gently. But Elena merely shrugged.

'She won't try to talk,' Joyce said, sounding tired and slightly exasperated. 'I've got nothing out of her at all this morning.'

'Elena,' Laura said more firmly. 'You understand you can't stay here for long. My grandmother can't keep you here. Do you understand that.'

The girl shrugged again and a single tear slipped down her cheek.

'You've been kidnapped and abused,' Laura said firmly, hoping the girl's grasp of English would cope with that. 'We need to get you some help and find the men who did this to you. Then we'll find some way to get you home to your family.' Laura was still not sure how much Elena understood of what she was saying but she suddenly put down her mug and covered her face with her hands and began to sob convulsively.

'Elena,' Laura said, putting an arm round her shoulders. 'We're trying to help you. But you must talk to us. We can't keep you here. And you need help to get home.'

Elena shrugged Laura off and eventually the storm of tears burnt itself out and she turned frightened eyes to Joyce and then to Laura. She had evidently recognised the word home.

'Not go home,' she said. 'Never go home.'

'Your family must be frantic with worry,' Joyce said. 'Your mother and father will be desperate to know what happened to you. You must tell your mother and father where you are.'

'No,' Elena said, her voice dull. 'Father, mother not to know. They kill me.'

For a second Laura thought the girl was trying to make a joke and then she realised with a shudder that she was deadly serious. She met Elena's eyes and saw only despair in them.

'Brothers kill me,' Elena said flatly and Laura believed her. 'Me bad girl.'

'Then you must get help here,' she said. 'You must talk to the police.'

If anything Elena's agitation only increased at that suggestion.

'No talk,' she said. 'Man say girl run, girl talk to police, then mother be killed. Bad men everywhere, men here, men at home. Men know village, know where mother live. They find. And here, men everywhere. First I was in London. Then new man came. He bought me and brought me here.'

'Where do you come from?' Laura asked quietly, hardly believing that what the girl was saying was possible in Europe in the twenty-first century.

'Albania,' Elena said. 'And now I Albanian whore. That is what they tell me, men who bring me here. I am whore. Go back, my brothers kill me. Or men kill my mother.'

'Do you believe that?' Joyce asked sharply. Elena looked at her with contempt.

'Of course,' she said. 'It is the truth. They say no good run away. I stay with them and they look after me. I can never go home. But I run anyway. I not stay more with these men and other men who come all day and all night and the things they do. It too bad there. If I stay I die. I get sick now. So I choose die my way. When I climb to the top of there...' She nodded briefly at the block of flats where she had taken refuge. 'I go there to jump.'

Laura glanced at Joyce, feeling close to despair herself.

'Can you let Elena stay another night?' she said quietly. 'I'll do a bit of research, see if I can find somewhere safe for her to stay, some sort of women's shelter, maybe. We can't sort this out ourselves. We need some help. She needs somewhere safe, she needs a doctor, she probably needs a lawyer, and she should certainly talk to the police eventually to see if they can track these bastards down.'

Joyce nodded bleakly, her face full of pain, and Laura thought that nothing in her grandmother's experience could have prepared her for this.

'See what you can do, love,' Joyce said without hesitation. 'She'll be fine here for another night. I'll take care of her.'

Elena looked at the two women intently for a moment.

'Not go home,' she said, her voice pleading now. 'Never go home.'

Laura hugged her briefly.

'You'll be safe now,' she said, wondering desperately how she could possibly deliver on that promise.

And as her grandmother came to the door with her she put a hand on her arm.

'You realise what we're doing is probably illegal?' Laura said.

Joyce smiled grimly. 'Happen it is,' she said. 'But it looks like the lesser of two evils to me. See what you can sort out for the poor lass, pet, and then we'll think about the legal niceties. I'd not want a suicide on my conscience, nor would you, because that's how it'll end if we're not right careful. She's right at the end of her tether, you can tell that just looking at her.'

Laura nodded and closed the front door gently behind her. Once in the car she buried her face in her hands for a moment, overwhelmed by the anger she felt at what Elena had said. In her job, she thought, she should be used to witnessing the inhumanity some human beings were capable of, but the depravity of men who could kidnap children – and Elena was even now little more than a child – and transport them across continents to sell them into the sort of slavery the girl had suffered, filled her with impotent rage. Eventually she swallowed down her emotions and drove slowly back to the office where, still simmering, she began to trawl the Internet to discover what she could about the rights of women who had been trafficked into the country for sex.

What she discovered was not encouraging. Outside London there seemed to be little help available for girls and women in Elena's situation, and even in the capital sanctuary was hard to find. In the end she rang an organisation that offered a small number of beds for women who had escaped the clutches of traffickers, and explained Elena's situation to a sympathetic official. But cold comfort was about all that she could offer.

'There's no money for this sort of thing,' the woman said. 'We could fill our beds twenty times over. Does the girl have her passport?'

'From what she says, I doubt she ever had a passport,' Laura said. 'She was kidnapped on her way to school, for God's sake.'

'But she says she's from Albania? Which adds to the problem, of course, because it's not in the European Union, so her immigration status will be automatically deemed illegal. I think the first thing to do, if you can, is find an interpreter, so that she can tell you in more detail what happened. You're lucky she can speak English at all. Many can't. Some make a break for it not even knowing what country they're in. But in her case deportation is a real threat.'

'Yes, I know that, and I'm sure all this legal stuff is very important, but what I really need right now is to find her somewhere safe to stay. We can sort the rest out when she's had time to see a doctor and build up her strength a bit. You don't seem to understand – she's in a desperate state.'

'You say your grandmother can't keep her?'

'She's only got the one bedroom,' Laura said defensively, guessing what would come next.

'And you're not able to give her a bed yourself?'

Laura swallowed hard, thinking of Thackeray's likely reaction if she brought even an abused illegal immigrant back to their flat. That was a moral dilemma she did not dare present him with.

'No,' she said. 'That's not possible.'

'Hang on a minute,' the charity officer said. 'The churches are involved in this work as well. It's just possible I can find you someone in Yorkshire who could help.'

There was a silence broken only by the rustling of paperwork at the other end of the phone, before the woman spoke again.

'Try Father Aiden Moran at the Church of the Sacred Heart in Arnedale. Arnedale is near you, isn't it?' Laura froze for a second.

'Yes,' she said quietly. 'It's not very far. There's no one else nearer, in Bradfield itself?'

'I don't think this has been much of a problem in your area so far. That's the only contact I have.'

'Right,' Laura said. 'I'll talk to him and see whether he can help. Thanks.'

'Good luck,' the woman said. 'Get in touch if you need any

more advice, won't you? We'll do our best to help.'

She sat and stared at her phone for a long time. Why, she wondered, did it have to be someone at the Sacred Heart in Arnedale, where, as far as she knew, Frank Rafferty was still the parish priest, a man who was as close to Thackeray's father as anyone in this world and one whose discretion she could not trust and on whose loyalty she personally could certainly not rely.

'Damn and blast,' she muttered under her breath, aware that Tony Holloway was watching her curiously from across the newsroom. 'I think that's a no-go area. Somehow I'm going to have to crack this one myself.'

CHAPTER NINE

DCI Thackeray tapped on Superintendent Longley's office door early the next day. He knew the Super was booked for another session with the inquiry team at County HQ later in the morning, but wanted to catch him for a briefing on the murder case before he left Bradfield. Longley was already at his desk, in full uniform, looking as grim as Thackeray had expected he might.

'Sit down, Michael,' he said, his expression abstracted. 'Any developments overnight?'

Thackeray shook his head.

'I've just had a briefing with the murder team, for what it's worth, which isn't much. We've had very little response to the television pictures.' The artist's impression of the dead girl had been broadcast the previous evening on both of the local TV news programmes and the detectives on the end of the phone lines the previous evening had nursed hopes of a breakthrough, which had not materialised.

'One woman thought she knew her but when we showed her pictures of other black girls this morning she got completely confused. Turned out she thought it was a young woman who works in Marks and Spencers and who's safe and well at home in Eckersley.'

'And that's all?'

'That's all. We've found her shoes but no handbag, though it seems inconceivable that a girl dressed like that for a night on the town wouldn't have carried some sort of bag, however small. She'd need some money with her at the very least. To all intents and purposes she seems to have dropped into Bradfield from another planet.'

'Aye, well, let's not get too carried away,' Longley said drily. 'What about the forensics? Anything new there?'

'Nothing more from Amos Atherton yet. They're running various tests, including DNA. Somewhere, of course, there's a man who fathered her baby, but he'll remain as mysterious as the girl herself unless we get some positive ID.'

'So it's running into the sand?'

'We've several lines of inquiry I still want to pursue. I'm not convinced that no one in the minority community knows her, African, Caribbean, whatever. But it's not looking like an easy one to crack so far.'

'I'll have to leave it in your hands, Michael,' Longley said wearily. 'I'm tied up at County again today.'

'How's that going, sir?' Thackeray asked cautiously. It had taken a DCI with a troubled career history and a superintendent with very definite ideas about how he liked his division run a long time to come to terms with each other, Thackeray thought, but he would be unhappy now to see Longley leave the service prematurely because of a case in which no one had covered themselves in glory.

'How the hell should I know how it's going?' Longley said. 'They give very little away. And I've no idea what the bloody spooks have been saying, or Val Ridley, for that matter, if she's given evidence. I don't even know that. She's out of our control now she's resigned, any road. She could be putting the knife right between my shoulder blades right now for all I know.'

'You think they've seen her already?'

'How the hell would I know,' Longley snapped again. 'They tell you bugger all. Just go through a long list of questions. Why did I do this, why did I do that, what were my priorities, what was the budget, what was the staffing...?' He hesitated, his face flushed. 'After this little lot, I'm not even sure I want to carry on any longer, Michael, and that's the truth. I've had it up to here.' He drew an angry finger across his throat where the flesh bulged over his uniform collar and grimaced. 'Is it worth the aggro, I ask you?'

'I'm a bit worried they'll ask me about my trip to Ireland,' Thackeray said quietly, suddenly back in a windswept Atlantic seaside resort in winter where he had faced a man as unapologetically ruthless as he had ever met before. He shivered slightly and forced his attention back to Longley's totally unexpected response.

'What trip to Ireland?' Longley asked. 'You were on holiday, weren't you? Who knows where you went?'

'You haven't told them?'

'I knew nothing about your holiday plans, Michael. Nothing at all.'

'And the information I picked up there?'

'Information received,' Longley said. 'Anonymous information received.'

'Right,' Thackeray said with a faint smile. 'I'd better tell Laura that.'

'You do that and you'll be fine. There's no reason why both of us should suffer for that bloody case. A lot of the blame for what went wrong rests somewhere else entirely and I'll make bloody sure the inquiry knows that, don't you worry. If you and your young woman are careful about what you tell the beggars, you'll be fine.' Longley glanced at his watch. 'I'd best be off,' he said. 'I know they're looking for a bloody scapegoat so I suppose I'd better give them one. If I end up on the golf course a few years before I expected I don't suppose there'll be many tears shed.'

Thackeray watched Longley march down the corridor to the stairs at a brisk military pace before he made his own way back to the incident room next to the main CID office, his head whirling. He might not shed tears for Jack Longley, but he would certainly regret his going, he thought. His replacement as a boss could be much worse.

The incident room was almost deserted as most of the detectives had set about fulfilling the tasks they had been allocated at the briefing earlier, but Sergeant Kevin Mower was still at his desk, his head close to his computer screen and a slight frown on his face. He glanced up as Thackeray approached and gave a wry grin.

'I've got some info on "disappeared" asylum seekers from immigration but there's no one I've found yet who fits our victim's profile. If she's as young as we think she is, she may have come here as part of a family group, of course.'

'In which case why haven't her family reported her missing?'

'Because if they're illegals they'll be too frightened?' Mower said, his tone matter-of-fact.

'I suppose there's a whole constituency out there living without any contact with the law, however much they need it,' Thackeray said.

'That's about it, guv,' Mower said. 'You know that. There's a whole underground economy based on something very close to slavery. The only time it surfaces is when something goes catastrophically wrong, like with the Chinese cockle-pickers who drowned in Morecambe Bay. So maybe that's what we're dealing with here. And we may never find out who the victim is because no one who knows her will come anywhere near us.'

'We know someone knows her,' Thackeray said. 'Not least the girl Karen Wilson saw her with before she died. Has nothing turned up on the CCTV tapes from the town centre? There's a good chance they'll have picked up the two of them somewhere.'

'Do you know how many hours' worth of CCTV there is to look at for one evening, guv?' Mower asked mildly. 'We've got two people still ploughing through it.'

'Good,' Thackeray said. He glanced round the office but its only other occupants both had telephones glued to their ears. He dropped his voice all the same.

'D'you know where Val Ridley is, Kevin?' he asked.

'I've got her mobile number,' Mower said with obvious reluctance. 'Do you want to talk to her?' Thackeray shook his head.

'I just wondered if she'd been to County to talk to the inquiry yet. It wouldn't do for me to contact her, but maybe you could find out?' Mower nodded imperceptibly.

'I'll see what I can do, guv,' he said. 'Strictly off the record.'

When Thackeray had gone back to his own office, Mower

went downstairs and out of the building and stood on a windy corner of the town hall square watching the passers-by blindly for a moment before he pulled out his mobile. For a long time he thought he was going to be switched to voicemail for the fourth time, but eventually Val Ridley's familiar voice responded, though the tone was not particularly friendly.

'Why are you hassling me like this, Kevin?' she asked. 'I got your messages but what I do or don't do is really nothing to do with you any more.'

'Look, I know how angry you are about what happened, Val, but I just want you to think about who you're going to damage in all this,' Mower said.

'I know exactly who you're trying to protect, Kevin,' Val said sharply. 'But I'm not sure he deserves all this heart on the sleeve loyalty. And I'm bloody sure his girlfriend doesn't.'

'I think she was taken for a ride in a particularly nasty way,' Mower said carefully. 'Listen, Val, please. You have a point about the child. That was unforgivable. But the rest was more cock-up than conspiracy, believe me. I just want to be sure you don't take the innocent down with the guilty on this crusade of yours, that's all.'

'Right,' Val said, though Mower could detect no conviction in her voice.

'Are you in Bradfield? Can we get together for a drink?'

'No and no,' Val said. 'They don't want to see me until next week, as it goes, so for the moment I'm staying well out of the way.'

'Let me buy you a meal when you get back?'

'Leave it, Kevin,' Val said sharply. 'This is something I have to work out for myself.'

'Fine,' Mower said. 'But remember what I've said, won't you. Please?' But she rang off without offering any reply to that and Mower stood for a moment, letting the wind swirl around him, before switching his own phone off and giving a shrug. He had tried, he thought, and he could not think of anything more he could do.

Laura put her phone down and glanced at her watch. It was four-thirty and the newsroom was beginning to fall silent as reporters packed up after a day that had begun for most of them at eight. Her chances of finding what she was looking for were becoming slimmer, she thought. Academics, on the whole, did not seem to work late into the afternoon. She had spent the last half-hour calling around the language departments of all the local universities and colleges on the off-chance of discovering someone who could speak Albanian, so far without success. All this, she thought wryly, to avoid asking the one person who could probably supply the answer to her problem off the top of his head: the priest in Arnedale.

But by now she was getting to the bottom of her list of possible language departments, and her prospects of success seemed to be dwindling. She had been kept on hold by the department at one of the Leeds universities for several minutes now and was on the point of hanging up when someone she had not heard before came on the line. The voice was male and gruff, with a local accent, but when he offered a name it was certainly not a native one.

'You want someone who can speak Albanian?' the stranger asked.

'I do,' Laura said, glancing around the now almost deserted office to make sure she was not being overheard. 'I've met a young Albanian girl who speaks almost no English and I need someone to translate for her. Is that something you could do?'

'My name is Ibramovic. I'm Bosnian myself, speak Serbo-Croat. But I did have a lot of contact with the Albanian speakers in Kosovo years ago before I came over here, before all the trouble, when Yugoslavia was still Yugoslavia. I'm a bit rusty, but I could probably help. What's it all about?'

'Well, that's what I'm trying to find out,' Laura said evasively. 'She has problems but she speaks so little English we can't really work out what they are. Could I bring her over to see you, do you think?'

'I don't see why not,' the voice said. 'When exactly?'

'I've got a day off tomorrow,' Laura said. 'Could you fit us in tomorrow morning some time?' There was a rustle of papers at the other end of the phone.

'About eleven? Do you know your way?' Ibramovic asked. The appointment made, Laura cleared her desk and was pulling on her jacket when her phone rang again.

'Laura? It's Jenna, Jenna Heywood. I hoped I'd catch you. I wondered if you fancied a drink after work?'

Laura hesitated, surprised by the invitation.

'I was going to see my grandmother before I went home...'

'I won't keep you long,' Jenna said, and Laura thought she heard a slight break in her usually confident voice. 'I'm at my new flat, right in town. If you just popped in on your way I'd be really grateful for your advice.'

'I'll be there in ten minutes,' Laura said, taking down the address of an apartment in one of the newly converted warehouses close to the canal. This, she thought, was too good an opportunity to miss, although she knew how furious another interview with Jenna would make Tony Holloway. Ten minutes later she had parked her car outside The Woolcomber building, the name and the towering stone walls by now the only reminder of its industrial past, and took the lift from the marble foyer to the top floor where Jenna was waiting for her at the door of one of the two penthouse apartments.

'This is very nice,' Laura said as she glanced around the stylish open-plan living room with its tall windows giving a vast view across the town, where lights were just beginning to flicker into life like scattered jewels, and a glimpse beyond of the dark, looming Pennine hills silhouetted against a stormy western sky.

'I'm only renting it,' Jenna said. 'I couldn't stand living with my mother again after all this time. But I'm not sure about putting down roots here again just yet.'

'You're very cautious,' Laura said.

'I had...have a life in London,' Jenna said. 'I'm not convinced yet I've got one here.' She half-turned towards the well-stocked drinks cabinet as if to hide her expression. 'What will you have?' she asked.

'A vodka and tonic, please,' Laura said. 'Light on the vodka, I'm driving.'

Drinks in hand, Jenna waved Laura into a seat close to the window, and sat herself in silence for a moment sipping her own drink and gazing out at the quickly falling dusk outside.

'I'm not at all certain I should be talking to you,' she said eventually. 'But to be perfectly honest I don't know anyone else up here I could talk to. Can I trust you to keep what I say strictly off the record? For the moment, anyway? I promise that when there's something to print you'll be the first to know.'

'That sounds reasonable,' Laura said. 'Though it won't please Tony Holloway.'

'I don't trust Tony Holloway,' Jenna said with some asperity. 'I think he's in the pocket of the old guard at United.'

'I wouldn't be surprised,' Laura said. 'He's been reporting on United for so long he lives and breathes the club just as much as the directors do. It's something that happens to sports reporters, isn't it? They lose their critical faculties where the local team's concerned.'

'Yes, well, when the local team's split into two factions, then that makes it impossible for them to do their job. Judging by how little you know about football, you're not in a position to take sides.'

'Thanks for that vote of confidence,' Laura said with a grin. 'I thought I'd done a reasonable job at concealing my ignorance.'

'Hardly,' Jenna said, without rancour. 'Anyway, that's all by the way. It's not what's going on *on* the pitch that's bothering me. It's what's happening behind the scenes. I was quite prepared for a fight when I came up here to take my dad's place, but not for this sort of nastiness.' She reached into her designer handbag and took out a sheet of paper, which she passed to Laura.

'Everyone gets furious letters from the fans in the so-called beautiful game,' Jenna said. 'It seems to generate more emotion than I could ever have imagined. But this is something else.'

Laura unfolded the single sheet of lined paper to discover a couple of sentences composed from words carefully cut from newsprint, very likely, she thought, as she took in the type-faces, cut from the *Gazette* itself. The message was short and succinct.

'STOP, bitch. Leave UNITED. We do not want YOU. Go BACK TO London. If YOU don't you will BE Sorry. We are not JOKING.'

'Surely this is just some overwrought fan taking it out on you because you're a woman, isn't it?' Laura said.

'I'd like to think so,' Jenna said quietly. 'But there's more.' She walked across to the kitchen and opened the fridge from which she took a small plastic box. She opened the lid and then the brown paper packet, encased in an extra layer of cling-film, which lay inside. 'It's not pleasant,' she said, opening the parcel very carefully to reveal what Laura identified by smell alone as a small but pungent turd. Jenna shrugged and wrapped her exhibit up again quickly and closed the box tightly. 'It arrived in the post yesterday,' she said. 'Someone must really hate me. But whoever it is sent it here. They knew I'd just moved.' She pulled a disgusted face and replaced the packet in her fridge.

'I'm keeping it as evidence, in case it's needed,' she said, and Laura marvelled at her composure.

'You should go to the police,' she said.

'Not yet,' Jenna came back quickly. 'That's why I wanted to talk to you. You know this town. You said you knew Les Hardcastle personally. I just wanted to pick your brains, just to find out who or what I'm up against before I make a move myself. I've been in some tough business battles myself over the years, but nothing like this, never with anyone who would get into these sorts of dirty tricks. It's unbelievable.'

'It's harassment. It's illegal,' Laura said.

'I won't be bullied,' Jenna said. 'What they're forgetting is that I'm my father's daughter, in that respect at least. The more they push, the more I'll resist.'

'What makes you think Les Hardcastle is behind it?'

'Les is the one who's putting up most opposition to my plan to build a new stadium out of town.'

'Can he stop you if you're the majority shareholder?'

'Unfortunately he can,' Jenna said. 'My lawyers tell me there's a covenant on that site and that it can only be sold for redevelopment with the approval of a two-thirds majority of the shareholders. I haven't got that majority.'

'Can you get it?' Laura asked, thinking of her father's holding, which he seemed willing enough to sell if the price was right.

'From what I've been able to discover Les has more than a third of the shares sewn up between himself and his mates.'

'So it's a stalemate? You can't move without help, but nor can he.'

'Which may be why someone is making a pretty strenuous effort to persuade me to give up on United and pack my bags completely. They must reckon if I can't make a difference here I'll sell my shares and let the old guard get on with whatever they want to get on with. Which as far as I can see is to get the club closed down so they can sell the assets and run.'

'And that would explain the rumours about a transfer for Okigbo? The last thing they want is a star player who might bring the crowds back and turn the club back into a going concern?'

'I've heard the rumours and they're nonsense. I told Tony Holloway that, but I haven't seen anything in the *Gazette* yet. The last thing I want to do when we're in the middle of a Cup run is sell OK Okigbo. Though I must say, Minelli is as ambivalent about it as usual. I don't understand that man.'

'How did OK get here in the first place,' Laura asked. 'He seems an unlikely recruit for a team like Bradfield United.'

'He was,' Jenna said. 'My father said he and another Nigerian turned up at the club one day asking to see him. OK had been playing for some obscure country team in Nigeria and no one had ever heard of him, apparently. Dad gave him a trial and took him on. Then an agent turned up, of course, and demanded more cash, but by then OK had started scoring goals and the fans loved him, so Dad had to pay up and look as if he was enjoying it. But it cost him. It's still costing us. But like Dad I reckon it's worth it, at least in the short term. We'll get our investment back when he moves on, which eventually he will, of course.'

'What does Paolo Minelli think about all this? How much say does the manager have?' Laura asked.

'What did you think of Minelli when you met him,' Jenna asked. Laura smiled.

'I thought he was a slimy creep but that doesn't mean he isn't a good manager. I've no way of judging that.'

'He's OK as a manager, I suppose,' Jenna said. 'But I find his attitude to OK a bit surprising. You'd think he'd be only too delighted to have a player like that in the team, but all he seems to do at the moment is find fault most of the time.'

'Do you think he's a racist?'

'I don't think so. I don't think officials with that sort of prejudice can last long in football these days. It's an international game and they have to get on with people on that basis. Players are coming in from all over the world.'

'Maybe it's just personal then?' Laura suggested.

'Or maybe Minelli lost out because my father recruited Okigbo, and there was no cut in it back then for the manager,' Jenna said. 'I think that's the most likely explanation and the reason he wants rid of him now. He wants OK in the short term to win a few games for him and then fancies a cut of the second transfer fee because he lost out on the first.'

'Is this game completely corrupt?' Laura asked, thinking that Tony Holloway had hinted as much.

'Maybe not completely,' Jenna said. 'But I'm beginning to learn just how polluted it can be.' She glanced at the fridge for a second. 'I won't give in, you know. I won't be bullied by these bastards. My father and I weren't close after I went to London, but he was a man I respected. I'll stick with United for his sake. I won't let his successors carve it up for their own profit. No way.'

Laura was feeling weary by the time she pulled up outside her grandmother's house, and nothing Joyce told her made her feel much better. Elena was asleep in Joyce's bed, where, her grandmother told her, she had spent much of the day.

'She's still not eating properly,' Joyce said. 'Whenever she wakes up she keeps peering out of the window looking for someone, but she won't even try to tell me who.'

'We need to get her away from here,' Laura said. 'I called this rescue service they've got in London again today, but even if we could get her there they say all their beds are full. As far as I can see they always are. And it's the only charity in the country that has beds and is approved by the police and all the other authorities. Everywhere else it's left pretty much to the police to treat the problem as they like. Some are sympathetic to the victims, some less so. It's a bit of a lottery.'

'Have you talked to your man about it?' Joyce asked.

'Not yet,' Laura said. 'But I'm going to have to. We can't go on like this. It's probably illegal, what we're doing, and it's not actually doing Elena any good. She needs help, medical help, legal help, whatever.'

'She'll run again,' Joyce said grimly. 'You haven't seen the look in her eyes when she sees someone across the road, or coming towards the house. She's petrified. Last time someone knocked on the front door she tried to run out the back. Fortunately I'd turned the key in the lock. It was only one of my neighbours bringing me a letter that had gone to the wrong house.'

'Someone will see her here sooner or later and wonder who she is,' Laura said. 'She can't stay here, but I've no idea where she can go. Let's see what we learn tomorrow with this interpreter and think about it then. We may get some answers.'

'And we may not,' Joyce said.

CHAPTER TEN

Itzak Ibramovic was a huge grizzled man who seemed to fill his small office with barely restrained energy when Laura arrived at the university the next morning with Elena clinging defensively to her arm. The girl seemed to flinch as she took in the lecturer's bulk and she moved sharply away from him as he bustled about organising two chairs for his visitors in a space barely large enough for his own desk and chair and the piles of books and papers that tottered on every flat surface. When they were settled he reached up to a shelf behind him and pulled down a brimming coffee pot, which he waved in the women's direction.

'Thank you,' Laura said for them both, thinking, as he took his time fussing with mugs and offering sugar and milk before loading his own cup with four heaped teaspoonfuls, that any chance for Elena to draw breath and maybe relax would be a good thing. But as Laura took an experimental sip of the intensely strong brew, Elena merely gazed at the mug she had accepted, and avoided the big man's eyes.

Ibramovic looked at his visitors with undisguised curiosity.

'It's a bit unusual, this,' he said. 'Is your young friend here legally?'

'I doubt it,' Laura said. 'But that's the problem. Her English is so limited that we can't find out who she is, or where she comes from or what to do to help her. My grandmother found her half frozen in her back garden and, I guess, saved her life by taking her in.'

'But you think she's Albanian?'

'She says so,' Laura said, glancing at Elena doubtfully. The girl was shivering, her fragile hands wrapped around the coffee mug for comfort.

Ibramovic turned his brown eyes to the girl and spoke to her surprisingly gently in a language Laura could get not the slightest aural grip on and, in spite of her nervousness, it was obvious that Elena understood some of what he was saying. For the first time since she had met her, Laura saw a spark of light in her eyes.

Ibramovic went on for some time, with the girl occasionally giving the slightest of nods and murmurs in response to what were obviously questions, and the lecturer making an occasional note on a pad in front of him. As the conversation went on his face darkened although his voice never wavered from the low patient tone he had adopted from the first. Eventually, as tears began to roll down Elena's cheeks, he stopped and placed his hands flat on the desk with a heavy sigh.

'It's as you suspected,' he said. Laura glanced at Elena and put an encouraging arm round her shoulders.

'Tell me,' she said.

'She comes from a remote village in the mountains near Korce close to the border with Greece. Unusually she comes from a Christian, not a Muslim family, though she won't tell me her family name. She says she can't go back because of the shame she will bring. And it's true. It is not just the Muslims who guard their daughter's honour in that region.'

'And she was kidnapped?' Laura said, her mouth dry.

'On the way to school. After that she never knew where she was, except that she travelled long distances, usually in the back of a lorry with other girls.' Ibramovic hesitated, his expression darkening. 'They were cold and hungry and terrified, she said. Men who spoke Albanian kept her for what seemed like a very long time as they travelled. They raped her, of course. Many times, she says. They raped all the girls.' For the first time, Ibramovic's voice faltered and he took a shuddering breath before he felt able to continue.

'Until they learnt to do as they were told. And if they didn't rape them they beat them into submission. They were made to work in a bar for a time, as prostitutes. She thinks that was in Serbia. Then she thinks the girls were sold on because more men took over. Different men, different languages, but still they had no idea where they were taken. And eventually she realised she was in England because she knew enough English to recognise a few words she had leant at school. But she still kept being moved on, until eventually she managed to escape. And she hid in some flats and then at your grandmother's house.'

Elena was listening to Ibramovic with rapt attention and she suddenly grabbed Laura's arm.

'Thank you,' she whispered. 'Thank you, thank you.'

Ibramovic stood up suddenly and turned to the window where he stood for a long moment looking at the misty city below. Eventually he shrugged and turned back to Laura.

'I'm sorry,' he said, his face strained. 'I have a daughter her age.' He shrugged helplessly and sat down again and lit a cigarette.

'Ask her if she knows where she was being held,' Laura said quietly. 'She must have been in Bradfield somewhere. It seems unbelievable but where else could she have been kept if she ran away on foot? And ask her if she can remember anything about the men. Names, descriptions, anything. Someone's got to find these bastards and lock them up for a very long time.'

But even Laura could tell from Elena's stumbling answer that she had little idea where she had been held, or who her captors were. Ibramovic shrugged again and ground out his cigarette angrily in an ashtray full of half-smoked stub-ends.

'She says it was an old house. They were locked in and the windows were boarded over so they couldn't see out. They stayed there most of the time, three or four to a room, until they were called for. Some girls were taken to another place where men came all day and all night.'

'Many many men,' Elena whispered, obviously half following what Ibramovic was saying. She carried on urgently in Albanian and Laura waited impatiently for the translation.

'Sometimes some of the girls, the younger prettier ones, she says, were given special treatment. They were cleaned up and given pretty clothes and taken to meet men somewhere else, a smarter place, and they stayed with them longer, were given food and drink and sometimes presents – though the men took those away later – but always they had to sleep with the men they visited. It was just a bit, what would you call it, a bit more up-market?'

'A sort of call-girl system?'

'Something like that.'

'Could she identify any of the men involved? Could she describe them?' Laura whispered, but when Elena heard the question she flashed a glance at Laura that was more desperate than ever and then shook her head before launching into a another long response.

'There were different men all the time at the house,' Ibramovic said. 'Big men who didn't hesitate to use their fists or worse if the girls stepped out of line. But she only saw the boss once. When she went out for the last time he went with her and some other girls in a car driven by one of the guards. She doesn't think she could recognise him again. She's not sure, but she knows he was the boss because of the way he gave orders, and she thinks that she had heard his voice once or twice at the house and at the brothel they were taken to. She might recognise his voice, she says.'

'So how did she get away?'

Elena obviously understood the question because she glanced at Laura fiercely.

'I run,' she said. 'My man sleep in bed and I go down. Out door. And I run and run. And hide. High up, I hide. Man come, I jump, I think.' She lapsed into rapid Albanian then and Ibramovic translated slowly, his face sombre.

'She was dressed up that night and taken to meet a man she had slept with before. She recognised him. But she stayed awake when he went to sleep and made her escape down the back stairs of wherever it was they were staying. She only had flimsy clothes and no coat but she found herself in a town centre, bright lights, busy roads so she tried to get away to somewhere where she would be less noticeable. She spent the rest of the night hiding in some undergrowth and then the next day found her way to the flats that are being pulled down and stayed there a couple of nights. But she was very cold and hungry and eventually got frightened by some young men and found her way to your grandmother's house. She found her there and took her in? Is that right?'

'That's right,' Laura said. 'I think she probably saved her life.'

'The police?' Ibramovic asked quietly. But the word made Elena grab Laura's arm in a frantic grip.

'No police,' she said.

'She's afraid of being sent home,' Laura said. 'She thinks her family will kill her. Is that possible in this day and age?'

Ibramovic's face darkened.

'It's possible,' he said. 'I got out of Yugoslavia because I had the wrong sort of politics at the time. I've never been tempted to go back because there are different sorts of fanaticism at work there now. And Albania is even worse, especially in the country districts where Elena comes from. In a remote district she was lucky to be going to school at all. Many girls are kept at home; Muslim, Christian, it makes no difference. Family honour is everything. A woman who is raped is blamed for it. They might not kill her but they certainly wouldn't want her back. She'll be unmarriageable now.'

Laura drew a sharp breath and put her arm round Elena.

'We'll keep you safe,' she said, although she had absolutely no idea how she was going to achieve that objective. Just then her mobile rang and she was surprised to hear Joyce's voice at the other end, a voice which, even with a poor connection, was filled with distress.

'What is it, Nan?' Laura asked quietly.

'There's men searching the estate,' Joyce said. 'I watched them from the window. They went all round what's left of the flats, and then started banging on doors where people are still living. They got to me eventually and said they were from immigration. I asked them for some identification. You know they're always on about people not letting anyone in without identification?'

'Did you let them in?' Laura asked, filled with anxiety.

'No, I didn't,' Joyce snapped. 'I may be a bit decrepit but I'm not a complete fool, you know. Anyway, they flashed some sort of card at me, so quick I couldn't read it, and then they showed me this picture and it was her, our lass. They said she was an illegal asylum seeker and if I saw her anywhere I was to ring a number. They gave me a number.'

'An office number?' Laura asked.

'No, a mobile, which made me even more suspicious. She's not been telling us a pack of lies, though, has she? I'd not like to believe that.'

'No, she's not been telling us lies,' Laura said quietly, glancing at Ibramovic as if for confirmation, although he could only hear half the conversation. 'Write down what these men looked like, Nan, in case we need to describe them.'

'It's not safe to bring her back here,' Joyce said, her voice sounding desperate now. 'You only have to say the words "asylum seeker" and half the folk round here start spitting blood. I don't know what happened to the brotherhood of man, I really don't. If anyone sees her they'll fall over themselves to tell – what is it they say these days? – grass her up?'

'I'll sort it out, Nan,' Laura said, although she felt a lead weight settling on her shoulders as she wondered how she could fulfil that promise. 'I'll call you later.' She broke the connection and turned back to Ibramovic.

'Trouble?' the lecturer asked.

'Someone's looking for her and it's not the police,' Laura said. 'When you think how much she knows it's not surprising, is it? I don't think it's safe to take her back to my grandmother's house.' Elena herself was looking at the two of them in increasing agitation, obviously half understanding what was going on.

'And you can't keep her with you?'

'No, my partner's...' she hesitated, not wanting to scare Elena any more than she had to. 'Let's say he's in law enforcement,' she said with a faint smile. 'I can't involve him.'

Ibramovic nodded slowly.

'She can come home with me,' he said. 'We live in Ilkley, well out of the way of your Bradfield thugs. My wife, myself and my daughter. We can look after her for a little while to give you time to find something more permanent. I thought there were charities that deal with this sort of problem?'

'There are, but they seem to be mostly in London, and they've no beds free anyway. I've tried.'

'So it's settled then,' Ibramovic said. He glanced at his watch. 'I have one class to give now. Beginners Russian. I never thought when I had to study Russian as a schoolboy and resented it so much that it would enable me to make a living in another country. Nobody wants to learn Serbo-Croat, as you can imagine. Can you wait here and I'll talk to my wife and take you home.'

'You're sure she won't mind?'

'We were both refugees in this country in more generous times,' he said. 'Why would we mind?'

Laura drove back to Bradfield thoughtfully and alone. She had followed Itzak Ibramovic's car slowly through the afternoon traffic, heading north out of Leeds, with Elena sitting at her side, her hands clenched anxiously on her lap. Before the main road along the river Wharfe reached Ilkley's busy town centre, Ibramovic turned off into a quiet suburban avenue in the shadow of the steep hill leading up to the famous moor and pulled up on the drive of a stone semi-detached house, locked his car and unlocked the front door. Laura and Elena followed uncertainly, only to be met in the narrow hallway by a fair-haired middle-aged woman with a welcoming smile.

'This is Elena,' Laura said, drawing the girl forward. 'It's very good of you...'

'Is not a problem,' Ibramovic's wife said warmly. 'We will look after her. Has Itzak explained what's happening to her? I don't speak Albanian myself.' She took Elena's arm and drew her into the sitting room and sat her down in an armchair.

'I am Lilijana,' she said. 'I am from Belgrade. And you are very welcome in my house.'

Laura had stayed long enough to be plied with tea and cakes and watch as Elena visibly relaxed in the warm glow of Lilijana's care and Ibramovic's translation. She left feeling reassured that the girl would be well looked after, although she knew with a sick certainty that the haven she had found her could only be temporary. The couple did not seem at all concerned about the legal implications of what they were doing, but Laura knew that Elena's situation would have to be regularised, sooner rather than later, and that would involve more stress and trauma for the girl. The immediate future might look better, but long term it could probably only get much worse.

She sat at traffic lights waiting to take the turn off the main Leeds road towards Bradfield wondering what to do with the rest of her day off. She glanced across the valley towards her home town, dominated by the massive bulk of Earnshaw's mill, now being redeveloped as luxury apartments, and wondered just where the 'massage parlour' that Elena said she had been forced to work in was situated amongst that grey expanse of narrow Victorian streets and more modern estates. You could hide a dozen illegal operations inside Earnshaw's, she thought, or even in the still standing remnants of The Heights on the hills beyond. But it was much more likely to be concealed behind some relatively harmless shop-front close to the city centre.

And then there were the more up-market assignations Elena had described, when she and other girls had been dressed up by a woman who had supervised their toilet before putting them in a car with a couple of minders who had taken them to what the girl guessed was a hotel, with carpeted corridors and big rooms with huge TVs and beds larger and softer than she had even dreamt could possibly exist. The men there had been younger, she had said, young and good-looking enough to have wives and girlfriends, she thought, but still not averse to forcing themselves on the girls they paid for, sometimes alone, and sometimes three or four of them at a time, wallowing in sex until they and she were exhausted, and they would send for her minder to take her away again, back to the prison house where all she could do was curl into a wretched ball and try to sleep and forget until someone decided to use and abuse her again.

Feeling sick and almost frantic with outrage, Laura went home and phoned Joyce to make sure she was safe.

'They seem to have given up, the so-called immigration men,' Joyce said.

'Did you make a note of what they looked like? We'll end up telling someone official about all this. We'll have to. And it'll be best if we don't forget anything.'

'She's going to need a lawyer, that lass,' Joyce said.

'Yes, she is. I'll keep on pestering the charity in London to see what they can do to help. In the meantime she's safe where she is, and she can get her strength back before she has to face any more questions.'

'Your policeman won't be best pleased if he finds out what you're doing,' Joyce said. As a long-time enthusiast for demos and picket-lines in her younger days, Joyce had always been ambivalent about Laura's relationship with Thackeray.

'I know,' Laura said. 'But I can't bear the thought of her being arrested and flung into some awful immigration detention place. Not after what she's been through. If there's no official way of giving her some time and space we'll have to do it the unofficial way.'

'You're a good lass,' Joyce said.

But Laura knew she was skating on very thin ice, and she

sat for a moment wondering if she could talk Ted Grant into allowing her to spend some time investigating prostitution in Bradfield, on the off-chance that she could find out more about who might be exploiting girls like Elena. But before she could give any more thought to her next move, the phone rang and she was surprised to hear her father at the other end, with a querulous note in his voice.

'I'm in a right quandary here,' he said peremptorily. 'I thought you'd keep me in touch with what's going on at United.'

'I'm not sure what *is* going on at United,' Laura said. 'Though since we last spoke I have talked to Jenna Heywood and I know someone's trying pretty hard to get rid of her. And they don't seem to be too fussy about the methods they use either.'

'Well, what's all this about selling their best player, the black lad, what's his name?' Jack Ackroyd insisted.

'Okigbo. Where did you hear about that?' Laura asked, surprised.

'There was a little snippet in the *Mail* this morning, round-up of the bottom divisions, sort of thing. We get it a day late down here, so it's not today's news. Surely your sports people know about it.'

'I've had a day off today and haven't seen this afternoon's paper,' Laura said, glancing at the copy of the *Gazette* she had bought on the way home and flicking over to the back page where, sure enough, Tony Holloway had indulged in three columns of speculation about the future of United's star player.

'Jenna Heywood will be furious,' Laura said. 'She certainly doesn't want to lose him.'

'I tried to speak to Les Hardcastle on the phone but he's very elusive. I wanted to know what he'd give me for my shares.'

'If you want the club to survive I wouldn't sell them to Les,' Laura said. 'But Jenna might buy them. She needs a two thirds majority to get her rescue plan off the ground and she's not got it yet. You could do a crafty deal there.' She smiled to herself, knowing that crafty deals were what her father still enjoyed best.

'Oh aye?' Jack Ackroyd said. 'She'll be paying over the odds then, will she?'

'So will Les Hardcastle and his cronies, I expect,' Laura said. 'They want to get hold of more than a third so they can stymie Jenna's plans.'

'An auction then?' Jack said and Laura could imagine the gleam in his eyes.

'Something like that,' she said.

'Well, I'll tell you what you can do for me, love. Try and contact Les for me, would you? It's costing me a fortune from here. Ask him to ring me. I want a quiet word. And try to find out from your sports editor just what's going on with this black lad and the manager, what's his name? He's an Eytie, isn't he? Does he want him to go, or is it all going on over his head? I need a bit of background on this one, pet. Can you do that for me?'

Laura smiled to herself.

'You're an old rogue, Dad,' she said.

'Aye, well, to tell you the truth it gets a bit bloody boring out here, just your mum and me and the golf course. There's not much excitement. She sends her love, by the way, and wants to know when you're coming out.'

'Before Christmas, maybe,' Laura said, thinking that a break might be what she and Thackeray needed to sort themselves out. 'I'll see if I can catch up with Hardcastle for you, but I don't reckon he'll tell me much. The last thing I did was a fairly sympathetic interview with Jenna Heywood, so I reckon that will put me firmly in her camp as far as the old guard are concerned.'

'Aye, well, see what you can do.' And Jack rang off abruptly, no doubt after calculating the cost of his call, Laura thought wryly. Her father had made a fortune by counting the pennies and she did not reckon that he was going to stop now. And he would undoubtedly sell his shares to the highest bidder with not a shred of sentimentality, even if it meant the closure of the football club he had once professed to support. In many ways Jack was more in tune with twenty-first century Britain than she was herself, and in a totally different world from his mother, who would still storm a few barricades in pursuit of what she believed was right if only her arthritic knees would let her.

Thackeray came home soon after seven, more appreciative than usual of the meal Laura had cooked and apparently more relaxed.

'A good day?' Laura asked.

'Better than some recently,' he said. 'We've had a bit of a breakthrough in this murder case at last. We've got some CCTV footage of the dead girl in the town centre the night she was killed, which gives us a better estimate of the time of death. The only witness who saw her was pretty vague about the time, but she was filmed at half past midnight alive and well in Kirkgate, hurrying in the direction of the canal. It also gives us a much better description of the second girl. We'll be able to circulate the footage and maybe find out who she was.'

'The second girl?' Laura asked.

'Of course, you weren't at work today. We've already released it to the Press. The dead girl had someone with her, a white girl, quite young, not wearing a coat though it was a chilly night. We've put out an appeal for her to come forward. It'll be in the *Gazette* somewhere tomorrow.'

Laura suddenly felt very cold. There could be little doubt, she thought, that the second girl must be Elena, although she had carefully avoided mentioning that she had not been alone when she ran away. By tomorrow one of those smudged images of the two of them would be released to the world. She had always known that Elena would have to face the police at some point, but the point was obviously much more imminent than she had hoped or expected. She swallowed hard and thought fast. She would have to contact Ibramovic tomorrow morning and ask him to break the news gently to Elena. For the moment, she would say nothing and let the child rest.

'How many brothels do you reckon there are in Bradfield,' she asked brightly. Thackeray looked slightly startled.

'Why do you ask?'

'I told you. I'm trying to get Ted to let me do something on these charities that help girls trafficked into prostitution.'

'I'd stick to the charities, if I were you,' Thackeray said, his eyes anxious. 'You don't want to go poking around the sex trade, here or anywhere else. There's some very unpleasant characters involved.'

'I'm sure there are,' Laura said, hoping the acknowledgement did not sound too heartfelt.

'I don't want you dressing up as a tart again,' Thackeray said.

Laura grinned, recalling one of Ted Grant's more outrageous enterprises which had involved her doing just that and ending up in a police cell for her pains, to Thackeray's intense embarrassment.

'I'm older and wiser now,' she said. But as she cleared away the dishes, she wondered if that were strictly true. Her rash adoption of Elena, she thought, might turn out to be as ill-advised as her pretended soliciting had turned out to be years earlier. Whatever happened, she was somehow going to have to explain just why she and Joyce had failed to report the girl to the authorities as soon as they found her. And that, she thought, was not going to be a conversation she was going to enjoy.

CHAPTER ELEVEN

The sergeant on the front desk at Bradfield's main police station gazed in open admiration as the two young women draped themselves over his desk, long blonde hair curling seductively over their expensive jackets, which were unbuttoned just enough to reveal the skinny tops and ample cleavage beneath.

'Can I help you, ladies?' he asked with unconcealed fervour, and all three of them were well aware of how his imagination was suggesting very interesting ways of achieving that objective. Both women smiled, but faintly, as if his open-mouthed admiration was too boring to attract more than a moment's attention. The older of the two tapped slightly imperiously on the counter top with long puce fingernails, the same shade as her liberal lip-gloss, and offered as much of a frown as her artificially smoothed brow would allow.

'It's that girl, innit?' she asked, her accent more Essex than local. 'The girl in the canal. We think we saw her, didn't we? And the other one. The one you're looking for in the paper.'

The Sergeant swallowed hard and straightened up from his position leaning across the counter like an eager Labrador. Whatever he had expected from the two visitors, it was not this, and his hormones went into a rapid retreat.

'I'll tell CID,' he mumbled reaching for the internal phone. 'Can you take a seat and someone will be down to see you.'

Within five minutes the two young women had flounced into seats across an interview room table from DCI Michael Thackeray and Sergeant Kevin Mower and had introduced themselves, confirming Thackeray's immediate impression that he had seen both of them somewhere before. The older of the two, in her mid-thirties, he guessed, and by far the more confident, had clearly appointed herself spokeswoman for the pair, and even before she spoke for the first time Thackeray had half-recognised her as the person who had escorted the younger woman, weeping and distraught, from the Bradfield United party Laura had taken him to the previous weekend.

'I'm Jolene Peters. My husband, for my sins, is Bradfield United's first-choice goalie, and this is Katrina Jones. She's engaged to Lee Towers, who plays midfield.'

'I remember you,' Thackeray said, to the evident surprise of the women and the Sergeant. Kevin Mower's reaction to the unexpected visitors had been much the same as the desk sergeant's, although he was wily enough to keep his expression, if not his roving eyes, firmly under control.

'We've not met.' Thackeray went on. 'But I saw you both at the party after United's draw with Chelsea. You seemed to be having some trouble with Lee that night, Katrina, as I recall.'

Katrina flushed faintly under her make-up and glanced at the diamond ring that still sparkled on her left hand. The drink throwing episode hadn't led to a ring throwing sequel yet, Thackeray deduced, although he supposed there was still plenty of time for that.

'Yeah, well, that's partly what this is all about,' Jolene said. 'Bloody men.'

'I don't think...' Thackeray began, but Jolene interrupted him quickly.

'We saw them two girls,' she said quickly. 'The one who's dead in the canal and her little friend. Little tart more like. We saw them with our blokes and some of the other players a couple of weeks before at the country club. And then again, after the Chelsea game. At least we think it were the same two that night. We didn't get such a close look at them and it were dark in the car park. But I know for a fact that my Dave slept with one of them, he's admitted it, and we think Lee did too, the little one. That's what the row was about at the party. That's why Katrina chucked her bubbly at Lee. He was just laughing at her, like he'd done something clever, wasn't he? And now one of them's dead, like, and we don't know what the fuck to do, do we? But it wasn't the black one our lads slept with. We reckon she went with OK, didn't she? Like with like, like. So Dave reckons. She slept with Okigbo.'

Thackeray felt the surge of adrenaline that came with a breakthrough in a case, especially one as unexpected as this.

'I think you'd better go back to the beginning,' he said, more calmly than he felt. 'Tell me exactly what happened and when.'

The two women, it appeared, had gone on a shopping trip to Leeds on a Saturday afternoon two weeks earlier, a day when United were playing away at Rochdale, just across the Pennine hills, and they had decided not to make the trip with the team. A little light pillaging at Harvey Nicks had been followed by more than a few drinks at a smart Leeds bar and the two had not got back to Jolene Peter's home with their loot until well after nine that evening, somewhat the worse for wear, only to find the house dark and empty, with no sign that the first-choice goalie had even been home to feed the two hungry Dobermans as agreed.

Drunk, hungry and somewhat miffed, Jolene had tipped dog-food into bowls with ill-grace and then rung around some of the other team wives to discover that most of the men had repaired to the West Royd country club to celebrate an unexpected win over a normally stronger team.

'So you went to find the men at the club?' Mower prompted, as Jolene temporarily ran out of steam.

'Course we did, if they were having a party,' Jolene said, as if dealing with a backward child. 'I had this new dress, didn't I? Prada?' She glanced at the men as if expecting them to be impressed.

'And I had this new handbag, gorgeous, and a sexy new top, though in the end I don't think Lee even noticed,' Katrina said.

Mower glanced sardonically at Thackeray, who looked bemused by this turn in the conversation.

'So you went up to the country club?' he said sharply.

'In our new gear,' Katrina said.

'We got a cab, didn't we? I was a bit pissed by then,' Jolene said. 'Can't be too careful, can you, Inspector?'

'And what happened when you got there?' Mower broke in, worrying for his boss's blood pressure.

'They were all there, weren't they? Most of the lads and a few of the wives. No one had effing bothered to contact us though. Bastards. Anyway, when someone had bought us drinks, we began to wonder where Dave and Lee had got to. They weren't in evidence anywhere and some of the other lads were giving us funny looks, like they were trying to distract us. So we began to wonder what was up.'

'OK wasn't around either,' Katrina said. 'And that were a bit funny because he loves to party, that lad. *And* he'd scored the winning goal, apparently. But he were nowhere to be seen.'

Jolene and Katrina exchanged a quick glance, as if to confirm that what came next was really what they wanted the police to know. But Katrina did not hesitate.

'There's some rooms upstairs, for people to stop over the night, like,' she said, her face pinched and waspish with emotion. 'If they lose it, and can't get home. They must have taken the girls up there. That's why I were so furious at the second party. Someone made a joke about it and Lee gave me such a cheeky bloody look, so I threw my champagne at him. It turned out later that those bloody girls had been there again that night, too, though because me and Jolene were there, our lads kept away from them.' She twisted her engagement ring around her finger and Mower wondered if she was going to take it off there and then.

'You saw the girls clearly, at the first party?' Thackeray asked, and both women nodded.

'You could positively identify them?' And they nodded again.

'It were them two, I'm sure it were. Or two very similar. The first time, after the Rochdale game, we went looking for our blokes and the two lasses came scuttling out, a black lass and a skinny white girl. Looked half starved. Someone must have rung upstairs and tipped Dave and Lee off,' Katrina said. 'We saw them going out to the car park, looking right scared, and then the three lads came back.'

'Looking like cats who'd stolen the cream,' Jolene said. 'Bastards.'

'Of course they said nowt had happened, but we knew it had,' Katrina said. 'One of my mates said it's an open secret. If anyone wants a woman, it's arranged for them. And then we saw them again at the Chelsea party. Two girls were just leaving as we arrived, legging it across the car park again wi'a couple of big blokes, and Lee and Dave didn't know where to look. That's why we were so fed up that night, an' all. When someone started joking about it, I just lost it.'

'And it was the same two girls?'

'Well, I wouldn't swear it were t' same two,' Jolene said. 'It were a bit dark to see much. But it were two young girls so we thought they must be t'same.'

Thackeray thought it better not to tell the women that there was no way it could have been the same girls, as one of them by that time was already dead and the other had disappeared. The fact that they had been so quickly replaced and the footballers evidently content with the new arrangement would only fuel their fury.

'Do you know who does the arranging if these girls turn up?' Thackeray asked, stony-faced now.

'Minelli, of course.' Jolene's face was hard as she spoke the name of a man she obviously hated. 'Minelli controls everything about the players. Even their sex lives.'

'So he's a pimp?' The word dropped into the conversation like the crack of a whip.

'When it suits him. Other times he's telling them to lay off sex at home before a big game,' Jolene said, passing on advice from the team manager that obviously rankled. 'Thinks he's some sort of God, that man. You wouldn't believe it.'

Thackeray took a deep breath. To say that he had disliked Minelli on sight would be an understatement, he thought, although he knew this was an instant reaction to the Italian's too close proximity to Laura. But he knew that he was walking on thin ice here, and might be too ready to believe the women's vindictive and quite possibly fanciful allegations about United's boss. He must watch his objectivity, he thought. That morning he had received his own summons to an interview with the inquiry team at County HQ, scheduled for the following week, and he was only too aware of how searching their questions would be about his abandonment of procedure when Laura had been in danger. He knew that making a habit of unpredictability would be fatal to his career within a very short time.

'Has anyone you've spoken to suggested where these girls come from?' Thackeray asked as neutrally as he could manage, but both women shook their heads at that.

'She was foreign, the white girl, someone said,' Jolene said. 'But the other one, the black bitch. She spoke English all right. Someone said she and OK were getting on just fine.'

'Did you see Paolo Minelli with them at all?' But both women shook their heads at that.

'And did he seem to be involved in getting them off the premises when you two turned up? On either occasion? Did he hustle them out to the car park or anything like that.' But again they shook their heads.

'They were with two other blokes the second time,' Jolene

said. 'They were heading to a car on t'far side of the car park. By the time we got inside the lads were all present and correct but they looked a bit shifty. The first time we got a better look because they passed us in t'corridor when we went upstairs. After that there was a bit of mayhem, wasn't there? Hardly surprising. Then after we'd seen them again, running off when we arrived for the Chelsea party, it all kicked off again.' And in spite of pressing on with their questions, that was about as much as Thackeray and Mower could elicit in the way of eyewitness evidence about what had gone on the night of the celebration parties.

When the women had gone, having checked and signed their statements, Thackeray called Mower into his office and waved him into a chair.

'Well, we'll have to check all that out,' he said. 'We know it can't have been the dead girl they saw the second time because her body had already been found. So it looks as though there's a regular supplier of a number of girls no doubt as and when they're called for.' He glanced away, his face bleak.

'I'll come with you to interview Minelli,' he said. 'We're going to be about as popular as a couple of suicide bombers once it gets out we're investigating Bradfield United. And it will get out. You can be sure of that, once we start working our way through the players.'

'A pity it's happened when they're on a winning roll,' Mower said. 'The fans'll think we're going to damage their chances in the Cup.'

'Never mind the bloody Cup,' Thackeray said with unusual vehemence. 'There's a girl dead and another one missing. We're talking life and death here.'

'That's what the fans think too, guv,' Mower said, with a crooked grin. 'You don't talk proportion with football fans in a situation like this.'

'Then it's time they grew up,' Thackeray snapped. 'That's a game, this is a murder, and by the looks of it a whole lot more viciousness as well.'

'Can we believe anything those two bimbos said?' Mower asked. 'They obviously hate Minelli.'

'We can't necessarily believe anything they said without corroboration,' Thackeray said sharply. 'So that's our next step. We'll talk to Minelli now, straight away, and then work our way through the players, starting with Okigbo, who told me to my face he'd never seen the victim before. It sounds to me it's quite possible he was lying, and he may not be the only one if all these girls were on the game. The town's probably full of men who know them and won't want to admit it.'

'Right, guv,' Mower said equably.

'And there's something else that may be significant,' Thackeray said. 'When I went to the United party with Laura I was surprised to see our old friend Steve Stone there, living it up with the best of them. His sister's Minelli's girlfriend, apparently. It may be an innocent connection, or it may not. Stone's not come to our attention again, since the last time, as far as I know, but we know what he was into back then, even though the Crown Prosecution Service wouldn't have it. If Minelli's procuring girls he may be using Stone's services to source them.'

'Whoa, guv,' Mower said, looking alarmed. 'That's jumping a few guns, isn't it? I know you weren't best pleased when the CPS threw the case out, but he does have legitimate businesses. We gave him a fright back then. But we'll need something rock solid to take Stone on again.'

'Well, let's give Paolo Minelli a fright, shall we?' Thackeray said. 'And then we'll tackle young Okigbo. It looks as if he's lied about knowing the dead girl, and in the absence of any other suspects, that makes him number one in my book. Unless he's got a very convincing alibi indeed.'

Paolo Minelli had been summoned from the training ground to meet DCI Thackeray and Sergeant Kevin Mower and did not look best pleased about it when he came into his own office, hot and sweaty and wearing a muddy tracksuit and trainers. He glanced at the two officers who were sitting waiting for him, and then closed the door to the outer office, where a secretary was sitting at her desk with an ill-concealed expression of curiosity on her face. He tried to smooth down his dishevelled hair irritably and wiped his face with a tissue.

'Gentlemen?' he said, when the officers had introduced themselves. 'What is so urgent that I have to leave my team just now?'

Mower took the artist's impression of the dead girl from his file and offered it to Minelli.

'We're are investigating the death of this young woman,' he said. 'And we have reason to believe that she was at a party for your team members a couple of weeks ago. Do you remember seeing her?'

Minelli wiped his brow again, still breathing heavily, and took his seat behind his desk before taking the picture from Mower and studying it for a moment in silence.

'No,' he said at length. 'I don't know this girl. I've never seen her before. *Certo.*'

'This would be the party two Saturdays ago at the country club, after you won your game against Rochdale and Okigbo scored the winning goal.'

Minelli shrugged as eloquently as only an Italian can, and spread his hands wide.

'I remember the party,' he said. 'Of course, we had a good win and the team were excited that evening. What is the phrase? Over the moon? But I didn't see this girl.'

'Could she have been with Okigbo? Is she his girlfriend?' Mower asked. 'A black girl? I don't suppose there are too many black girls at your parties.'

'I don't think OK has a girlfriend. He's not been in Bradfield very long.' Minelli shrugged again. 'I didn't see her, but I spent a lot of time at that party with the chairman in another room. We had a lot to talk about.'

'It's been suggested to us that girls are sometimes provided for your team members, invited to parties for their entertainment, as you might say. And that you might be doing the providing,' Thackeray broke in harshly, although he had asked Mower to take the lead in the interview. Mower glanced at his boss anxiously, wondering if there was something going on here he did not know about. He was certainly offering Minelli more information than he would have done himself at this stage in the interview.

Paolo Minelli bunched his fists on the desk in front of him for a moment, gazing at Thackeray's disdainful face, before he replied, his features contorted with anger. He launched into what the police officers guessed was a string of Italian expletives before switching back to English.

'That is an outrageous suggestion,' he said, almost choking

with emotion. 'You make it sound as if I provide prostitutes for them?'

'The suggestion's not true, then?' Thackeray persisted.

'Is not true,' Minelli said. 'I don't know where these girls came from or who they might be. But you should be aware, Inspector. I have enemies here who would like to get rid of me, who have other plans for the club. I know that. I didn't realise they would go this far.' He took a deep breath to calm himself before he continued more quietly.

'You know what young men are like, especially young men who have plenty of money and lots of testosterone. There are always girls around, just like round a pop group. It is natural. But I am their coach, not their father. I don't interfere in their private life unless their private life is interfering with their work. Drink, drugs, girls... You know the problems. But at the moment we are quite lucky here. I do not have any difficulties with the players at the moment.'

'I'm pleased to hear that,' Thackeray said drily. 'But I think you may be running into problems with Okigbo. He was allegedly seen with this girl, and now she's dead. Show Mr Minelli the picture of the other girl we're looking for, Kevin.' Mower did as he was told, but again Minelli, after staring for a moment at the blurred CCTV image, shook his head angrily.

'I'm sorry,' he said. 'I've never seen her before either. But these young men – there are lots of girls, you know? They come and go.' He smiled faintly at the two officers, as if soliciting their sympathy, and glanced away again, wiping his brow, when they did not respond.

'Black girls?' Mower asked bluntly.

'Not so many black girls,' Minelli said. 'But half the team

are unmarried. The girlfriends come and go. What do you expect?'

'So it would surprise you to know that it has been suggested that these two girls are prostitutes, call girls, apparently, who were brought to the party by a couple of men?' Thackeray said.

Minelli took a sharp breath and visibly paled beneath his tan.

'It would surprise me, yes,' he said. 'I told you. I know nothing of girls like that.'

'You wouldn't expect your players to make use of services of that sort?'

'No, I wouldn't,' Minelli said. 'There is a risk, a risk of diseases... I would be worried about that, yes. Who suggested this, anyway? Who is telling you all these lies?'

Thackeray smiled grimly.

'You know I can't tell you that, Mr Minelli,' he said. 'But the source is reliable.'

He looked at the coach bleakly for a moment.

'Your own partner is Angelica Stone, is that right?'

Minelli nodded, with what appeared to be genuine surprise.

'Is that relevant, Inspector,' he asked faintly.

'Only in so far as she is the sister of Stephen Stone, who has come to the attention of the police at one time or another, in the context of prostitution.'

'Steve?' Minelli said, looking astonished. 'He is Angelica's brother, but I hardly know him... He's a businessman, as far as I know, a legitimate businessman. He owns clubs. What has Steve Stone got to do with any of this?'

'Probably nothing at all,' Thackeray said. 'It may just be a coincidence that he was at another party for your players at the West Royd club last weekend. Nothing to do with these girls at all?'

'That is where I saw you, too,' Minelli said suddenly, as if something that had been bothering him had suddenly fallen into place. Thackeray nodded but did not elaborate.

'Right, that's fine then, Mr Minelli,' Thackeray said, sounding suddenly uninterested and conscious of Mower's worried look. He guessed that he had probably gone further than he should down that avenue. 'And you can confirm again that you have never seen either of these girls.'

'Never,' Minelli said fervently.

'So all that remains is for me to ask you to arrange meetings for us with your team members, starting with Okigbo, Dave Peters and Lee Towers.'

Minelli gazed at Thackeray for a moment, looking appalled.

'All the team?' he asked, almost choking on the words.

'Eventually,' Thackeray said, his expression implacable. 'But those three young men first, starting with Okigbo. This afternoon if possible.'

'This will get into the papers,' Minelli said, licking his dry lips. 'This place is like a – what do you call it? – a sieve?'

'I dare say it will,' Thackeray said. 'There's very little I can do about that.'

Back outside the stadium, where a few desolate looking fans were queuing in the rain in the hope of still getting a ticket for the match against Chelsea the following week, Mower glanced at his boss with curious eyes.

'You were pushing it a bit with the Steve Stone issue, weren't you, guv?' he asked.

'Steve Stone and the possible presence of prostitutes in the same place would make anyone wonder,' Thackeray said shortly as they walked back to the car. 'We know he was involved three years ago and got away with it. Why should anything have changed. After the balls-up by the CPS he probably thinks he's invincible.'

'Do you want to talk to him?'

'Not yet,' Thackeray said. 'You're right. If we move on Stone we'll have to be extra sure we've got something very solid to go on. I don't want another case chucked back at me for lack of evidence. But if he was at one Bradfield United party, when I saw him, he might well have been at the previous one, when these girls were also seen. So we can legitimately ask him about that. But first we'll talk to these young footballers. If some of them were in bed with the murdered girl and her friend once, they could well have been with them again the night our victim died. They could easily have arranged to see them again. It's the only real lead we've got so far.'

'Did you believe Minelli was as squeaky clean as he claimed?' Mower asked as he started the car and drove back towards the town centre and police HQ.

'Not really,' Thackeray said. 'I think he's a very good actor. At the very least he knows more about the girls than he's prepared to admit.'

'What we really need is the second girl,' Mower said. 'And what really worries me is that she may be dead as well and we just haven't found her body yet.'

As he pulled into the police car park Thackeray's mobile phone rang and Mower watched as he listened to the caller and his face hardened.

'Thanks for letting me know, Amos,' he said, before disconnecting. He glanced at Mower.

'Amos Atherton,' he said. 'He's just got blood test results on our victim. She was HIV positive.'

'Well, that'll come as glad tidings to whoever she's slept with,' Mower said quietly. 'Including the father of her child. And if that includes any of the footballers, Minelli will do his nut.'

'And if she really is a tom, there could be hundreds of men,' Thackeray said. 'Not least, Bradfield United's star player. I think Paolo Minelli's troubles have only just begun.' And Mower could not understand why Thackeray allowed himself a faint smile of triumph at that.

CHAPTER TWELVE

For the hundredth time that morning Laura Ackroyd's hand hovered over the phone on her desk and then moved abruptly back to her computer keyboard as she tried without much success to concentrate on work. At her side was a copy of the day's first edition which included on its front page the slightly blurred image of the girl the police wanted to interview, the girl she knew as Elena, which had arrived in the office the previous afternoon. She knew, with a feeling of sick horror in her stomach, that she would have to tell Thackeray, sooner rather than later, where Elena was. Concealing her whereabouts now she was wanted as a witness in a murder case was indefensible, morally and legally. The police needed to know what Elena knew about the dead girl and the longer Laura stood in the way of that, the more trouble she knew she, and the Ibramovic family and Elena herself, would be in.

But still she hesitated, with her hand half on and half off the telephone. She could not bear to send the police to Elena's safe haven in Ilkley unannounced, she decided. The least she owed the girl she and Joyce had tried to help, and the family who had offered her shelter, was that she should tell them face to face what they had to do. She would go out there as soon as she finished work, she thought, and then tell Thackeray what she and Joyce had done. A couple more hours would not make much difference to the police inquiries she decided, and it would be kinder to the girl if she offered to take her to police headquarters herself rather than letting the police pick her up and quite likely terrify her more than she was terrified already.

She turned back to her computer again with a sigh, only to be interrupted again within minutes by Tony Holloway, who approached her desk looking furious.

'Did you know about these police inquiries?' he asked. Laura looked at him blankly, her mind racing at the thought that Tony had somehow found out about Elena.

'Inquiries about what?' she asked, her mouth dry.

'I've just had a call from a contact at United. Apparently the police have been up at Beck Lane interviewing the coach, and they're planning to talk to the whole bloody team later. And I don't just mean the police. I mean your bloody DCI boyfriend, in person, apparently. What the hell's all that about? And why didn't you tell me something like that was going on.'

Laura flushed slightly, conscious of how her own guilt had misled her.

'I might possibly have told you if I'd known the first thing about it,' she said with some asperity. 'Do I have to tell people on this wretched paper one more time? Michael Thackeray doesn't confide in me about his cases and I don't confide in him about my stories. I haven't the faintest idea why he might want to talk to Paolo Minelli. You'll have to ask him yourself.' The latter statement was true, she thought, even if the first was not strictly accurate. She and Michael did often talk about their work, and judging by the dilemma she had just landed herself in over the Albanian girl, talking to him might have been the more prudent option this time too. But Tony was not to be mollified.

'It seems a bit of a coincidence to me,' he said. 'You wheedle your way into Jenna Heywood's good books, get invited to matches and parties, and then all of a sudden your bloody copper's all over the team like a rash. Are you telling me there's no connection?'

'I'm telling you exactly that,' Laura said. 'I don't know why Michael should want to talk to Minelli. As far as I know he's investigating the murder of a girl who was found in the canal. Though you probably know as well as I do there's some odd things going on at United at the moment. Perhaps someone's complained to the police about that. Jenna Heywood certainly doesn't seem to be very happy. But that's your province, Tony. You're supposed to have eyes and ears up at Beck Lane. I suggest you use them.'

'What are you saying? I'm not doing my job properly?'

Laura hesitated, knowing that she could not share Jenna's confidences but quite keen that the harassment of a woman she liked should be exposed to the light of day, even if it had to be through the medium of Tony Holloway.

'I'll tell you one thing, which came from my father, who still has some United shares, apparently,' she said. 'He reckons there's quite a vicious auction going on to prevent Jenna getting the two thirds majority she needs to push through her plans for the club to leave Beck Lane. My dad's been approached to sell, by more than one buyer, I think. You'd get a good story if you did some digging around in that area. I'll give you his phone number in Portugal if you like.'

But Tony still looked mutinous and Laura wondered again why he seemed to be taking so little professional interest in what seemed to her might turn out to be the death throes of the club. Once she had sorted out the problem with the Albanian girl she would talk to Jenna again, she thought, to see if she could persuade her to talk publicly about the pressure she was under. Suffering that sort of abuse in silence was self-defeating, but she guessed that until the big Chelsea match was over Jenna would be very reluctant to risk blackening the club's name and possibly demoralising the players. Once the inevitable defeat in London arrived, things might be different.

OK Okigbo was a stocky young man, with a cheerful round face, on whom an Italian suit sat uncomfortably. His physique gave little indication of his magical ability to dance and weave around opponents on the football pitch and crack the ball into the net from seemingly impossible angles with uncanny accuracy. More a potential Maradona than a Beckham, Mower thought, as Okigbo came into Paolo Minelli's office that afternoon, accompanied by a white man the Sergeant did not recognise. To his surprise, Thackeray, who had commandeered the office for the rest of the day, evidently did.

'We won't be needing you, Mr Jenkins,' the DCI said brusquely to Okigbo's agent.

'That right?' Jenkins said, his own aggression barely under control. 'Isn't my client entitled to have anyone here to look after his interests, then?' The smile on Okigbo's face faded slightly as if he only now realised the seriousness of what was happening.

'He's entitled to have a solicitor with him if he feels he needs one,' Thackeray said. 'But I'm only here to ask some preliminary questions. Mr Okigbo isn't under arrest or even under caution. We simply want to clarify some facts with him at this stage.'

'What facts?' Jenkins asked, his face flushed. 'What's this in connection with?' Okigbo was watching him now, still relaxed but hanging on every word, as if he was used to Jenkins talking on his behalf.

'It's in connection with the death of a young woman we have reason to believe your client has met,' Thackeray said. 'Now, if you would leave, we would like to get on.'

Okigbo flashed a pleading look at Jenkins, suddenly anxious, but the agent had paled under his tan, and he ran a hand around his collar as if it had become too tight. He put a hand on the footballer's shoulder.

'I'll get you a brief,' he said. 'D'you want him here now? What about your mate Emanuel? Isn't he a lawyer? You can do that, you know. *They* can bloody wait.' He glared at Thackeray but Okigbo shrugged.

'I'll answer their questions. I'll be fine,' he said, not sounding totally as if he believed the statement himself. As Jenkins spun on his heel and left, Thackeray waved the young man into the chair facing the desk and he sat down, leaning forward slightly as if to hear the police officers better. To Mower's surprise, he was the one who spoke first.

'Do I know you?' he asked, smiling tentatively again. Thackeray looked grim as he introduced himself and Mower.

'We met at the West Royd club last Sunday. You were with Emanuel Asida, as I recall.'

'Ah, yes, I remember now,' Okigbo said, leaning back in his chair again, suddenly looking much happier. 'The policeman at the party looking for the name of a Nigerian girl. And are you still looking for her name?'

'I'm afraid we are, Mr Okigbo. She's dead and we still haven't succeeded in identifying her. And now I have information that leads me to believe that you did know her although you said you didn't when we met.'

'No, I don't think so,' Okigbo said easily. 'I would remember a Nigerian girl. There are not so many here. We would have lots to talk about, you know? Where she came from, who she knew, what she did in Lagos or wherever...'

'You do understand the seriousness of what we are asking you?' Thackeray asked, irritated by the footballer's casual attitude. 'We are investigating a murder here.'

Okigbo looked at him blankly for a moment.

'A murder?' he said. 'I didn't understand that. A murder is serious, yes? This girl you are talking about is murdered?'

'Let me take you back to another party,' Thackeray said. 'The party at West Royd after your game against Rochdale.'

'Ah, yes, Rochdale. That was a very good game. I had a very good game.' Okigbo smiled at the recollection.

'Not the game, Mr Okigbo, the party,' Mower broke in, as taken aback as Thackeray evidently was by OK Okigbo. 'You were at that particular party at West Royd. Is that right?'

'Oh, yes, it was a good party too,' Okigbo said with a satisfied smile and a slight giggle. 'I had too much to drink that night, you know? Everyone was buying me drinks that night.'

'And girls? Or a girl?' Thackeray snapped, and for the first time he thought he saw a flash of anxiety, if not fear, in Okigbo's eyes.

'I understand you spent some time that night with a young black girl,' Thackeray said. 'There were two young girls at the party that night and one of them could well have been the girl we have found dead. Have you anything to tell me about that?'

Okigbo shook his head.

'It is difficult to remember what happened,' he said. 'I had a lot to drink that night. Too much to drink.'

'Are you saying you don't remember these girls?'

The footballer shook his head again.

'Maybe,' he said. 'I think there was a very friendly girl. But she was not your Nigerian girl. She was not Nigerian. She said she was a Jamaican girl, a West Indian.'

'You slept with her?' Thackeray asked.

'Yes, I think I did. I recollect I did.'

'And you're sure she said she was West Indian?'

'We didn't talk much,' Okigbo said, looking slightly shamefaced now. 'I was drunk. You know how it goes?' Mower smiled slightly, knowing that his boss was the last person to know how that particular scenario went.

'Did she tell you anything at all about herself?' Thackeray ploughed on, ignoring the question.

'Her name,' Okigbo offered eagerly now. 'She said she was called Grace. A nice name. A very nice name. She was a very nice girl.'

'Was she a prostitute?' Mower asked flatly, and Okigbo flinched slightly. 'Were the two girls prostitutes?'

'I don't know,' Okigbo said. 'I don't think so.'

'Oh, come on, Mr Okigbo,' Mower pressed him. 'You know how to define a prostitute. Did you pay this girl for sex that night or not. Did anyone pay either of the girls for sex?'

'I don't know,' Okigbo muttered. 'I don't remember. I was very drunk. I am ashamed at how drunk I was. Paolo was not happy about it.'

'But Paolo didn't complain about you sleeping with the girl?'

'No, he didn't complain about that,' Okigbo whispered. 'Was she really a whore?'

'I would have thought you could have worked that out for yourself, Mr Okigbo. According to our information two girls were brought to the party by car, spent some time upstairs with you and several other players and were then taken away again. What does that sound like to you?' Thackeray asked. The player shook his head, his eyes moistening and his bravado punctured.

'I was very drunk,' he said again.

'Do you remember what arrangements you made with this girl, Grace?'

'No, I truly don't remember.' Okigbo's eyes flickered away from his interrogator again.

'Had you ever met her before?' Thackeray asked. 'And I should tell you before you answer that question that the girl was pregnant and DNA can give us a good idea of who the father was.'

'No, I had never met her before,' Okigbo said fiercely. 'If she was a whore... I don't do that, not often. I don't usually go with whores, sir. And that is God's truth. I was brought up a good Christian back home. But now...' He shrugged, looking momentarily desolate.

'And she told you nothing about herself, apart from the fact that she was West Indian?'

'Nothing.'

'And did she consent freely to having sex with you?' Thackeray asked, seeing the immediate shock on Okigbo's face again and very aware of how little sympathy he felt for the man he was questioning.

'You mean did I rape her?' he asked, his eyes full of horror. 'Of course I didn't rape her. She was willing. Of course she was willing.'

'It's just that if a girl is forced into prostitution, as many are these days, and if they tell the man that they are with them under duress, then having sex with the girl could be construed as rape. Do you understand?'

'I understand,' Okigbo said very quietly. 'I am not a fool, Chief Inspector. Before I became a footballer I had planned to be a lawyer.'

'Did Grace suggest she was being forced?' Thackeray persisted.

'No, no, of course not,' Okigbo said fervently. 'There was nothing like that. I think... I believed she was willing. But I was drunk. I can't be sure. She seemed like a nice girl. As far as I can remember.'

'Did you see her again?'

Okigbo hesitated and then he shrugged.

'Yes, I saw her again. I was at the club with some other players one night last week and both girls were there again. I slept with her again. I liked her very much. That night she did ask me to lend her some money. I gave her a hundred pounds.'

'Is this the girl?' Thackeray asked, putting the drawing of the dead girl on the desk in front of Okigbo. The footballer nodded.

'I think so, yes,' he whispered.

'Did you arrange to meet her again?'

'No,' Okigbo whispered, and Thackeray was almost certain he was lying.

Thackeray hesitated before he spoke again, and Mower, guessing what was coming, looked at the young man opposite them with a hint of sympathy in his eyes.

'There is one thing you need to know about these encounters with the girl you knew as Grace,' Thackeray said. 'If she is in fact the same girl who was found dead in the canal, you have to know that she was infected with the HIV virus. In the circumstances, you may want to have a medical check yourself. I'm sorry.'

'Dear Jesus,' OK Okigbo whispered, his eyes filling with tears. 'What have I done?'

Laura Ackroyd got away from work early that afternoon and arrived at the Ibramovic's house just as a tall dark-haired girl in school uniform with a heavy bag over her shoulder was letting herself in through the front door.

'Hi,' Laura said. 'You must be Itzak's daughter.'

The girl nodded gloomily.

'Jazzy,' she said. 'You're Elena's friend?' Laura nodded and to her surprise the girl turned and took hold of her arm in a bruising grip.

'Can you find the men who did all that to her?' she asked fiercely. 'It's disgusting what happened to her. Horrible. She told us all about it. And I bet my dad left the worst bits out when he translated.'

Laura extricated herself gently from the girl's hand.

'I know,' she said. 'But unless Elena is willing to help the police it may be difficult to pin the men down.'

'But the police will send her back home. That can't be right. They might come for her again. Or kill her. Or her family will.' It was obvious that Jazzy had been overwhelmed by Elena's story.

'Let me talk to your mother,' Laura said gently. 'Something else has happened that I need to talk to Elena about, and then we'll have to see what we should do next.'

Jazzy pushed the front door open and went inside, calling for her mother as she did so. Lilijana came from the kitchen to greet her, closely followed by an anxious looking Elena.

'We need to talk,' Laura said, seeing the anxiety deepen in the eyes of all three of them.

'Come in,' Lilijana said quietly, waving Laura into the sitting room where she sat in a chair facing the other three, Elena between the mother and Jazzy, who put a protective arm around the other girl's painfully thin shoulders. The two girls, not that much different in age, had obviously become friends.

'Elena,' Laura said, hoping that without Itzak to translate she could make herself understood. 'The night you ran away you were not alone, were you? You ran away with someone else, another girl? There were two of you. You had a friend with you?'

The girl looked at her with blank eyes for a moment before the tears came and she nodded.

'She lost,' she whispered. 'Grace lost. Men come and I run. Grace run.'

'Did they catch up with Grace?' Laura asked, reaching out a hand as if to seize her by way of illustration and Elena nodded dumbly.

'Was Grace a black girl?' Laura asked, but Elena shook her head, not understanding.

'Black? African?' Understanding dawned and Elena nodded again.

'African. Yes. She say African.'

Laura sighed, knowing that the answer made Elena's position untenable and her own probably even worse.

'You must talk to the police, Elena,' Laura said. 'Your friend Grace is dead.'

Elena gave a slight moan and clutched Jazzy for support as tears flowed down her cheeks. Lilijana put a protective arm around both girls.

'Go upstairs you two,' she said. 'Jazzy, look after her. I want to talk to Laura alone for a minute.' The girls left, without glancing back, although Jazzy looked mutinous, and Lilijana stood up angrily to face Laura.

'I need to talk to my husband,' she said. 'Elena needs to have things explained to her in her own language.'

'There's nothing you can do, any of you,' Laura said. 'There's no choice, believe me. Either Elena comes back to Bradfield with me to talk to the police or I send the police here to talk to her. I'm sure you'll be able to continue to look after her, if that's what you want, but she's a witness in a murder inquiry. She must tell them what she knows. There's no choice. Honestly there isn't.'

'How did her friend die?' Lilijana asked quietly.

'She was pulled from the canal in Bradfield last week. She

was attacked and then either fell, or was pushed, into the water. The police are looking for Elena as a witness. Her photograph is in the evening paper. I don't suppose you see the *Bradfield Gazette* out here, but the two girls were caught on street cameras. She and her friend are quite recognisable. It won't be long before someone sees her here and realises who she is. The photograph will get into the national papers, perhaps be on TV...'

'They don't think she did it?' Lilijana asked, looking horrified at the idea.

'No, I'm sure they don't, but she may have seen who did,' Laura said. 'She must make a statement to the police.'

The other woman nodded slowly.

'Let her stay here,' she said. 'I will get Itzak to explain all this to her when he comes home. Give us a little time to prepare her, and then send your policemen here. It will be kinder that way.'

Laura sighed.

'There's one policeman I know quite well,' she said. 'I'll tell him when I see him this evening. That should give you time to prepare Elena. I'm sorry to have to put you through all this. I didn't realise there might be a connection between her and the dead girl until yesterday myself, and it was as much a shock to me as it is to you. But you must see, it changes everything.'

'Yes,' Lilijana said. 'Poor girl. As if the other things she's been through are not enough. We sat up late last night while she told Itzak more details about her life since she was kidnapped. For some of the time she was in some dreadful bar in Belgrade. I feel ashamed that she was abused in my own city. Then she was sold, like a slave, sold and sold again.

How can this happen in this day? What is going on in the world?'

'I spoke to a charity in London that helps these girls and they said there are thousands of them being trafficked around Europe,' Laura said. 'They are kidnapped, or else tricked into believing they're being offered a legitimate job in a more prosperous country. And if they try to run away their families are threatened. It makes me sick to think about it.'

'She must tell the police everything she knows. It's the only way these men can be stopped,' Lilijana said with sudden determination. 'Itzak and I will tell her what's happening. Prepare her. And Itzak can translate for her.'

'Fine,' Laura said, with a feeling of immense weariness. 'I'll leave it to you and Itzak. I'm really sorry to have landed you in all this.' Lilijana put a hand on her shoulder as she got up to go.

'We all have to do the best we can,' she said.

Laura drove back to Bradfield slowly, and when she got home poured herself a large vodka and tonic and flung herself down on the settee before calling her grandmother to fill her in on the latest developments. Joyce listened in silence until she had finished, and when she spoke her voice sounded strained and Laura wondered if she was crying.

'Some decisions are hard to take, pet. But I think you're doing the right thing. You've no real choice.'

'Michael will be furious we've kept her under wraps as long as we have,' Laura said.

'Aye, well, you're going to have to face him down on that. We did the right thing in the beginning. We couldn't know how it would turn out.'

'No,' Laura said, not really believing herself. 'I'll let you know what happens.'

For a long time she sat watching the clock creep round from six o'clock to seven, feeling too sick to think about cooking a meal, merely refilling her glass to bolster her courage. Just after seven she jumped as the phone rang, and she answered it expecting to hear Michael Thackeray's voice telling her, as he often did, that he would be late home. But the voice at the other end was that of Ibramovic, and she could tell immediately that his news was not good.

'I'm sorry,' he said. 'Have you spoken to the police yet?'

'Not yet,' Laura said.

'It's just that Elena has gone. She and Jazzy have packed a bag and disappeared.'

'Oh hell,' Laura said, as she heard Thackeray's key in the front door. 'That is all I need.'

CHAPTER THIRTEEN

Thackeray found Laura sitting on the sofa staring into an empty glass and could tell from the lack of response to his arrival that something was seriously wrong. He took his coat off and hung it up carefully, trying to control the feeling of dread that almost overwhelmed him.

'Bad day?' he asked, putting a tentative hand on her shoulder. She shrugged slightly and turned towards him with eyes full of tears.

'I've messed something up big time,' she said. 'You're not going to like this.'

He sat down beside her and took her hand.

'What's happened?' he asked, and slowly she told him how she had met Elena at her grandmother's house and everything that had followed. She would have found it easier to struggle through her story if Thackeray had responded in any way, but once he realised that what she was telling him was related to the case he was working on he got up and went to the window, where he stood with his back to Laura, gazing into the wintry garden outside without saying anything at all while he listened to her halting explanation of what she had done and why.

When she had added as a post-script the devastating news

that Elena and Jazzy Ibramovic had apparently run off together rather than allow Elena to face the police, Laura paused briefly. When Thackeray still did not respond, she sighed.

'I'm sorry, Michael,' she said. 'I'd really no idea what we were getting into with this. It just seemed like the right thing to do at the time. I'm really, really sorry.'

Thackeray spun round to face her at that, his face white and drawn and his eyes angry.

'Sorry hardly seems to cover it this time, does it?' he said. 'I can hardly believe that you and Joyce could have been so stupid. To think that you could hide someone who was so obviously here illegally was one thing.'

'The girl was half starved when Joyce found her,' Laura said.

'Right. But to try to hide someone who had been trafficked by thugs who you must have guessed would stop at nothing to keep Elena quiet is something else entirely. Even if you didn't make the connection to the dead girl, you knew Elena was being hunted by men who were running a vicious illegal racket. You must have known that she was in danger. And if she was in danger, you were too. And so was Joyce. And now, to cap it all, you've lost her. You could have brought her to see me this afternoon but you warned her you wanted her to talk to the police and then you left her in Ilkley. Wasn't it obvious to you that she would run away again? Surely you could see that? So just at the moment when we've gone public with her picture as a witness to the killing, she's haring around Yorkshire, barely able to speak English, with no means of support, a prey to anyone who recognises her. And she's got another child with her. So in the end, all you've achieved is to put two girls at risk. And me in an impossible position. How the hell do you think I'm going to explain all this to Jack Longley, who's at the end of his tether over this inquiry we're involved in. How am I going to tell him that we've got to start a massive hunt for a witness whose whereabouts have been known to my girlfriend for the last four days?'

'The last thing I wanted to do was embarrass you,' Laura said, her voice so quiet that Thackeray could barely hear her.

'Again!' Thackeray said bitterly. 'The timing couldn't be worse, could it? Just when the inquiry is going to rake over the embers of the last case you got inadvertently involved in.'

'That wasn't my fault,' Laura said, stung into vehemence now. 'Vince Newsom stole that document. You know he'd do anything for a story. He's completely ruthless.'

'So you say,' Thackeray said.

'That's not fair, Michael,' Laura said. 'You know what happened.'

'You didn't have to go drinking with Newsom that night,' Thackeray said. 'You didn't have to get so drunk that he had to drive you home. Why was he so keen to do that, anyway? Did he think he could sneak into your bed for old time's sake while I was away? I've always wondered.'

'Michael,' Laura cried, terrified at where Thackeray's anger was taking him. She had seen him furious before, and depressed and distant, but never overtly jealous. And the fact that he could well be right about Vince Newsom's motives that night only frightened her the more. 'I was worried about you. I had a drink too many. It wasn't the end of the world.

He must have found the paper in my bag when he looked for my door key.'

'Right,' Thackeray said, tight-lipped. Laura had not realised how the incident still rankled but she knew it would hurt far more if he ever discovered that Newsom had in fact claimed to have slept with her that night, and although she denied it to him and to herself, there was still the niggling doubt left at the back of her mind that it could be true. She could not remember.

'Never mind all that,' Laura said, desperate to change the subject, however uncomfortable that might also be. 'It's water under the bridge. What can we do about Elena?'

'You can't do anything about Elena,' Thackeray said flatly. 'You've done far too much already. Tomorrow I'll want formal statements from you, and Joyce, and this translator and his wife, chapter and verse about what's been going on from you all. In the meantime, I'll have someone talk to the family in Ilkley tonight so we can put out descriptions of the two girls across the county. The parents must be seriously worried by what's happened. How old is the daughter?'

'Sixteen or seventeen, I think,' Laura said. 'She's still at school.'

'I want the two of them found, and the sooner the better,' Thackeray said. He glanced at his watch. 'I'll get straight back to the office and set it all in motion.' He looked again at Laura who had slumped back in her seat gazing at him with a stricken expression and tears in her eyes, but his face did not soften.

'I won't come back tonight,' he said. 'So don't wait up. I need to think. In fact I reckon we both need some space.

Tomorrow is not going to be a good day.' And with that he pulled on his coat again and went out, closing the front door very deliberately behind him. Laura gazed at it for a long time, until she could no longer hear the engine of his car as it made the long descent into the town centre. She wondered if he would ever come back and she sat for a long time without moving, feeling totally drained of all emotion. Then she rang Joyce to tell her what had happened.

'If the girls turn up at your place, call the police, Nan,' she said urgently. 'Michael's right. If she was a witness to a murder, or has information about the men involved, she's in real danger. She didn't tell us half of what she knew. And now she's on the loose with another girl who's got absolutely nothing to do with anything.'

'You can't blame Elena,' Joyce said with some heat. 'She's got very little English and she was terrified, suicidal in fact. She said as much.'

Laura ran a hand wearily over her eyes and sighed.

'Michael is furious with us,' she said. 'It's all a horrible mess. I don't think he'll ever forgive me.'

There was a silence at the other end of the phone for a moment before Joyce spoke again.

'I'm sorry, pet,' she said eventually. 'You know I've never thought he was the right man for you, but I'd not want to be the one to drive you apart. Give it time. If he loves you he'll come back.'

'Maybe,' Laura said quietly, feeling a cold chill inside. 'And maybe not.'

She spent the rest of the evening wandering restlessly around the flat, drinking coffee and nibbling at a sandwich, which was all she felt she could eat but in the end she found it choked her. She hurled the remnants into the bin, and poured herself another vodka and tonic as a nightcap, only to find her heart thumping when the phone rang. She grabbed the receiver hoping that Thackeray might have calmed down enough to call her, only to find an angry Itzak Ibramovic at the other end.

'We're worried to death about Jasmin and I've just had the police round,' he said. 'Did Elena tell you anything about this other girl, the girl they've found dead.'

'No,' Laura said. 'She never mentioned her. I had no idea. If I'd known I would have insisted she went to the police. I'm so sorry about all this. Have they found any trace of them?'

Ibramovic snorted.

'I've rung round all Jasmin's friends, youth hostels, anything I can think of. She's taken her post office book and I know she had several hundred pounds in there that she was saving up for a holiday. If she's drawn that out they could be in London by now. Anywhere. I don't think the police know where to start looking to be honest.'

'I'm sure Jazzy will contact you,' Laura said. 'She'll know how worried you'll be. Has she got a mobile phone?'

'She has, but she's switched it off,' Ibramovic said. 'She's not stupid. She probably knows she can be traced via the mobile. In any case, she's left the charger in her room so the battery will run down eventually.'

'Perhaps she's switched it off to conserve the battery. In case of an emergency.'

'Like when these animals catch up with them, you mean,' Ibramovic said bitterly.

'What can I say?' Laura asked helplessly. 'Elena fooled us all.'

'Me most of all,' Ibramovic conceded. 'I was the one she talked to most, in her own language. She gave no hint that she had run away with someone else. I blame myself.'

'The police will pull out all the stops to find them,' Laura said, trying to sound reassuring. 'They really need her as a witness.'

'And the traffickers really need to prevent her becoming one,' Ibramovic said. 'Who would you put your money on finding them first?'

'The police,' Laura said firmly. 'They've far more resources. They will find them. We just have to hope it won't take too long. What did they say about publicity? Are they going to launch an appeal for the two girls to come back?'

'Apparently,' Ibramovic said. 'Given that they've already released information about Elena in connection with the murder case they can't back down now to protect her and Jasmin, can they? The traffickers must already be out looking for Elena and that puts Jazzy at risk as well.'

'Elena must have known that,' Laura said. 'She must have been very frightened of talking to the police.'

'She was very frightened,' Ibramovic said flatly. 'That was obvious. And now we are very frightened too.' And with his voice breaking, he hung up.

Guilt, Laura thought, as she flung herself back into her chair trying to control the despair that threatened to overwhelm her, was an emotion that had never tormented her greatly before, but it had stormed into her life now, and in a way that revealed more clearly than she had ever understood how it had distorted Thackeray's life for so long. If these girls were harmed in any way by the mistakes she had made today, she thought, she would never forgive herself.

The phone rang again suddenly and again she seized the receiver with a hope that was dashed this time by her father's voice.

'I've been trying to get through for an hour or more,' Jack Ackroyd complained. 'Your phone's been permanently engaged.'

'I've been busy,' Laura said irritably. Jack was the last person she wanted to talk to this evening.

'Aye, well, I thought I was doing you a favour by letting you have the latest on the United situation.'

Laura hesitated, not registering for a moment what her father was talking about.

'Oh, Bradfield United?' she said dully, neither knowing nor caring now what happened now to the football team and all its works.

'I told you about the share offers,' Jack said sharply. 'Well, I've decided to sell to Les Hardcastle after all. It were the better offer, marginally, but I reckon he's a better bet in the long run. I can't see how Sam Heywood's lass is going to make a go of it. She knows less than nowt about football.'

'Right,' Laura said listlessly, without the energy to argue. 'And does that give Les his blocking share, do you think?'

'I don't know if it clinches it, but it'll certainly help,' Jack said.

'Dad, this isn't a good time,' Laura said. 'Let's talk about it another day, shall we. Give my love to Mum.'

'Oh well, if you're not interested...'

'Goodnight, Dad,' Laura said, and hung up abruptly, adding another ounce of guilt to the burden that already weighed her down. And the worst thing was, she thought, as she got ready to go to bed alone, that there did not seem to be any way now that she could undo the events she had inadvertently set in train. She was impotent, and that was the hardest thing of all to bear.

Sergeant Kevin Mower, who had been hauled away by DCI Thackeray from a contented evening with a six-pack of lagers and a DVD, was not in the best of moods when he reported back to his boss at police HQ at eight o'clock that evening. But when he saw the look in Thackeray's eyes when he strode into the main CID office, just as Mower was carefully hanging up his leather jacket, he decided that even the mildest complaint about unwanted overtime would be too dangerous to indulge.

'Guv?' He was, he could see from the empty desks, the only person Thackeray seemed to have summoned. 'Do we have a problem?'

'The second girl,' Thackeray said. 'You won't believe this.' And he repeated the gist of what Laura had told him in staccato sentences, which told Mower all he needed to know about the state of his domestic relationship. And by tomorrow, Mower thought grimly, his professional standing would not be in much better shape when he passed on the news to Superintendent Longley.

'We need to find the pair of them,' Mower said when Thackeray had finished.

'I've asked Ilkley to interview the parents this evening, but I want you to go over there tomorrow first thing and talk to them in more detail, take statements, look at both the girls' rooms, and anything else you can think of. Take Sharif with you. I imagine Ibramovic is a Muslim so it might be reassuring. We're not gunning for him. Laura obviously talked him into it.'

'And Laura?' Mower asked tentatively.

'I'll ask Jack Longley to organise interviews with Laura and her grandmother tomorrow. You and I will keep well out of that.' Mower did not think he had ever seen Thackeray look so bleak. His recent brush with death had aged him but this personal calamity seemed to have added another ten years.

'Right,' Mower said. 'And tonight? What more can we do?'

Thackeray glanced at his watch.

'I've asked Ilkley to let us have a photograph of the Ibramovic girl. That should come soon. When we've got that we'll put out a county-wide alert for the two of them. At the same time you can get the pictures down to the train station and the coach terminus, here and in Ilkley, and see if they've bought tickets out. Apparently Jasmin had money in the post office bank, so they could have left the area completely. If we find out where they've gone we can widen the hunt out of the county – London, Manchester, wherever. And start on hotels and B&Bs. I can't imagine they'll try to sleep rough. There'll be a trail somewhere and the sooner we find it the better.'

A uniformed constable came into the room with a sheet of paper in his hand.

'Marked "urgent", sir,' he said as he handed it to

Thackeray. Thackeray glanced for a moment at the faxed photograph of a dark-haired, serious-faced young girl before handing it to Mower.

'Jasmin Ibramovic,' he said. 'Do some copies of this for circulation. Let's find them, shall we, before anyone else does?'

Mower photocopied the photograph of Jasmin and the image of Elena taken from the CCTV tape, which was lying on his desk, and took his jacket back off its hanger by the door.

'With a bit of luck we'll trace them, guv, before any harm's done.' But as he left the building to begin his inquiries he knew that he was probably whistling in the wind and he guessed that Thackeray felt much the same.

Thackeray himself went back to his own office, closed the door and lit a cigarette with his customary contempt for the building's no-smoking rules. He felt weary to the marrow of his bones and his back was beginning to jab with the pain he was trying to become accustomed to. He took a painkiller with a swig of mineral water and, leaning back in his chair, he closed his eyes. Somewhere in the swirling mist of panic that suddenly filled his mind he could see Laura's stricken face. It was only just over a week since Jack Longley had suggested the option of early retirement to him and he had angrily rejected it. But now? he wondered. He knew that Jack's own career could end in ruins very soon if the inquiry found him culpable for the last of the division's cock-ups, and he wondered if his own could possibly survive if Laura's catastrophic intervention in this murder investigation ended as badly as it seemed it might.

He stubbed out his cigarette and desperately lit another. He could just about imagine life without his job. He had spent nearly a month in a hospital bed contemplating that contingency. Life without Laura, and after this evening that no longer seemed such a remote possibility, was much harder to get his mind around. And life without the job and without Laura filled him with an all-consuming dread. Somehow, he thought, he had to find a way through this nightmare or it would undoubtedly destroy him. But where the path to salvation lay he had, at this moment, no idea at all.

By nine-thirty Mower had exhausted all the lines of inquiry which remained open to him. No one in the ticket offices at the almost deserted railway station or the long-distance bus station had recognised either of the two girls he was seeking when he had shown them their photographs, and the train station in Ilkley, he had ascertained, had already closed for the night. He sat in his car drumming his fingers anxiously on the steering wheel before driving off towards the north of the town where Aysgarth Lane, the hub of the Asian community, doubled as the focus for the sex trade after dark when most of the chattering shoppers in *shalwar kameez* had made their way home and drawn the blinds against the weather and the mysterious ways of the West. He drove slowly down the main artery, just as slowly as some of the other cars with a single male occupant cruising the Lane. On every corner a handful of women, shivering in mini-skirts and skimpy tops, stood watching carefully to see which car would slow down as it passed and offer the opportunity for them to dart to an open window as a driver drew to a halt.

The trade, Mower thought, was as old as time and as relentless. But he was looking for someone in particular and when he saw her he stopped sharply, bringing a hoot of protest from the car behind. A tall black woman, in thigh-length boots and very short shorts, with a fake fur jacket clutched around her neck to protect her from the wind, came up to the car and then hesitated.

'Come on, Jackie, I don't bite,' Mower shouted through the open window. 'Get in and keep warm for a minute, why don't you?' The woman glanced around at her companions, and then at a couple of men in leather coats who were leaning against a wall a little further up the street, before giving a shrug and doing as she was told.

'I didn't recognise you for a minute, Mr Mower,' she said, pulling the door closed and sitting shivering in the passenger seat. 'I've not seen you for a while. Are you looking for business?'

'I'm not so desperate I need to pay,' Mower snapped. 'I need some help.'

'Oh aye?' Jackie said, glancing out of the window at the shadowy figures on the street, and Mower considered how he had almost not recognised her either. When he had first met her, in the course of an investigation soon after he had arrived in Bradfield from the south, he recalled thinking how she had seemed too attractive and far too young to be travelling down the road she was already set on. He knew that even now she was still in her twenties, but she looked forty in the poor light, heavy make-up failing to conceal the ravages of an addiction she sustained on the street.

'Let's go for a little drive,' she said, turning back to Mower with dead eyes and an attempted smile that looked grotesque through the bright red slash of lipstick. 'It looks better, doesn't it? I do have my reputation to think of.' Mower shrugged and slipped the car into gear and drove up Aysgarth Lane until they reached the suburban semis that lined the main road a mile or so further out of town, where he parked in a bus-stop layby and switched the engine off.

'We need some help, Jackie,' Mower said. 'What have you heard about foreign girls here on the game? Brought in illegally, probably against their will?'

Jackie looked out of the side window of the car for a long time before she answered.

'Rumours is all,' she said. 'And even repeating them to you might be dodgy. There's some right vicious characters muscling in these days. Foreigners.'

'You read about the girl we fished out of the canal?' Mower said quietly.

'A black lass? Aye, we heard about her. Were she one of 'em?'

'We think so. And there was someone with her. An Albanian girl we're trying to find. Only looks about fifteen or sixteen...'

'They're not on the street, them girls,' Jackie said. 'They daren't let them out of their sight. They're kept in back rooms somewhere, massage parlours, clubs, you know the score.'

'Do you know where?'

Jackie shook her head slowly.

'No names. Just a hint,' Mower persisted.

But Jackie shrugged.

'I'd tell you if I knew,' she said. 'It's one thing to make your own mind up to do this. Summat else entirely to be forced. That's disgusting. But I've not heard owt definite. Just that it's going on. Now you'd best drop me back. I've a living to make.'

'Couldn't you try rehab?' Mower asked, wondering how quickly the living she was making would kill her. 'Get out of all this?'

'And then what? Live on t'dole? Even without the smack I've got expensive tastes, me. It's simple economics, Mr Mower, isn't it? I make more in a night this way than I'd make in a month on t'bloody minimum wage.'

Mower started the car again and did a U-turn to head back to town.

'If you hear anything, you'll let me know?' he asked as Jackie opened the passenger door when he stopped at her particular street corner.

'If I hear owt, pet,' Jackie said, staggering upright on the pavement again in her stiletto boots. 'Take care.'

'And you,' Mower said as he drew away.

CHAPTER FOURTEEN

DCI Thackeray called a meeting for his murder team early the next morning and briefed them on the overnight developments. Leaving Laura Ackroyd's name determinedly out of his description of how Elena had evaded their attention and been given shelter in Ilkley, he was aware of one or two knowing looks between his detectives when he necessarily mentioned Joyce Ackroyd as the girl's initial rescuer. When he had to admit that Elena and her new friend were once more on the run, there was a collective sucking in of breath around the room.

'I've got a call out for the two girls,' Thackeray said deliberately, quelling the murmur of speculation. 'So far we've found no evidence that they've left the area by train or coach, although Jasmin does seem to have drawn out some money from her post office account. But for the moment we'll have to assume they're still in West Yorkshire, unless we find evidence to the contrary from the CCTV tapes from the train and the bus stations. But if they're still here, they're at great risk. The Albanian girl is a crucial witness and we need her found. But whoever brought her here is also undoubtedly looking for her. We've evidence of that already. Immigration say they had no one seeking information on The Heights when Joyce Ackroyd says she had a visit from two men claiming to be their officers, so we can only assume it was the traffickers looking for the girl. They've killed once and will undoubtedly kill again to protect themselves if they find her before we do. Or smuggle her out of the country by the same route they use to smuggle girls in. The same applies to the girl she's with. So finding them is urgent. A top priority. Their lives are at risk. I've got Jasmin's father coming in at ten to go through all possible places she could seek refuge. He's understandably going frantic. Kevin, I want you and Sharif to talk to him when he arrives, and Omar, you take over as family liaison officer when he goes back home. They're going to need a lot of support. It's all arranged with the Ilkley police.'

Mohammed Sharif, known generally as Omar, nodded, his dark eyes sympathetic.

'Are there other kids?' he asked. Thackeray shook his head.

'She's an only child.' His face remained impassive and he hoped no one could guess how sick that made him feel.

'Right,' he said, knowing that he had to press on to save his own equilibrium. 'We have made some progress. We know now that the dead girl is called Grace, and that she told the missing girl Elena that she was African, regardless of what she told the footballer she slept with. We still have some of the footballers to interview today, including Lee Towers, whose fiancée is sure that he slept with one of the girls, and the goalkeeper, Dave Peters, who's admitted as much to his wife. They're coming in later and I want to find out everything they can remember about their encounter with the two girls. And if they're having memory problems, we'll remind them that to sleep with someone who's offering services under duress can be legally regarded as rape. That should put the fear of God into them. I'll talk to both of them myself, and you can sit in Pete.' He nodded to a young detective who was sitting at the back of the room, looking slightly sickened by what the meeting was being told.

'The rest of you,' Thackeray went on implacably. 'I want every massage parlour and dodgy venue that opens during the day visited this morning and searched for signs of prostitution on the premises. Then there'll be overtime tonight as we work our way through all the clubs. We're getting some help later from John O'Malley and the vice unit at County. I want every single one of the obvious places raided, and if that turns up nothing useful we'll have to start looking for the less obvious. I don't believe these two girls are the only trafficked women in the town. From what Elena has already said there are ten or a dozen she knows of hidden away in a house somewhere and taken out from there to work. I want them found.'

When tasks had been allocated and most of the grim-faced detectives had bustled away, Thackeray gestured for Mower to follow him into his office. The Sergeant closed the door carefully behind him and watched as his boss sat heavily down behind his desk, lit a cigarette and drew the smoke greedily into his lungs.

'We're up to our necks again,' Thackeray said bleakly.

'How did the Super take the news,' Mower asked. Thackeray shrugged wearily.

'How do you think?' he said. 'Incandescent hardly does it justice. If he gets his hands on Laura I think he'll strangle her himself.'

And you too, Mower thought, noticing how Thackeray's hands shook as he flicked the ash off his cigarette. He could still scarcely credit himself how naïve Laura had been in her dealings with the Albanian girl, and he wondered how rocky her relationship with Thackeray had become for her to fail to give him even a hint about what she had become involved in. But those were questions he had more sense than to even whisper with his boss in his present state. He glanced at his watch.

'Lee Towers is due in shortly,' he said. 'I take it you're planning to give him and his mate a hard time?'

'Oh yes,' Thackeray said. 'I want chapter and verse about what these footballers were up to that night, and any other night they entertained Elena and Grace, or girls like them. They must have some idea who's organising that particular service. I'll tell them that if they can't put their finger on a source we'll have to assume that they're hiring the girls themselves and face the consequences of dealing in trafficked women. That should sharpen their minds a bit.'

'And I'll prod Ibramovic into recalling everything Elena told him, as well as trying to work out where she and Jasmin could have gone.' Mower hesitated for a moment. 'Who's going to talk to Laura, guv?' he asked eventually, and was shocked at the sudden flash of anger in Thackeray's eyes.

'The Super,' he said flatly. 'He's agreed to that, insisted in fact. And he'll organise something with Joyce Ackroyd as well. He wants us out of it.'

'Right, guv,' Mower said, feeling relieved for himself and the DCI, and apprehensive for Laura at the same time.

'In his present mood he'll be looking for something to charge the pair of them with,' Thackeray said, his face like stone.

'That'd be a bit harsh if they didn't know we were looking for the girl,' Mower said carefully.

'I don't think so. Not really,' Thackeray snapped, and Mower wondered if this time there was going to be any way back.

Ten minutes later Michael Thackeray and his young DC, Peter Hodge, found Lee Towers and a solicitor waiting for them in an interview room on the ground floor. Thackeray nodded grimly at the lawyer, then concentrated on the footballer, who was sitting bolt upright on his chair looking distinctly uncomfortable. He was an athletic-looking young man, in a suit and an open necked black shirt, which revealed a heavy gold chain around his neck. He was tanned and sporting blond highlights in his fashionably tousled dark hair, which occasionally flopped into his curiously pale eyes, but he fiddled nervously with a gold ring on his finger as he watched the two police officers take their seats and Hodge switch on a tape recorder and announce who was present in the room.

'My client is here voluntarily to assist in any way he can,' the lawyer said quickly.

'I'm aware of that,' Thackeray said. 'But this is a murder inquiry and I have reason to believe your client knew the victim and her friend, whose whereabouts are at present unknown. I'm sure he has no objection to this interview being taped?'

Towers glanced at the solicitor and then shook his head.

'That's OK,' he said in little more than a whisper.

'Right,' Thackeray said. 'Then perhaps we can start by your

telling us how you first met the two girls we now know as Grace and Elena, and how your relationship, if you can call it that, developed.'

Towers swallowed hard and opened his mouth, but for a moment nothing came out.

'In your own words, Lee,' his lawyer offered sympathetically. 'You've done nothing illegal.' Thackeray raised an eyebrow at that but said nothing, and eventually Lee Towers leant across the table towards him and began.

'They turned up at a couple of parties at the country club,' he said.

'A bit louder for the tape,' DC Hodge said sharply, and Towers repeated himself.

'OK really fancied the black lass but I liked the other one better, Elena she said her name was.'

'Did they give you any other names?'

'No, just Grace and Elena. That's all you need, isn't it? They were both up for it, no problem. Didn't object when we asked them to come upstairs.'

'Who, exactly, went upstairs on which occasion?' Thackeray snapped.

'The same both times. OK and the black lass took one room, me and Dave, Dave Peters, went with the other one.'

'Singly or together?' Thackeray's tone was contemptuous now, and Towers flushed and glanced away, while his solicitor's lips tightened in distaste.

'Together,' he said. 'She said she didn't mind.'

'Let's leave that on one side for now then,' Thackeray said, to the obvious relief of everyone in the room. 'Did these girls tell you anything at all about themselves?'

'Not really,' Towers said.

'You didn't chat them up, then? Spend any time getting to know them?'

'Not really,' Towers said again. 'There was a lot of drink around and I thought they were only there for one thing.'

'So you knew they were prostitutes?' Thackeray snapped.

'Not really,' Towers said again, looking sick. 'There's always a lot of girls around, girls ready to go to bed with you if that's what you want. I wouldn't call them prostitutes exactly, just an easy lay.'

'Did you pay her?'

Towers glanced at his solicitor for help but the lawyer's face was not sympathetic.

'Not the first time,' he said. 'But later, the last time I saw her last week she asked for a hundred quid. It were a bit unusual that. They didn't usually ask for money.'

'They?'

'Different girls, they come and go. There were another two little tarts at the Chelsea party. That's what upset our women so much.'

'And you were sure the girl – or girls – you slept with were willing? They gave their full consent to whatever you and Dave asked them to do? The foreign girl you met at the Rochdale party, especially? Anyone can see she's very young.'

'Of course she did,' Towers said, angry this time. 'What are you saying? That we raped her? That's rubbish. She was willing. She didn't seem to enjoy it much...' He stopped suddenly realising that he had perhaps gone to far. But it was too late. Thackeray's voice took on a note of controlled fury.

'I think you need to understand the law, Mr Towers, before

you go any further. Firstly, you need to be sure that a girl is over the age of consent. We don't know how old Elena is, but we do know that some girls are being brought to this country for prostitution well under the age of sixteen. Secondly, you have to be sure that consent is given on each and every occasion you sleep with a woman. In the case of Grace and Elena we have reason to believe that they have been brought into the country illegally and have been forced into prostitution by violence and threats. In that case consent is always and every time in doubt. I'm told that Elena at least speaks very little English so it's difficult to know how you can be so sure she was willing. Do you understand what I'm saying?'

Towers swallowed hard and nodded, giving his solicitor a desperate glance, but he too was looking pale and seemed unable to find his voice.

'Do you understand?' Thackeray repeated.

'Yeah, yeah,' Towers said. 'We didn't know they were on the game. We thought they were out for a good time. There were often a few girls like that there.'

'So how exactly did they get to these parties?' Thackeray snapped. 'Did you or the other players ask for girls to be provided?'

'No, of course not,' Towers said. 'My fiancée would kill me if I tried anything like that. They just turned up.'

'But who arranged for them to turn up? We have evidence that they were brought by car and that there were men, minders, with them. Someone must have invited them to come. Was it Paolo Minelli? Was it a little perk he provided when you'd had a good result? Did he pay them if you didn't?'

Towers' eyes widened in horror.

'Hell, no,' he said.

'So if not him, who? Who was paying for the whores to make themselves available, Mr Towers? Who was the pimp?'

'I don't know,' Towers said. 'I swear to God I don't know.'

'Do you know a man called Stephen Stone?' Thackeray asked, but Towers shook his head.

'I don't think so,' he said.

'He was at the last party you had at the West Royd club after the Chelsea game,' Thackeray said. 'I was there myself and I saw him. He's the brother of Angelica Stone, Minelli's girlfriend.'

Towers nodded as if to indicate his pressing desire to be helpful now the focus had shifted slightly from his own behaviour.

'I know Angelica,' he said. 'She's often around. But her brother? No.'

'And girls were there that night, as well? Girls you knew would be willing and eager to go upstairs with you?'

'Most of us had our wives or girlfriends with us that night. You know how it is? The previous party was a bit impromptu. Just the lads. But at the Chelsea party I couldn't do owt. Dave were in the same boat. But I think OK got his end away wi'one of them, though not the black lass he really fancied. I didn't see her or her friend that night. OK was really taken with the lass he met after the Rochdale game. I'm pretty sure he saw her again. But I didn't see her, certainly not at the Chelsea party. But you need to ask him not me.'

'So you two couldn't find an opportunity to cheat on your wife and girlfriend that night, then?' Thackeray's voice was loaded with contempt.

'I think that remark is a bit unnecessary, Chief Inspector,' Towers' solicitor said faintly.

'Do you?' Thackeray said. 'How would you describe it then?' But he didn't wait for an answer. 'I'm seeing your team-mate Dave Peters later,' he said to Towers. 'I shall expect your stories to tally. In the meantime you can go, but I fully expect to need to talk to you again.'

'There's one thing,' Towers said suddenly, his voice half strangled. 'OK Okigbo said you told him his tart had Aids.' His solicitor drew a sharp breath again, evidently still capable of being shocked by what he was hearing.

'I didn't say that,' Thackeray snapped. 'I told him the murdered girl, Grace, was HIV positive. We don't know about the other girl because we haven't made contact with her yet.'

Towers said nothing but he seemed to have difficulty getting to his feet, and when he did he looked faintly green beneath his expensive tan. His solicitor followed him to the interview room door looking almost as distressed.

'You know where to contact me, Chief Inspector,' he said.

'Oh yes,' Thackeray said and, to DC Hodge's surprise, when the door had closed behind the footballer and his lawyer, he thumped his fist down so hard on the interview room table that they both winced.

'Boss?' the younger man said cautiously. Thackeray looked up and shook his head briefly, his eyes opaque.

'Better than thumping that over-paid, incontinent young bastard, which is what he deserves,' he said. 'Come on, let's see if the next one has arrived. If the CPS would wear it, I'd like to charge the lot of them with statutory rape, but I don't suppose they will. We'll just go on persecuting the women. There's not much obvious correlation between the law and justice, is there?' And he led his bemused young colleague out of the room.

Laura arrived at the *Gazette* office that morning late, tired and thoroughly deflated. She had slept badly, alone in the bed she normally shared with Michael Thackeray, and had then been roused from her semi-stupor as she sat in the kitchen, hunched over a large mug of coffee, by a call from police headquarters asking her to see Superintendent Longley as soon as she could that morning. Feeling slightly sick, she had made an appointment and presented herself in Longley's office, where she found the Superintendent alone, in full uniform, gazing out of his window at the wind-swept town hall square below. Eventually he turned and held out a hand for her to shake with an expression that was about as far from welcoming as she could imagine.

Laura felt she knew Longley well enough, having lived with Thackeray's take on his boss for so long, but she had met him only a couple of times, and never in circumstances remotely like this. She took in his portly shape encased in navy blue with buttons gleaming, his shiny, almost bald head, and the fleshy, slightly grey, creased face and chilly blue eyes, and recognised an unhappy and seriously embarrassed man.

'Ms Ackroyd, sit down,' Longley said, waving her into a chair and lowering himself into his own with ponderous dignity.

'Laura, please,' she said, flicking the cloud of copper-coloured hair she had not had time to put up out of her eyes, and crossing her legs, encased in her red leather boots. Confession, she thought, might be the best, possibly the only, form of defence, although she doubted she would be offered much in the way of absolution, either here or anywhere else this morning. While Longley hesitated, she waded in.

'You don't have to tell me that I've been involved in something very stupid, and I don't have to tell you how sorry I am,' she said. 'I don't regret having helped this girl Elena when she was obviously sick and in trouble, but once I realised the police wanted to interview her in connection with the death of the other girl, I know I should have brought her straight here, not given her the chance to run off again.'

Looking rather less than disarmed, Longley leant across his desk.

'Concealing an illegal immigrant is an offence, Ms Ackroyd,' he said.

'She was half-starved, sick and unable to communicate very much,' Laura said. 'I regarded her as a victim not a criminal, and I wanted to get hold of a translator and find out a bit more before I persuaded her to talk to the authorities. Not such a big deal.'

'With a story for your newspaper in mind, no doubt?'

Laura flushed slightly.

'That wasn't my top priority,' she said. 'But it was a consideration, yes. I was shocked by what Elena told me. It's something that's largely hidden. I thought *Gazette* readers should know that the trafficking of young girls was going on right here in Bradfield. And I knew that if she was arrested there was a strong chance that she'd be shipped off to some immigration detention centre and I'd not be able to speak to her easily again. Was I wrong? Were you even aware of this horrible trade on your doorstep?'

But Longley refused to bat that one back.

'We have a special unit dealing with this sort of thing at County,' he said. 'But that's hardly the point. This was a murder investigation that your own...' He hesitated, old and conservative enough for the word he was looking for not to come easily to his lips. 'That your own *partner* was investigating. I'm amazed you didn't tell Michael about the girl your grandmother had taken in.'

Laura glanced away. There was no way she was going to confide in Longley about the state of her relationship with Michael Thackeray.

'My grandmother and I decided we should find out a bit more about Elena's circumstances. What she was saying was very vague and garbled. We needed her to get her strength back and I needed to find a translator. Speakers of Albanian are a bit difficult to track down. It took time. Once I'd learnt the full story I knew we would have to talk to the authorities – the immigration people, the police, whoever. But I thought it was kinder to let her have a bit of peace with the Ibramovic's. They're good people. They were keen to look after her, and I knew she'd be safe there, well out of Bradfield. I didn't know you were looking for her then.'

Laura pushed her unruly hair away from her face and leant towards Longley, putting all her considerable powers of persuasion into her voice.

'It was pure bad luck that I wasn't at work when you issued the picture and the appeal for Elena,' she said. 'If I'd known on Wednesday, of course I would have told Michael then. You have to believe that.' But Laura knew that it was not Longley that she had to convince, it was Michael Thackeray himself, and however sceptically the Superintendent might look at her, Thackeray would take even more persuading.

'So you went back to Ilkley on Thursday when you realised we were looking for the girl, but you still didn't bring her back to Bradfield,' Longley said, real anger in his voice now. 'You left her there and gave her and the Ibramovic girl the chance to run off. You'll forgive me if I suggest that was criminally careless of you.'

'Yes,' Laura said. 'That was stupid. I was hoping Michael would go out to Ilkley to talk to her rather than her having to be taken to the police station. You've no idea how fragile she is. It never crossed my mind that she would run away.'

'A lot of things seem to have never crossed your mind, Ms Ackroyd, not least the fact that if this girl has been used in the way she claims, the people who have abused her, who may well be the same people who have murdered her friend, will be extremely anxious to get her back. Being arrested as an illegal immigrant may be unpleasant, but believe me, having her fall back into the hands of the people traffickers could be much, much worse.'

Laura nodded, feeling sick and numb, knowing she could not argue with that, and Longley leant back in his chair and sighed.

'I'll arrange for one of my officers to take a formal statement from you,' he said. 'I've already asked a detective and a woman officer to visit your grandmother to do the same. I understand she's not very mobile.'

'Thank you,' Laura said.

'I think I should warn you that I may have to pass what you've told me to the Crown Prosecution Service. You seem to have interfered pretty disastrously in a murder investigation, and not for the first time. They may decide to pursue it further.'

'Whatever,' Laura said dully, thinking how furious her friend Vicky Mendelson's husband David, who worked for the CPS, would be when he found out what had happened. She wondered where she could find a friend and ally in all this mess.

Longley hesitated for a moment.

'When are you due to talk to the inquiry at County HQ?' he asked.

'Next week,' Laura said, and the Superintendent nodded.

'I think,' he said carefully, 'that you and the DCI need to discuss just how your private and your professional lives intersect, don't you? This is the second time it's been a major problem.'

'I'm sure we do,' Laura said non-committally, biting her lip to prevent herself blurting out that her main fear this morning was not statements or inquiries or even the possibility of prosecution but the fact that she and Michael Thackeray would not intersect again in any significant way at all.

Half an hour later she had left the police station, having signed her statement. She had felt even more drained than she had when she got out of bed that morning as she had walked slowly across the town to the *Gazette* office where she was met, before she took off her coat, by an evidently over-excited Tony Holloway.

'Where've you been? I need to talk to you,' he said,

following on her heels to her desk. 'All hell's broken loose at United and Ted Grant's doing his nut.'

'What's happened now?' Laura asked wearily. 'You may think I'm muscling in on your territory, Tony, but I can tell you honestly, nothing's further from my mind.'

'Never mind all that now,' Tony said. 'You can help, actually. I can't get much sense out of the press people at Beck Lane, and I know you've managed to inveigle your way into Jenna Heywood's good books, so Ted wants you to call her and see if we can firm up the rumours that are flying around.'

'What rumours are they?' Laura asked.

'Just that OK Okigbo, and possibly some of the other players, have been sleeping with tarts and have picked up something nasty from them, probably AIDS. And that they've been interviewed by the police because one of the girls is the one who ended up dead in the canal. I dare say lover-boy may just have mentioned that in passing, but we know where your loyalties lie, don't we? So – we could have our star player banged up as a murder suspect just before they're due to go to London for the Chelsea replay. How major is that?'

Laura felt very cold suddenly. She shook her head.

'I know absolutely nothing about all that,' she said. 'And I doubt very much that Jenna Heywood will tell me anything, even if it's true. It's the sort of thing they'll put a very tight lid on. You know that.'

'It could finish the club off if it's true,' Tony said. 'The shareholders'll do their nut. Will you call her?'

'Is that what Ted wants?' Laura asked, glancing towards the editor's glass-walled office where, unusually, the door was tight shut.

'That's what Ted wants,' Tony said.

Laura sat down at her desk and picked up the phone to call the football club and, to her surprise, was put straight through to Jenna. But when she spelt out the reason for her call Jenna interrupted her coldly.

'We've got no comment on that,' she said. 'I'm sorry, Laura. You'll have to ask the press office at police HQ what's going on.'

'I think we've already tried that,' Laura said, glancing at Tony, but thinking of Elena. A place like a hotel, she had said, but why not the country club? 'You realise that the girl who was murdered and her friend could have been at your team parties, don't you? And that they were probably prostitutes in the country illegally.'

'No comment,' Jenna said.

'Have you seen the photograph of the girls?' Laura persisted. 'You might even recognise them.'

Jenna seemed to hesitate for no more than a split second, and seemed to be weighing her words very carefully.

'If I do, I'll be talking to the coach about it and telling the police, not you. Now I must get on.'

Laura hesitated, absolutely sure that Jenna knew more than she was telling her.

'You recognised her, didn't you?' she said. 'Do you also know who arranged for the girls to be at those parties? Was it Minelli?'

'No comment,' Jenna said sharply. 'I've nothing to say to the *Gazette* about the players' private lives.'

'There's one other thing, Jenna,' Laura said impulsively. 'You might like to know that my father's apparently sold his shares in United to Les Hardcastle.' She heard Jenna draw a sharp breath at the other end of the phone.

'Thanks for telling me that,' she said. 'I'll give it some thought over the weekend. I'm going down to London tomorrow for a bit of peace and quiet before the big match. The team travel down on Sunday. Give me a call after it's all over, Laura, next Wednesday, say, and we'll have a chat then. In the meantime, I want out of Bradfield for a bit. I've had more than enough of it.'

Laura put the phone down and shook her head at Tony Holloway.

'Nothing doing,' she said. 'Whatever she knows she's not telling me. By the sound of it she's still more worried about the in-fighting amongst the directors than she is about any problem with the players. I think maybe your rumours are just that – rumours.'

'No way,' Holloway said, looking obstinate.

'Wouldn't it be more productive to do some digging around Les Hardcastle's plans for the club?' she suggested. 'If anything's a threat to its future it's that, not the sexual antics of the players.'

'Give me a break, Laura,' he snapped. 'If only half what I'm hearing about OK Okigbo is true the whole Press pack from London will already be halfway up the M1. I need to break this story and I need to break it before they arrive. It's mega.'

'If you say so, Tony,' Laura said wearily as she logged onto her computer. 'If you say so.'

CHAPTER FIFTEEN

Sergeant Kevin Mower put his head round DCI Thackeray's door later that morning and found his boss more or less as he had left him several hours before, his room fuggy with cigarette smoke and a pile of unopened files on the desk in front of him. He glanced up lethargically as Mower came in and closed the door.

'Developments, guv,' the Sergeant said. 'I've had a long talk with Ibramovic and pretty well wrung him dry. He's not unhelpful. He knows we're doing our best. But he was more useful on what the girl told him about the trafficking racket than he is on where she and his daughter may have gone. He doesn't seem to have any idea about that.'

'Did Elena give him a family name?'

'Nope, and she never gave any hint that Grace even existed.'

'We may never find out who the dead girl really is,' Thackeray said. 'An anonymous death in a faraway country. Her family will never know what happened to her.' Thackeray seemed to look bleakly straight through Mower for a moment before he shook himself slightly and returned to the present.

'And the trafficking? What did Elena say about that?' he asked.

'She told Ibramovic about the house where she was kept. Quite a big house, she said, although coming from where she comes from he said anything with more than two or three rooms would seem big to her. He's a Bosnian, so he should know. Anyway, he reckons three floors at least and some sort of cellar. She said when girls got hysterical or stroppy they'd be put underground in a room without windows and left there for a couple of days. The whole house was dark, apparently. Elena said that the windows all round the house were generally covered up with what sounded like wooden shutters. Which means it has to be an old house, Victorian probably, with those shutters that close on the inside.'

'There's a few of those still about in the older parts of Bradfield,' Thackeray said. 'Mainly around Aysgarth Lane.'

'Right, and that would be a good area to choose if you're going to put women on the street. But I did speak to one of my contacts and she said she didn't think foreign girls were being run on the street. She'd heard rumours but never met anyone like that, and didn't know anyone who had.'

'The vice team from County are going to do a sweep of the red light districts tonight,' Thackeray said. 'We haven't the numbers to do it ourselves. I want every woman on the game questioned.'

'That sounds good,' Mower said. 'It may turn up some sort of corroboration of the rumours. But Jackie reckons that they're being run as call girls. Kept under close guard and taken out to clients. Or possibly offered in some of the clubs.'

'That would fit with what we know about Grace and Elena being taken to West Royd,' Thackeray said. 'Tomorrow I want to start interviewing every single person who was at the

United parties at the club over the last few months. Find out from Minelli how many there've been. It seems to be after they've won a match and I understand they've been doing that unusually often recently. Someone must know how those girls got there, who brought them, who asked for them to be brought.'

'You'd best make a start quickly,' Mower said. 'Everyone connected with United will be going to London for the big match, don't forget. That's on Tuesday evening.'

'Plenty of overtime over the weekend then,' Thackeray said. 'I'll fix it with Jack Longley. Start by asking the football club for a list of all those who were invited, including wives and girlfriends. We'll start with the legitimate guests, but ask them all if they saw anyone they didn't recognise or didn't expect to find there. It'll be tedious but necessary. A lot of people must have seen those two girls at least at one club party, and maybe other girls we haven't identified, if what Jolene and Katrina said about seeing girls leave the Chelsea party was true. I want a picture of how they arrived, who they spoke to, who they went upstairs with – it may not be only the three players we know about – and how they left, and who with, who ordered them and who paid for them. We'll interview the whole team, if necessary. Girls have been seen coming and going in the car park. What sort of car were they in? What were they wearing? Who were they with? I want a complete picture of each night, and particularly the night the two girls ran off, after asking the men they were with for money. They ran, but who, if anyone, followed? Someone may have noticed.'

'Guv,' Mower said, making copious notes as he listened to Thackeray. 'We could ask the beat coppers in the older areas of town about the house, too,' he suggested. 'Somewhere old and large, with windows more or less permanently shuttered up. There can't be too many places like that. If we find a likely house we can ask the neighbours what they've seen.'

'Yes, organise that too, would you, Kevin?' Thackeray said, tiredly. 'Any other leads?'

'Possibly,' Mower said. 'Joyce Ackroyd has turned up trumps. She's here now looking at mug shots for the two men who knocked on her door claiming to be from immigration. She reckons they went round most of the estate so there's a good chance we'll get a good description, if not a positive ID. And she made a note of the mobile phone number they were giving out. I suppose the chances are that it's a pay-as-you-go with no registered owner, but you never know. Someone may have been stupid enough to give their own number. I'm having it checked out. Anyway, if it's switched on we may be able to pinpoint its whereabouts. That might help us find the house too.'

'If they've any sense they'll have ditched the phone by now, and quite possibly moved their base,' Thackeray said. 'But give it a try. We can't afford not to. Have there been any sightings of the two runaway girls?'

'Nothing yet,' Mower said. 'We're still wading through the CCTV tapes. The *Gazette* and local TV want to know if you want them to go with the pictures of the two of them?'

'If we do, we risk alerting the traffickers to the fact that Elena's still in Bradfield.'

'If we don't, we get no feedback from the public.'

The two men's eyes met in shared anxiety for a moment.

'Go with Jasmin's picture,' Thackeray said. 'But ask them

not to make any connection between her and the other girl. Missing schoolgirls are common enough, and if we find her we'll find Elena as well, obviously. Tell her parents what we're doing and why. They'll understand. The fact that Elena's with her makes Jasmin's situation all the more dangerous. They'll know that.'

'Right, guv,' Mower said.

'Anything from the sweep of massage parlours?'

'Nothing so far,' Mower said. 'There's plenty of girls who will admit, if pushed, to offering a lot more than the standard massage, but we've not found anyone who knows anything about foreign girls being brought into their establishments. No one who'll admit it, anyway.'

'Right, well, keep going with that but softly, softly, especially in the clubs. I don't want to panic these bastards and have them leaving town, taking their girls with them.'

'Right, guv, I'll work on the trawl of the clubs myself tonight. Take someone with me, look like punters, and make some discreet inquiries. If what Elena says is true these girls must be offered for sale somehow, somewhere. We'll find them.'

'Let's hope so, before someone else gets killed,' Thackeray said. 'Or they're all shipped out to Manchester or London or Belgrade. I don't think we've got much time.'

Laura finished work that afternoon and sat at her blank computer screen for a long time, wondering what to do with the long empty evening that stretched ahead of her. She knew without being told that Thackeray would not come back that night. In fact she guessed that he would not come back at all unless they found some way of discussing and resolving the chasm of misunderstanding that now lay between them. Thackeray had never sold his own flat in Bradfield, and she knew that he regarded it as a bolthole for the moment when their affair finally crashed in flames, as she guessed that he had always thought it might. Maybe that moment had come at last, she thought. She desperately wanted to talk to him, but she knew from past experience that he had the capacity to bury himself in his work when he needed to, although if that failed, there was always the other route to emotional oblivion he had largely resisted since she had known him but which lurked like a rabid tiger in the dark undergrowth ready to consume him if he showed the slightest weakness.

Still debilitated by his spell in hospital, she knew he was finding the present case difficult. The next week, when they both had appointments with the inquiry team probing Bradfield CID's last horrific murder, would be worse. Together they might have withstood the pressure. Apart, she was not at all sure they could.

She sighed and had walked across the deserted office to get her coat when the phone on her desk rang. She hurried back and grabbed the receiver, her heart thumping, hoping against hope that it might be Thackeray, and was surprised to hear Vince Newsom's voice at the other end of the line. She had never found the emotional energy to follow Kevin Mower's advice and talk to her former colleague and lover about the evidence he proposed to give to the police inquiry, and now, she guessed, he had decided to take the initiative himself.

'Hi, doll,' Vince said, with his customary lack of charm. 'As you probably know, I'm up in your neck of the woods on

Monday, courtesy of the cops, and thought we might get together for old time's sake.'

'I don't think so,' Laura said. 'Not after what you did to me last time. What exactly do you intend to tell the inquiry?'

There was a short silence at the other end.

'That rather depends on you, darling,' Vince said.

'What do you mean?' Laura asked, although she had a good idea what was bothering him.

'Well, it did cross my mind that neither of us has much to gain by slagging each other off in front of these nosy coppers. What do you think?'

'I'm not sure what you're suggesting,' Laura said, as much to gain time as because it was true.

'Let me spell it out then, babe,' Vince said, an edge of irritation making his voice harsher. 'I'm sure you don't want to go into lurid detail about what went on that night and I'm bloody sure I don't want to be accused of nicking that crucial sheet of paper from you. I've a fiancée now whose family is already a bit sniffy about what I do for a living. A bit more *Telegraph* than *Globe* inclined, my future in-laws. I thought that if you said you had lost the document that was in your bag and I said I found it in my car after I'd dropped you off we would both be better off. What do you think?'

'You want me to lie to the inquiry to cover up for you?' Laura asked angrily, filled with fury that Vince Newsom should be trying to manipulate her yet again.

'You wouldn't be lying,' Vince snapped back. 'Can you honestly say how I found your precious piece of paper? Did you see me take it? Of course you didn't. You were out of it, baby. You know you were. I had to put you to bed, for God's sake. And you don't remember that, either, do you?'

Laura caught her breath, feeling as cold suddenly as she had felt hot a moment before.

'Do you really want everyone – and I do mean everyone – to know just how pissed you were that night?' Newsom persisted. 'Much better all round if we keep it simple. You couldn't drive home because you were over the limit, I kindly dropped you off, and later on I found this very interesting note in my car that you were supposed to deliver to lover boy. And surprise, surprise, I jumped on the gift-horse and rode with it before giving you the note back the next day. How's that? Suit you, does it? No hint of theft on my part, no hint of hanky-panky when you invited me in on yours. A win-win situation, if you ask me. Is it a deal?'

Laura desperately wanted to say no but she knew she couldn't. Vince's offer would take the dead weight off her shoulders that had been there ever since the day DC Val Ridley had given her that note for Michael Thackeray, the contents of which had found their way onto the front page of the *Globe* under Vince Newsom's by-line, the next morning. He was in no position to deny that he had got hold of the information but he would be as happy to say that he had found it by accident as she would be to see the suspicion that she had deliberately given it to him dispelled. And she would be even more grateful not to have Vince's visit to her flat explored at the inquiry. She knew he had come inside with her, she knew he had put her to bed, and when he had claimed to have gone further there was no way she could deny it. It would be deeply embarrassing to have Newsom tell the inquiry any of that, but much, much worse when Thackeray heard her ex's most lurid version of events, which was undoubtedly what would happen if she pushed an allegation of theft.

'It's a deal,' she said quietly to Newsom at last. 'You're a bastard, Vince, but it's a deal.'

'Good girl,' Vince said. 'So let's get this straight. The note could easily have fallen out of your bag in the car?'

'Right,' she said.

'And I gave you your key and dropped you at your door.'

'As far as I can remember,' Laura agreed.

'Just stick with your hazy memories and we'll be fine, baby,' Vince said. 'We'll be just fine. As far as I can find out I'm the first to give evidence on Monday so I'll stick to that. You make sure you do the same.'

With her coat round her shoulders Laura sat at her desk for a few more minutes, wondering again if she could or should try to contact Thackeray. But in the end, she shrugged and pulled her coat on and wound a scarf around her neck, and walked slowly out of the building, hesitating again in the foyer where she could see sleety rain lashing against the plateglass windows. She did not want to go home, and she toyed for a moment with the idea of going up to The Heights to see her grandmother. But although she knew that would please Joyce, she did not feel strong enough to spend an hour or so rehashing the mistakes they had both made that had so infuriated Thackeray. She also ruled out a late call on her friend Vicky Mendelson, who would be putting her children to bed. Vicky would, as always, be a comfort, but she did not want to risk seeing her husband David at the moment. As a Crown Prosecution Service lawyer, she knew that he would be as appalled as Thackeray was when he learnt of the mess she had got herself into.

But her own empty flat seemed less than enticing, and in the end she left her car in the car park and walked across the town centre, dodging the homeward bound shopping traffic, and strode up the stone steps to the imposing entrance of the Clarendon hotel, where she knew she could find an armchair in a quiet corner of the bar and sink into anonymous comfort with a vodka and tonic.

The Clarendon had been a favourite haunt of her father's, a place where Bradfield's surviving businessmen conferred, successors of the textile millionaires who had built solid monuments to themselves like the Exchange, the Italianate town hall and the town's major hotels, which still stood, although their mills and warehouses had fallen silent long ago. The place was still opulent and when she walked in there was a handful of prosperous looking men in suits at the bar taking their Scotch prior to the long drive home to the more salubrious dormitory towns in the Yorkshire Dales. One or two looked at her curiously as she sought out a seat and nodded to the waiter. This was still not a place where a woman on her own was a common sight once afternoon tea had ceased to be served in the lounge to elderly ladies in hats.

Service was quick, and she took a sip of her drink, leant back in her seat and closed her eyes for a second, trying to blot out the day completely. She felt sick at the thought that Thackeray might be trying to do the same with a bottle of Scotch. But she was not left in peace for long. She had only half finished her vodka and tonic when she was aware of a heavyweight figure making its way across the thick carpet towards her.

'Laura? Laura Ackroyd?' said the man she quickly recognised as her father's acquaintance Les Hardcastle. 'I thought it was you, Laura, and lovelier than ever.' Hardcastle dropped into the chair on the other side of the table and beamed at her, a florid man in his late fifties with silvery hair and calculating eyes. 'Have you spoken to your dad recently? I was only talking to him the other day, as it happens. We still keep in touch now and again, me and Jack. Sold me his shares in the end, you know.'

'I heard you'd had some dealings over Bradfield United,' Laura said, trying to summon some interest in the obsessions of the football fanatics. 'Are you going down to London for the Chelsea match?'

'Oh aye, I'll be at Stamford Bridge,' Hardcastle said, his eyes ablaze. 'It'll be good to take a close look at a club that's found an investor like they've got, the Russian fellow, you know? I'm trying to get someone like that on board at United. We'd be up in the Premiership in no time with that sort of investment in some decent players.'

'Is that what you're aiming at?' Laura said, trying not to look too sceptical as she recalled Jenna Heywood's conviction that Les would sell the club down the river for a suitable financial return. Les tapped the side of his nose and tried to look mysterious, although to Laura it merely made him seem shifty.

'It's not beyond the bounds of possibility,' he said. 'There's feelers out of a very encouraging sort. Can't say any more, especially as you're with the *Gazette*, my dear. But it'll all come out in the fullness of time. You'll see.'

'Well, make sure our sports editor's the first to hear of it, won't you?' Laura said. 'He's very keen to discover which way the club is going. I interviewed Jenna Heywood last week. Does she play any part in your plans?' Laura knew the answer to that question and she was not surprised when Hardcastle scowled.

'She's got no idea about football, that young woman,' Hardcastle said, with real venom in his voice, making Laura suddenly feel cold. 'Just as soon as the investor I've got in mind is fully on board, she'll be out on her ear, I make no secret of that. She won't be able to turn the deal down, believe me, even though my man won't want to keep her on as chairman. You wouldn't catch this lad leaving a woman in charge.'

'Any particular reason for that, Les?' Laura asked sweetly. 'Smaller brain, perhaps, or the lack of a willy?'

Les flushed, and leant across the table towards her angrily.

'There's no need for that,' he hissed. 'But it'd not be something a Muslim would do, is it?'

'A Muslim millionaire then, is it?' Laura asked.

'I'll say no more,' Hardcastle said, hauling himself back to his feet. 'Give my regards to your parents when you speak to them.' And with that he headed back to the bar where he was soon absorbed by a group of middle-aged men in suits who glanced in Laura's direction in response to something Hardcastle said, and then turned in on themselves again with knowing smiles. Irritated, Laura drained her glass and left the bar, which suddenly felt inhospitable, without a backward glance. On the steps of the hotel she paused for a moment and pulled out her mobile.

'Tony?' she said when her call was answered by voicemail. 'I've just had a chat with Les Hardcastle and his plans for the club. From what he says, you should be looking for a Muslim millionaire with an interest in football – or maybe just in football grounds. According to Les, he's going to get Bradfield United into the Premiership and give Chelsea's Russian a run for his money. Don't say I never do anything for you. If you want any more, give me a call.'

She rang off with a wry smile and pulled her scarf up tighter round her chin. It was a bitterly cold evening and she wondered where Elena and her friend were hiding. She hoped they were somewhere warm. For a second she gazed at her mobile before speed dialling another number, but again all she got was the impersonal tones of voicemail.

'Michael, it's me,' she said. 'Can we talk?' But as she flicked the phone off she felt the dread she had tried to banish in the bar return with full force. He won't call, she thought. This time, he really won't call.

CHAPTER SIXTEEN

Sergeant Kevin Mower had to admit that Stephen Stone had spared no expense on the décor at his new club, The Manhattan, a glossy art deco extravaganza in chrome and shiny red and black lacquer and leather. And it was already busy at nine-thirty on a Friday evening with a bustle of men in the ubiquitous smart casual dress of the affluent young. Wives and girlfriends were less in evidence, Mower thought as he sipped his extortionately priced cocktail, but there was a cluster of scantily dressed young women at the bar who seemed very ready to have drinks bought for them, and a couple of floor to ceiling poles that promised more exotic entertainment to come.

Mower leant back in his black leather and chrome chair and surveyed the scene benignly. If only more assignments were like this, he thought. He had planned to bring a colleague with him but the trawl of all the clubs in Bradfield that evening had soaked up officers and in the end most had been sent out alone. But he was not alone for long, as he had guessed he would not be. One of the girls at the bar, a willowy blonde in a slinky satin dress that revealed much more than it concealed, made her way over to his table with a bright smile.

'Hi,' she said. 'My name's Melanie. Would you like some company?'

'Sure,' Mower said. 'It's the first time I've been here. Some mates are coming in later but for the minute I'm all alone. Can I get you a drink?'

'Do you like champagne? Champagne's my favourite,' Melanie said eagerly, but Mower glanced at his own garishly coloured drink and shook his head.

'Start with a cocktail, why don't you?' he said, knowing that his expenses would not cover a bottle of bubbly at the sort of prices The Manhattan was likely to charge. 'This is nice.' He held his glass up enticingly. Melanie pouted slightly but nodded when the waiter came over to their table.

'One of those,' she said, pointing at the drink which Mower was sipping as slowly as he dared. Mower leant back again, admiring Melanie's undoubted charms but knowing that there was no way she had been smuggled into Bradfield from anywhere further east than Cleckheaton.

'You work here then, do you?' he asked, with what he hoped was an expectant leer.

'I'm a hostess,' Melanie said. 'Here to help you enjoy yourself.'

'Oh, you could do that all right,' Mower said, giving the girl's silky leg a stroke under the table.

'Well, we'll have to see about that, won't we, cheeky boy,' Melanie said. 'But I'm not allowed to get into any naughtiness on the premises, am I? They're very, very strict about that.' She nodded towards the disco at the far end of the room where a black-clad DJ had clamped headphones to his ears and was messing about with his decks.

'There's dancing later,' she said. Her drink arrived and she took a sip from a glass where the contents looked suspiciously paler than Mower's own. Her cocktail, he guessed, was probably little more than coloured water.

'Do you live local?' Melanie asked. 'Have you got your own place?'

Mower nodded.

'And you?' he asked.

'Only shared,' she said gloomily. 'It's not the same as having your own place, is it? What do you do then? Good job, is it? Must be if you can afford to come here.'

'Not bad,' Mower said cheerfully, realising that this was a girl totally out of her depth in what purported to be Bradfield's most sophisticated night-spot. She had the looks and the style but by no stretch of the imagination had she the sophistication or the wit. And whatever else she was, she was not an obvious tart. Her eyes were too bright and genuinely interested in him for that.

'How long has this place been open, then?' he asked. 'Have you been here since the start?'

Melanie giggled.

'It opened about two months ago, I think. But this is my first week, would you believe.' Oh yes, Mower thought, I'd believe that. Just his luck to get landed with a complete novice.

'So it's a good job then, is it, being a hostess? Good pay and all that?'

'Oh, not bad,' Melanie said. 'But then, they say there's tips?'

'For extra services?'

The girl glanced away, looking embarrassed.

'I told you. There's nothing like that. If that's what you and your mates are expecting you're going to be disappointed.' Mower looked across at the gaggle of girls by the bar, who were beginning to disperse amongst the tables, picking out men on their own, like him, or small groups without women, and gave Melanie a sceptical glance.

'I bet there's private rooms upstairs somewhere,' he said. 'Or round the back.'

Melanie suddenly looked annoyed and drained her drink with a flourish of her long blonde hair.

'There's nothing upstairs,' she said, her voice suddenly shrill. 'We're underneath a whole lot of offices, if you must know. And nothing anywhere else either. Aren't you listening? If you want that sort of girl you need to go down Aysgarth Lane and you won't have any problem.'

Mower was suddenly conscious of a looming presence behind him and he turned to see one of the club bouncers, eighteen stone of solid muscle compressed into a dark suit several sizes too small for him and an unfriendly look in his piggy eyes. The eyes of clubbers at other tables had also swivelled in his direction and he realised he had pushed his luck too far.

'You got trouble here, Mel?' the doorman asked. Melanie shrugged and got to her feet, then flounced back to the bar without a backward glance.

'Don't annoy the girls, if you know what's good for you, mate,' the bouncer said.

'No offence meant,' Mower muttered. 'I'm waiting for some friends.'

'Well, I'm watching you, mate. All right?' The man turned away but Mower was suddenly aware of someone else he did not particularly want to talk to making his way towards him through the increasingly crowded tables.

'Sergeant Mower,' Stephen Stone said, with a smile that reminded Mower of a lazily cruising shark. He sat down in the chair Melanie had vacated and glanced at Mower's glass. 'Another drink? On the house?'

'No thanks,' Mower said. Stone glanced around the room proprietorially as the DJ's speakers crashed into life and conversation became difficult for a moment until the music faded again as quickly as it had begun.

'You like it?' Stone mouthed, through the bass line.

Mower nodded, knowing that he would get no further with his inquiries that night.

'Very nice,' he said. 'Good décor.'

'Are you meeting someone?' Stone asked. 'Please be my guest, if you are. I'll tell the bar staff to put you on the list.'

'Thanks, but no thanks,' Mower said, getting to his feet.

'You must be looking for someone, then?' Stone persisted, no smile now. 'That little slag whose picture's all over the papers, maybe? I can assure you, you're wasting your time here. This is a legitimate business, all above board. No tarts are going to get through this door, believe me.'

'I just came in for a drink,' Mower said. 'I'm having a meal somewhere else. I'm off duty, for God's sake.'

'Be my guest next time, then,' Stone said with that glitteringly cold smile. 'Nice to see you again, Sergeant. And give my regards to Inspector Thackeray, won't you? I know he's not much of a clubbing man, but maybe you'll bring him with you next time. We could find him a bottle of pop, I dare say.'

Mower gritted his teeth and turned away, making his way through the tables with his hands clenched in his pockets. The final humiliation would be to be thrown out of The Manhattan, he thought, and he would say and do nothing which risked that. But as he pulled on his leather jacket and made his way out into the frosty street he promised himself that he would be back, with a warrant and back-up, if only to take that grin off Stephen Stone's face.

Back at police HQ, Mower found Thackeray still in his office, the air thick with cigarette smoke, and an expression of desperation in his eyes. Mower closed the door behind him and took a seat uninvited.

'Are you OK, guv?' he asked. Thackeray looked at him blankly for a moment and then shrugged but did not answer.

'How did you get on?' he asked. So Mower told him about his visit to The Manhatten.

'It's not too hard for Stone to work out who we're looking for,' he said tentatively when he'd finished. 'It's been all over the media. But calling her a slag? Was that just the way he always refers to women, or does he know? And if he knows, how does he know? We've never suggested in public that Grace or Elena were on the game. We're just looking for a friend of the dead girl as far as the Press is concerned. A missing witness. Why a slag?'

'He knows,' Thackeray said. 'He could have found out that Grace was HIV positive through his contacts at the football club, though I wouldn't have thought anyone is bandying that bit of information around. It's far too damaging. But it's just possible he's found out accidentally. Much more likely is that he knows because he knows the girls. If it wasn't for what happened last time I'd have him in so fast his feet wouldn't touch the ground. But in the circumstances we need more, or his solicitor will be screaming harassment as soon as we've got him over the threshold. As it is, Elena's out there like bait in a trap, which in one way is good for us, but desperately dangerous for her.'

'So what now? Surveillance?' Mower asked.

'Maybe. We're seeing Minelli again in the morning, before he goes off to London with the team. Let's see where we are after that, shall we? We can ask him what he's told his girlfriend Angelica so we know what she might have told Stone himself.'

'Right, guv,' Mower said. He glanced at his boss anxiously as he got to his feet but he was met with such an uncompromising stare that he turned away with a slight shrug.

'Night,' he said. But back in the CID office he pulled out his mobile and speed dialled Val Ridley's number. To his surprise, this time it was answered.

'Kevin?' the familiar cool voice said. 'You have to stop this, you know. You're becoming a nuisance.'

'Are you coming to Bradfield, Val?' Mower said quietly. 'That's all I want to know.'

'Probably, on Tuesday,' Val said.

'Are you sure you want to do this? Are you still so angry that you want to destroy people over it? The guv'nor looks as though he's going to crack up any time. That's not a good outcome.'

There was a long silence at the other end. 'Leave it, Kevin,' Val said eventually, and she hung up.

'Bloody woman,' Mower said as he pocketed his phone. He ran a hand across his closely cropped hair and sighed. The ignominious end to his evening's work still rankled. If Thackeray would not authorise surveillance of Stephen Stone, he thought, maybe there was scope for a little freelance work. He would, at the very least, find out where Stone went when he left The Manhattan that night. Somewhere in Bradfield there was a safe house where illicitly trafficked girls were imprisoned and for his money Stone was a prime candidate for gatekeeper to that particular hell. He pulled on his coat again and went out into the icy evening air determined to follow his hunch for as long as it took.

The next morning, with a feeling of liberation, Jenna Heywood filtered onto the M1, put her foot down and the BMW purred effortlessly up to eighty, eighty-five and then ninety in the outside lane. The sense of freedom was not just at getting away from Bradfield for the first time in two months, and from all the stress and unexpected anger that her new role had brought, but also because the twenty mile slog from home to the main motorway south had taken what seemed like for ever. Happy families heading in people carriers to the White Rose shopping centre for an afternoon's credit card excess, and football fans packed into cars of all shapes and sizes and pushing against time to get to Leeds United's stadium had clogged the M62 trans-Pennine motorway until Jenna had felt that she would scream in frustration. But to the south, after the M1 junction, the three-lane road seemed thankfully clear and she hoped to be at home in London in a couple of hours.

She switched on the radio and tuned into Five Live to pick up the afternoon's football prognostications and excitements, knowing that her own team's chances of glory would not be headline news this far ahead of the game on Tuesday. She could relax in the luxury of neutrality as the relative strengths and weaknesses of the Premiership contenders were probed by the usual array of inarticulate or incomprehensibly Scottish pundits. She smiled faintly at the tales of management jealousies, thankful that Bradfield United was too obscure for anyone to know or care about the tensions she had left at Beck Lane.

No one would care, except Tony Holloway, she thought, and his far more *simpatico* colleague, Laura Ackroyd. She wondered whether she should have invited Laura to come to the Cup match as her guest, but then dismissed the idea. She liked Laura, but was faintly suspicious of her obviously long-standing relationships with some of the old die-hards at the club. Just how close had Laura's father been to Les Hardcastle? she wondered, recognising her own resentment at the news that Jack Ackroyd had sold his shares to her rival for control of the club. The latest rumour, that Hardcastle was wooing an unknown millionaire sponsor for the club, had incensed her the previous evening when Holloway had passed the rumour on and asked for her comment. She had been foolish, perhaps, she thought, to slam the phone down on him. She might need Holloway as an ally in the difficult days ahead. But the mistake was made now, and could not be unmade, at least until the Chelsea game was over and the club had returned to their home ground either in triumph, or, more likely, in deep depression to lick their wounds. That was when the gloves would come off, she thought, and the *Gazette* would take sides in the war for the club's future, and Laura Ackroyd notwithstanding, she thought she knew exactly which way they would jump.

The traffic was thickening again as she approached Sheffield and a second wave of happy shoppers began to clog the inside lanes as they headed for Meadowhall, another temple of consumerism standing four-square on the ruins of nineteenth-century industry. She was not an economist but she wondered vaguely how long a country could survive if, as seemed likely, it ceased to produce anything tangible at all. Over the massive viaduct that gave a vast view of the city, the traffic thinned and she accelerated away into the fast lane again.

Suddenly she was aware that the car behind her was flashing its lights in her rear view mirror. She was tempted to put her foot down and leave him for dead, but thought better of it. She pulled into the middle lane to allow him to overtake, only to find the car still on her tail, swerving as she swerved and perilously close to her rear bumper. The traffic was light now and, feeling irritated, she pulled left again into the inside lane, braking as she did, slightly anxious in case there was some problem with her car that she had not become aware of and this was the following driver's somewhat eccentric method of warning her.

But as she slowed, she found herself boxed in by another car on her right, which suddenly nudged her BMW hard, making her swerve again, this time onto the hard shoulder, struggling with the wheel to keep control as panic kicked in. But it was a lost cause. Still travelling fast, and unable to hold her line, she felt the car clipped again from behind and then the roadside fence was beneath her wheels. It shattered into matchwood, offering no resistance to almost a ton of metal travelling at speed, and the BMW sailed over the embankment beyond and somersaulted into a field twenty feet below. The last thing Jenna Heywood remembered before darkness engulfed her was the look of triumph on the face of the driver in the car behind.

DCI Thackeray and Sergeant Mower arrived at the Bradfield United offices as arranged at noon to find the reception area piled high with suitcases and sports bags in readiness for the team's departure to their London hotel. United had been due to play a normal match that afternoon but the game had been cancelled because of the waterlogged condition of the pitch, to the evident relief of the club officials who seemed to be almost drunk with excitement at the forthcoming trip to London. Mower wondered cynically if maybe someone had arranged the waterlogged pitch deliberately.

When they were admitted to Minelli's office, the two police officers were surprised to find a second man present, a man Thackeray recognised vaguely but could not exactly place. Minelli spotted his puzzlement.

'Dennis Jenkins,' he said, waving towards his guest. 'OK's agent. He's got some questions he wants to ask you.'

'Has he?' Thackeray said. 'Well, I'm afraid that will have to wait, Mr Jenkins, until I've had my chat with Mr Minelli.'

Jenkins scowled but did not argue.

'I'll wait,' he said.

'Outside, please,' Thackeray insisted in a tone that left no room for argument, and Jenkins left, slamming the door behind him. Minelli shrugged eloquently.

'Agents are powerful people,' he said, a note of helplessness in his voice. 'He's very anxious about OK.'

'Perhaps he should be, Mr Minelli,' Thackeray said. 'Perhaps you both should be.'

Minelli subsided into his seat behind his desk and waved the two police officers into the chairs opposite.

'How can I help you, *signori*?' he asked. 'You know we go to London today for the big match? It is not a very good time.'

'It's never a very good time for murder, Mr Minelli,' Thackeray said, his voice sounding harsh even to his own ear. 'I want to take you back to the celebration parties at the West Royd club recently. We now have firm evidence that the girl who was murdered, and her friend, were both present at the club on several nights and had contact with at least three of your players and probably more. And by contact I mean sexual contact.' Thackeray handed the pictures of Grace and Elena across the desk.

'I have to ask you again, Mr Minelli, did you ever see either of these girls at the club?' Minelli barely glanced at the pictures.

'No,' he said. 'There are always a lot of people there. I haven't seen either of those girls. I told you that already.'

'Since we last spoke, have you heard any suggestion as to who invited them? Who brought them to the parties. Who took them away again. It must be a hot topic of discussion here in the circumstances, I should think.'

'No,' Minelli said. 'As I told you before, there are always girls around the players. It goes with the job. They are young men with a lot of money to spend and they attract pretty girls like moths to a flame.'

'Have the players ever given you any indication of where young women, young prostitutes in fact, might be found to come to their parties?'

Minelli swallowed hard. He looked pale and his hands were trembling slightly.

'It is not something I have ever talked about with my players. Casual sex is one thing. Using girls like that is another. It is dangerous, unhealthy. I would not put up with it if I knew about it. Never.'

'Right, let's go back to the parties. The young men who have admitted having contact with the girls so far are Okigbo, Peters and Towers. Can you recall anyone else the players were talking to on any occasion? In the case of Peters and Towers, it would have to have been before the wife and the fiancée arrived at the Rochdale celebration, a somewhat unexpected arrival, I'm told...'

Minelli shrugged again, his eyes taking on a slightly haunted look.

'The place was crowded that night,' he said. 'There was a lot of drink, a lot of excitement.' He licked his lips and glanced away.

'But?' Thackeray prompted, realising that Minelli had recalled something in that jostling crowd that he had not liked.

'Angelica invited her brother,' Minelli said. 'I don't like the man.'

'Stephen Stone? And who was he talking to?'

'I saw him chatting to Okigbo at the Rochdale party. I thought it was odd because I had heard him before making unpleasant comments about blacks. He didn't like them. It was obvious when you talked to him he was a racist.'

'Have you any idea what they were talking about?' Thackeray asked.

'No idea at all,' Minelli said. 'But Dennis Jenkins might know. He was in on the conversation, I think.'

'Did you ever talk to Angelica herself about the young men's sexual behaviour? Did you imply to her – or her brother – that they might be in the market for girls?'

'I told you I wouldn't encourage that. I certainly wouldn't discuss it with Angelica. No way. Why should I?'

'Where is OK Okigbo now, Mr Minelli?' Mower asked quickly. 'It sounds as though we need to talk to him and to Mr Jenkins right away.'

If anything Minelli looked sicker than ever.

'He went to London last night,' he said. 'I gave him permission to go early to see his sister, who lives somewhere down there. I was going to rest him today because he had a slight strain even if the rest of the team trained this morning. He'll be at the team hotel tomorrow tonight.'

Thackeray let his breath out with a faint hiss.

'That's a pity,' he said.

'Inspector Thackeray,' Minelli said urgently, leaning across his desk with his fists clenched. 'Tell me honestly. Do you think my best player killed that girl? Do you really believe that?'

'I can't answer that at the moment, Mr Minelli,' Thackeray

said. 'But I certainly need to speak to your best player again. When will you all be back in Bradfield?'

'The coach will bring everyone back immediately after the match on Tuesday evening,' Minelli said dully. 'I'm not expecting anything but a defeat, and it's best to get the players home afterwards, I think. Can you wait until then, Mr Thackeray? I don't want the team disturbed again...' It was as close to pleading as Minelli was likely to come.

'Do you know where Okigbo is staying tonight?' he asked. Minelli shook his head.

'I want you to let me know immediately if he fails to turn up tomorrow at your hotel,' Thackeray said sharply.

'It will be all over the papers if he fails to turn up,' Minelli whispered.

'And I hold you responsible for making sure he's on the coach back to Bradfield after the match.'

Minelli nodded, his face grey with anxiety now.

'And now,' Thackeray said. 'As Mr Jenkins is so conveniently here, perhaps I could borrow your office to talk to him privately.'

'Of course,' Minelli said, and he got up and brought Dennis Jenkins, who seemed to have been hovering outside the door, back into the room, before making his own exit with a palpable air of relief. Thackeray took Minelli's seat behind the desk and waved the agent into the chair next to Mower.

'Do you get hold of girls for your client Okigbo, Mr Jenkins?' the DCI asked.

'What the fuck's that supposed to mean?' Jenkins snapped, choosing to bluster where Minelli had wilted.

'Just what it says,' Thackeray said. 'Your client and other

players have admitted sleeping with prostitutes at the West Royd club on at least two occasions, and one of them has been murdered. I'm trying to discover how they made contact with these girls in the first place. Can you explain how it happened?'

'No I bloody can't,' Jenkins said. 'I may be OK's agent but I'm not his pimp.'

'Do you know who is?' Thackeray snapped.

Jenkins gulped slightly, his colour rising.

'No,' he said.

'I don't believe you, Mr Jenkins,' Thackeray said. 'You were seen talking to a man we think may be implicated in this unpleasant business. Do you recall the conversation?'

'Who saw me?' Jenkins snapped, and when Thackeray shook his head dismissively, he came back. 'Was it bloody Paolo? Was it Minelli? Did he say he'd seen me? That's the last time I do him any favours.'

'Did you have a discussion with Okigbo and another man about procuring girls?' Thackeray persisted. Jenkins drew a deep breath between his teeth, making a whistling sound that reminded Thackeray of a deflating balloon. Eventually he nodded.

'So what?' he said. 'OK said he fancied a black girl. He was sick of English girls. And this bloke said he thought he knew just the one. If he made it worth her while. And his.'

'In other words, if he paid her to prostitute herself.'

'He said she wouldn't come cheap but it could be arranged. He wouldn't be out of pocket personally. It's not illegal,' Jenkins said.

'No it's not,' Thackeray agreed. 'Unless she's underage. But the offer the other man made is certainly illegal. And the girl is dead. Who is he?'

Dennis Jenkins' gaze strayed wildly around the manager's office as if in search of help but in the end it came back to Thackeray's implacable face and the hostile eyes waiting for an answer.

'He's not connected with the club, not anyone I've seen around till recently,' Jenkins said. 'He's called Stone.'

Mower was watching Thackeray and guessed that only he noticed the briefest flash of triumph in his blue eyes.

'Thank you, Mr Jenkins,' Thackeray said quietly. 'Perhaps you'd like to explain in your statement why neither you nor your client felt able to tell us that sooner.'

'We didn't want OK harassed,' Jenkins said, as if that were explanation enough. 'He's an innocent, that lad. And Paolo and I are hoping to sell him on. When he's given United a bit of a boost. Though now there's this HIV thing, all that could go out of the bloody window. It's true, that, is it? She was infected, the black tart?'

'HIV positive and pregnant, assaulted and drowned,' Thackeray said angrily. 'Which is why I'll be wanting to talk to your "innocent" again just as soon as he's back in Bradfield.' At that moment his mobile rang and when he glanced at the caller display he came within an ace of switching off, but then he shrugged and got up to leave the room.

'Take Mr Jenkins' statement, Sergeant,' he said as he closed the door on the other two men. The outer office was empty and he took the call.

'Laura?' But the voice at the other end, hurried and outraged, did not offer the response he had been expecting.

'Jenna Heywood has been in an accident on the M1,' Laura said. 'She's unconscious in hospital. She told me she was being harassed, stalked even, and I'm wondering if it really was an accident. Ted Grant will be crawling all over the story. It's a major blow to the club and her plans for it. But I thought you ought to know what she told me last week. I think you may want to investigate.'

Thackeray took a deep breath before replying, with a hundred things flashing through his mind that he both wanted and did not want to share with Laura, but knowing that this was neither the time nor the place.

'I'll ask Kevin Mower to talk to you,' he said. 'Where are you? At home?'

'At the office,' Laura said. 'Tony Holloway was at work and rang me when he heard. We'll work on the story together for now.'

'I'll get Kevin to get back to you,' Thackeray said, and disconnected.

CHAPTER SEVENTEEN

Laura drove sedately down the M1 to Sheffield that Sunday morning, feeling slightly bewildered by the catastrophe that suddenly seemed to have overtaken her life. She was on the way to visit Jenna Heywood in hospital where she was confined with multiple injuries, Laura had been told when she phoned earlier, conscious but apparently lucky to be alive. Laura was driven by a genuine sympathy for a women she had come to like, but also by an intense curiosity to discover, if she could, whether her accident on the motorway could have been a part of the campaign of harassment Jenna had said she had been experiencing for weeks.

Laura found it almost impossible to believe that the affairs of United could possibly be a motive for attempted murder, if that was what it was. But when she had called the hospital that morning, the nurse had passed on a message from her still groggy patient to the effect that she would like to see her as soon as possible. So after a sleepless night, Laura had reluctantly set off through the clinging mist and patches of bright sunshine that were flitting across newly greened South Yorkshire with her brain too sluggish to make much sense of what had been going on.

Kevin Mower, she thought with irritation, had not been

much help the previous evening either. The Sergeant had picked her up from the office and they had gone to The Lamb for a drink and a sandwich after Laura's unsatisfactory phone call to Thackeray had been passed on to him.

'What's all this about, then?' he had asked, handing her a vodka and tonic and settling down with his own pint. According to the hospital in Sheffield, Jenna at that stage was still unconscious in intensive care and Laura could only assume that her life was hanging in the balance, although the nurse did not spell that out. In the circumstances, she felt no compunction about sharing what Jenna had told her with the police, recalling that she had been very clear that she intended to hang on to the evidence of harassment in case she ever made a complaint. If there was a time to complain about how Jenna Heywood had been treated it was now, Laura decided angrily and told Mower exactly what Jenna had told her.

'You'll find a dog turd in her fridge,' she said with distaste.

'Lovely,' Mower said.

'Well, wrapped up,' she added with a faint smile. 'If it'd been me, I'd have been terrified by all this, but Jenna seemed to be taking it in her stride.'

'She should have come to us straight away. Did she have any idea who was behind this campaign?' Mower had asked.

'Disgruntled fans upset by a having a woman in charge? Greedy directors whose plans she's thwarting by trying to make the club a success? Male chauvinist football pigs of one kind or another? She was guessing. She had no idea.'

'Not the beautiful game any more then,' Mower said.

'Was it ever?'

'D'you think she knew anything at all about this girl Elena who was at the club parties?' Mower asked. 'The young friend you kept very quiet about.'

'When she talked about all this I'd no idea that there was any connection between Elena and the club,' Laura said, defensively. 'I realise now Jenna might have known something about what was going on, but I never asked her and she never mentioned it. You'll have to follow that up yourselves.'

'There's not much we can do until – unless – she wakes up,' Mower had said sombrely, glancing at his watch. 'I checked with traffic down there, and they're looking for witnesses to the accident. Someone on the motorway must have seen what happened but no one's come forward. So far they're treating it as a routine RTA. There's absolutely no evidence to suggest anything else. She seems to have lost control and run off the road.'

'She's used to doing long distances in a fast car,' Laura said, exasperated by the routine nature of the police response. 'She can hardly be called a novice driver. And if she dies, does that mean there may never be any evidence?'

'There may not,' Mower agreed.

'But the fact she'd been threatened? That must carry some weight, surely?'

'Maybe,' Mower conceded. 'But we'll have to wait and see if she says anything herself or for any suggestion that it wasn't a genuine accident. Then we'll take it from there.'

Laura had drained her glass, discontented with that strategy but knowing that she would not be able to shift it.

'Thanks for the drink,' she said, getting to her feet and

pulling her coat on. 'I'm going up to see my grandmother. She's distraught because this girl Elena has disappeared again. I think, like everyone else, she blames me.'

'The boss doesn't seem very happy,' Mower said carefully.

'Neither of us is very happy,' Laura said dismissively. 'I made a stupid mistake and if this inquiry goes pear-shaped next week he's going to be even less happy because that's all about another stupid mistake I made. But just at the moment I don't think there's anything I can do about it.' Laura's tone was firm, but Mower could see from the strain on her face that she was close to breaking point.

'I'm sorry,' he said.

'Do you know if Val Ridley is coming up for the inquiry?' Laura asked, abruptly changing the subject, but Mower shrugged.

'I did manage to speak to her,' he said. 'But she wouldn't say one way or the other. If you're going to see Joyce, could I come with you? I've got another photograph, one your grandmother didn't see when she came in to go through the mug shots. It's important she has a look at it.'

'I'm sure she won't mind,' Laura said. 'I'm parked across the road. Why don't you follow me up there.'

But Mower's had been a wasted trip and he soon left, looking grim. Joyce had seemed tired when the two of them arrived, and she had glanced at Mower's photograph of Stephen Stone without any flicker of recognition. When the Sergeant had gone, Joyce sank into her chair close to the desultory flames of the gas fire and shut her eyes for a moment.

'There's no news of the girls, then?' she said.

Laura had shaken her head. 'If anything happens to them I'll never forgive myself,' she said quietly.

'And will your man forgive you?' her grandmother asked.

'I doubt it.'

Nearing her journey's end on the M1 the next morning, the sun suddenly dazzled Laura and she pulled the visor down and shook herself slightly as she felt her concentration slip. Was that what had happened to Jenna only ten miles or so further south on the same motorway? she wondered, as she realised she was approaching Sheffield, and took the turning for the city centre. The accident, if that's what it was, could have been as simple as a blinding flash of sunlight.

Within fifteen minutes she was standing at the foot of a high hospital bed where Jenna Heywood was still attached to numerous monitors but with her eyes wide open and bright, looking pale but remarkably unscathed after her narrow escape.

'How are you feeling?' Laura asked.

'The bruises are out of sight,' Jenna said, not sounding quite as breezy as she looked. 'I've got a broken leg, six broken ribs and a lot of internal bruising, and this bash on the head.' She fingered her hair gingerly and winced. 'It didn't break the skin – or the skull. Just knocked me out cold. I was lucky. The seat belt and the air-bag saved me from worse. They tell me my precious Beamer is a write-off. Someone must be seriously disappointed, though.'

Laura moved to the bedside chair and sat down, feeling breathless herself.

'You mean it wasn't an accident?'

'Oh no,' Jenna said. 'That was no accident. Some bastards deliberately ran me off the road.'

'Did you see them?' Laura asked, but Jenna shook her head bleakly.

'I got an impression of the cars, not who was in them,' she said. 'My memory's a bit hazy on the details but I'm sure it was deliberate and there were two cars involved, I think.'

'You'll tell the police now?'

'Yes,' Jenna said. 'Bring them on. This has gone way too far now. I want it stopped.'

'And do you really think Les Hardcastle is behind it? That he would try to have you killed?' Laura asked, trying to hide the incredulity she felt.

Jenna suddenly looked slightly forlorn against the white pillows and her eyes filled with tears.

'It's not what I want to think,' she said. 'I don't much like the man but I thought he and my father had been friends over the years.'

'Les came to our house once or twice when I was a teenager,' Laura said. 'He always seemed a friendly sort of bloke. Not as cuddly as your dad. I called him Uncle Sam. But I didn't think Les was friendly at all when I spoke to him this week. There was something much more unpleasant there, much more determined. He really seems to believe that he's got some millionaire to take an interest in the club and back his plans.'

'Did he say who?' Jenna said. 'Was it someone called Ahmed Firoz?'

'He didn't say. Who's Ahmed Firoz, anyway?' Laura asked.

'Well, he's a millionaire all right, but he's made his money by buying up run-down property, razing it and building shopping centres, cheap hotels, multiplex cinemas, and business parks, that sort of thing, anything that will make him a fat profit. He's been laying waste to sites right across the north of England, ripping down Victorian buildings, for years now. His motto seems to be never renovate if you can raze. He actually approached me just after my father died but I told him to get lost. I had my own plans for the club. So he may well have turned his attention to Les. But if Les seriously thinks Firoz is going to build him a new stadium on a prime town centre site he must be more stupid than I thought. The club's only hope is to move out of town altogether. That might just possibly save us. We're five million pounds in debt, for God's sake. And don't, whatever you do, print that.'

'You're going to tell me *when* I can print that,' Laura said with a grin. 'But according to Les, his investor will have the club in the Premiership in no time at all.'

'Pure fantasy,' Jenna said. 'Wishful thinking. But he won't listen to me. He's built me up into the enemy, the smart young know-it-all from down south, and a woman too, just to add insult to injury. He's obsessed.'

'Obsessed enough to try and kill you?'

'I don't know,' Jenna said, suddenly lying back against her pillows looking utterly frail and weary. 'I simply don't know. There seems to be so much going on at United that I knew nothing about.'

'You'll carry on, though?' Laura asked, not wanting to see Jenna defeated.

'I will, though now Paolo tells me there's a chance some of

the players may be infected with HIV. How the hell is the team supposed to cope with that?'

Laura gazed at Jenna in astonished horror, even as an anxious looking nurse came to the foot of the bed and indicated that she should go.

'How did that happen?' Laura asked. But Jenna did not respond. She turned her head away and closed her eyes and Laura instantly guessed exactly how it might have happened. To the nurse's relief, she said goodbye and made her way slowly through the ward and out of the hospital, her mind whirling. It must be Grace who had been HIV positive, she thought. The post-mortem would have revealed that. But if it was true of Grace, then what of Elena? Was that to be the indelible legacy of the abuse the girl had suffered? Laura felt so overwhelmed by blind fury that she sat motionless in her car for some time in the hospital car park before she dared trust herself to drive again.

Sergeant Kevin Mower, after he had spoken to Laura the previous evening and been left gloomily contemplating what looked like the wreckage two people he liked had made of their lives, had gone on to pursue his own inquiries. He had spent most of the night sitting in his misted-up car outside The Manhattan club, waiting for Stephen Stone to leave. Every now and again he had to switch the engine on to avoid hypothermia in spite of the sheepskin coat and woollen gloves he had dragged out of the furthest reaches of his wardrobe. He looked like a 1960s commercial traveller, he thought, as he glanced in his mirror before he left his flat. All I need is one of those little hats with a feather at the side. But for all his sartorial sacrifices, the night turned out to be a waste of time. Stone had finally left the club at about four in the morning, with a young woman Mower recognised as one of the hostesses on his arm, gazing adoringly up at him. They had gone into the car park at the back of the club and come out soon afterwards in a silver Aston Martin, which Mower seriously coveted as soon as he recognised its sleek profile.

It was only when he remembered how it had been earned that his anger kicked back in and he slid his own car into gear and followed at a discreet distance, which he knew was difficult on empty early morning roads, well lit and slick with rain. Whether Stone was aware of being watched, Mower never knew, but he guessed he probably was. Either way, his quarry drove at a strictly legal pace until he reached a leafy part of Southfield, where heavy gates swung open ahead of him as he swept into the drive of a large modern house. Mower pulled up a little way back and watched the gates swing shut again behind the car, the security lights come on and then go off and silence return to the sleeping neighbourhood. That, he thought, had been a complete waste of time, and he did an angry three point turn and roared back down into town to his own flat and a distinctly chilly and solitary bed.

He was back at police HQ at eight on Sunday morning and found Thackeray already there, looking marginally more cheerful than he had seen him for some time.

'Developments, guv?' he asked.

'The first bit of luck we've had in this wretched case,' Thackeray said. 'The mobile phone company have traced the location of the number Joyce Ackroyd was given.'

'It's still active?'

'It's still active, and it's somewhere in the vicinity of St Judes church off Aysgarth Lane.'

'Is that blasted place still standing?' Mower asked in surprise, thinking back to a catastrophic accident there some years previously that had almost cost Thackeray his life.

'Apparently, propped up with scaffolding and, like a lot of the streets around there, waiting for a major redevelopment scheme to start. Some of the houses are already boarded up, I'm told. I've already spoken to the beat bobby and he reckons there are squatters in a few of them, but he's not seen anything that makes him think anyone's running a brothel or anything like that.'

'But we're going to make sure?' Mower said with satisfaction.

'I want round the clock surveillance, starting now.' Thackeray turned to the street map of Bradfield on the wall behind his desk. 'I don't want as much as a mouse, let alone a rat, getting in or out of these streets here, Aysgarth to Inkerman, Blenheim to Austerlitz, without us knowing about it.'

'We'll need more troops than we've got on duty on a Sunday,' Mower said.

'I've cleared it with the Super,' Thackeray said. 'Call in anyone you need from CID, and uniform will assist. I want details of all vehicles arriving and leaving, all pedestrians on the streets, and which houses are occupied, officially or unofficially. I've asked the water company to set up some fake diversions so that traffic has to approach by a more limited number of streets, so that should help. But tell everyone to remain absolutely invisible. I don't want Stone and his mates scared off. I just want to know where they're holed up. As soon as we know that, we'll act.'

'Right,' Mower said, with some satisfaction as he turned to go.

'And Kevin,' Thackeray said sharply. 'I want updating as soon as anyone reports back. I'll be here all day. I want Stone pinned to the floor this time, with no wriggle room. He needs locking up for a long time.'

'Sir,' Mower said closing the door behind him with real relief. For the first time since he'd come back to work, Thackeray was showing some of his old decisiveness, Mower thought. He just hoped to God it would last.

Laura was surprised to find, when she returned from Sheffield and went to the *Gazette* office, that Tony Holloway was nowhere to be seen. In fact, the newsroom was deserted and distinctly chilly, the lights off and the computers down. She kept her coat on and sat at her desk gazing at her blank screen for a long time, her mind running endlessly over what she knew about the problems of Bradfield United and how that now seemed to mesh with the exploitation of the dead girl Grace and her friend Elena. How much of what she knew, or guessed, she could put in print the next morning she was not sure. Or even how much she should pass on to the police who, no doubt, would interview Jenna themselves as soon as the hospital allowed. Feeling unusually uncertain of herself, she wished she knew where Tony had gone.

She crossed the office to his desk, where a bundle of the Sunday papers was scattered around, most of them with the brief details of Jenna Heywood's accident prominently displayed, not just on the sports pages but at the front. United's unexpected draw with Chelsea had given the club a celebrity that not even a female in the chairman's seat had warranted until now. Laura scanned the papers and was surprised at how pessimistically Jenna's injuries were described. She wondered if Tony had checked out Jenna's more optimistic prognosis this morning. By the end of the day, she knew that between them they would have to produce a coherent version of the weekend's events for Ted Grant's early editorial conference, and it would be in both their interests to get the facts right.

Back at her own desk, she pulled out her mobile phone, which she had switched off for the drive back from Sheffield, and realised that there were two messages waiting. The first was from Holloway, telling her he was meeting Les Hardcastle at three for a chat about United's future. The second was an angry sounding call from her father asking her to ring him back. Laura glanced at her watch. It was five to three already. She could spare her father about thirty seconds. He answered the phone as if he had been sitting by it waiting for her call.

'Have I been sold down the bloody river by Les Hardcastle?' he said, without any greeting at all.

'Quite likely, Dad,' Laura said. 'What have you heard?'

'That he's getting into bed with that shark Ahmed Firoz.'

'I heard that too,' Laura said. 'Isn't it good news?'

'All Firoz will want is the land. He's about as likely to want to rescue the club as he is to bail out George Bush. Les told me nowt about this. The man's conned me. He's a bloody fraud.'

And quite likely a would-be murderer, Laura thought, but

it would be the fact that he had taken Jack Ackroyd for a ride that would really rankle down in Portugal.

'I'll see what I can dig up, Dad,' she said. 'Maybe they can be stopped.'

'I bloody well hope so,' Jack said, and hung up abruptly.

On a hunch, Laura buttoned up her coat again and walked across the town to the Clarendon hotel, where she glanced into the bar from the foyer. As she suspected, Tony Holloway was sitting at the far end of the room with Hardcastle, deep in animated conversation, the older man's face flushed with excitement. He thinks he's won, Laura thought to herself. He may even still think Jenna is dead or dying. He's going to get the most enormous shock when he finds out she isn't.

In two minds whether to march into the bar and tell the two men that she had just come back from Jenna's bedside, she was suddenly aware of a third man approaching their table, a tall, heavily built, grey-haired Asian wearing an expensive looking suit and an air of total self-confidence. Even without hearing anything of what was being said, Laura could see that the other two deferred to the new arrival, Tony half rising to his feet, and Les Hardcastle waving urgently to the waiter to attend to the newcomer's needs. Laura did not hesitate then. She marched across the thick pile carpet of the Clarendon bar with an enthusiastic smile on her lips and a cheery greeting for Tony Holloway.

'Here you are,' she said. 'I thought I'd lost you and would have to write tomorrow's story all by myself. Good afternoon, Les. You must be getting fed up with everything that's going wrong at that club of yours. But at least Jenna's not as badly hurt as they first thought. I've just come back from visiting her and she had some very interesting things to tell me that I'd like to check out with you. If that's all right?' She smiled invitingly at all three men.

To judge by the expressions on the men's faces, her intervention, as she had expected, was not remotely all right with any of them. Tony Holloway's face flushed with embarrassment and Les Hardcastle half rose in his chair with a flash of such naked rage that Laura took a pace backwards in case he decided to hit her. The third man remained seated and impassive, his dark eyes slightly hooded and full of curiosity as he watched the drama unfold before him.

Obviously thinking better of making a scene to upset the Sunday afternoon calm of the Clarendon, where people at other tables were already showing an interest, Les sank back into his seat and waved Laura into the fourth chair at the table.

'This is Laura Ackroyd, also from the *Gazette*,' he said to the silent onlooker opposite him, who took a sip of his iced water and nodded noncommittally in Laura's direction.

'She's helping me with this story,' Holloway added quickly.

'And you have been to see the unfortunate Ms Heywood?' the third man asked, his accent impeccably public school. 'How enterprising of you. The morning papers implied her life hung by a thread.'

'You shouldn't believe all you read in the papers, Mr...er...?' Laura said.

'Ahmed Firoz,' the big man said easily. 'I'm relieved to hear that the accident was not as serious as we were led to believe.'

'Are you?' Laura asked quietly.

'We all are,' Les Hardcastle said quickly. 'It would be a

tragedy for the club to lose our Jenna so soon after Sam. A real tragedy.'

'It wasn't an accident,' Laura said. 'It was an attempt to kill her.'

There was complete silence around the table for a long time before Hardcastle cleared his throat noisily.

'Is that what she's saying?' he asked.

'That's what she's going to tell the police. It comes after a lot of other harassment. All very unpleasant, and now positively murderous.'

Laura was aware of Firoz watching Hardcastle very intently as he drummed his fingers gently on the table.

'I think perhaps we need to continue this discussion without the help of the Press,' he said eventually. Laura watched Hardcastle's face darken to a positively dangerous puce before Tony Holloway got to his feet and Laura too pushed back her chair.

'I've missed my drink then, have I?' she said to Hardcastle sweetly. Firoz got to his feet with her and helped her on with her coat.

'It has been very interesting to meet you, Ms Ackroyd,' he said, his voice emollient but his eyes cold.

As the two reporters walked out of the hotel together, Tony gave instant vent to the frustration that had been simmering ever since Laura had entered the bar.

'You've lost us an exclusive there,' he said fiercely. 'I'm bloody sure Hardcastle and his friend were going to spell out exactly what they had planned for the club now Jenna Heywood's out of the way.'

'There's only one problem with that, Tony,' Laura said.

'Jenna's not out of the way. And as far as I can discover Ahmed Firoz is about as likely to rescue United as he is to become Archbishop of York. All he wants is the land. Les Hardcastle has been had. So has my dad. And so have you. And if Jenna can make her suspicions stick, Hardcastle may be facing a very long time in jail. If I were you, I'd keep very quiet about your cosy relationship with that gang of sharks or Ted Grant will have your guts for garters.'

CHAPTER EIGHTEEN

Laura Ackroyd dressed very carefully the next morning. She had time off work to attend the police inquiry at County HQ, and she wanted to give as sober and responsible an impression as she could to the officers from the Midlands. She chose a black suit over a not-too-revealing cream silk top, stuffed her red boots to the back of the wardrobe and slipped her feet into dark stockings and black shoes with a medium heel, before trying to discipline her unruly cloud of red hair into a neat chignon. She eyed herself critically in the mirror. She knew she stood to be accused of reckless impulsiveness, which had put her own life in danger and had almost cost Michael Thackeray his, but she hoped her almost nun-like appearance might help counter any preconceptions the inquiry team might harbour before she even appeared.

Nothing she had done was criminal and she was not the accused in the proceedings. She was not even likely to be the star prosecution witness. That honour would probably fall to the elusive Val Ridley. Even so, she knew that what she said this morning might affect future careers, and not just Michael Thackeray's. The least she could do was give an impression of sobriety and seriousness and try, in her evidence, to overcome the impression of recklessness that the inquiry might already have gained. But as she cast a final critical eye over her appearance in the mirror, she was suddenly filled with a crippling doubt that she could pull it off. When it came down to it, she had put the man she loved into an impossible situation, and even if the inquiry was less critical than she feared, even if he himself eventually forgave her, she doubted if she would ever forgive herself.

Two hours later she came out of the board room, where she had faced three sceptical and brusque senior police officers, feeling wrung dry, to find Michael Thackeray waiting for her in the foyer, his back to the inquiry desk, his expression grim. Her heart thudded uncomfortably and she gave him a wry smile.

'I didn't expect to see you here,' she said, her mouth dry.

'I had to come over anyway,' he said unconvincingly. 'How did it go?'

Laura shrugged. 'Difficult to tell,' she said. 'They listened to me but they didn't give much away. They said they might want to see me again when Val Ridley has given evidence, which she doesn't seem to have done yet. No doubt to compare our stories. Have you got time for a coffee? I think I need one.'

Thackeray glanced away. 'Not really,' he said. 'We've a big operation on this afternoon. That's why I'm here.'

'I'll get back to the office, then,' Laura said, pulling on her coat and hoping that Thackeray would not see the tears that welled up in her eyes. But he put a hand on her arm and she had to resist the overwhelming temptation to move so close to him that he had to take her in his arms. But that seemed to be very far from what he had in mind.

'I thought I'd talk to Vince Newsom,' he said. 'Find out what he's going to say. I don't see why he should implicate you in his nasty tabloid tricks.'

'Vince is OK,' Laura said dully, pushing emotion firmly out of her voice. 'He's given evidence already, I think. I've not seen him this morning but I'd already spoken to him about his evidence. He's already agreed to say he found the note accidentally in his car. That seems to be the best version of events for both of us, and as I told that lot in there, I really can't really remember very clearly what happened, so I can't dispute what he says.'

'You'd spoken to Vince?' Thackeray asked, an edge of angry disillusion in his voice. 'You did a deal with that bastard?'

'Oh, Michael,' Laura said desperately. 'He got hold of Val's note somehow. I didn't give it to him, but I can't prove that.'

'He stole it then, which is exactly what you'd expect.'

'We don't know that,' Laura said. 'I can't say that for sure either. He may have just found it. I could have dropped it. Anyway, that's what he's said, and I agreed just now that it's possible.'

'Right,' Thackeray said, his eyes stony. 'And what did you tell them about the hostage situation?'

'I told them that Christie was lapsing in and out of consciousness. I thought it was safe to go in, and I guessed you thought the same.'

'If they swallow that they'll swallow anything,' Thackeray said bleakly, turning away.

'Michael,' Laura said, putting a hand on his arm in her turn. 'We have to talk. We have to resolve all this.'

Thackeray shrugged her hand off and sighed.

'I'll call you when I've made arrests in this case I'm working on,' he said. 'That's my first priority. And we can't risk you and I getting tangled up in a live case again. It's stupid and dangerous and has got to stop.' He glanced at his watch. 'I'm due in a meeting five minutes ago,' he said, turning again and heading away before Laura had any chance to reply.

She watched him walk down the corridor without looking back and turn into one of the doors at the end and pass out of her sight. She drew a sharp breath and pushed her way out of the glass entrance doors, the wind buffeting her and searing her eyes so that by the time she reached her car, tears were running down her reddening cheeks. She sat for a moment with the engine running, gazing through the icy windscreen and waiting for it and her mind to clear. Thackeray, she thought, had spoken to her almost like a stranger, and she wondered if that was what she was destined to be in future; a stranger or even perhaps an enemy. Could all that passion have come to this?

At two that afternoon, four police vans followed by a couple of unmarked cars made their way slowly and silently up Aysgarth Lane, as if not wanting to draw too much attention to themselves. They turned at traffic lights into the maze of dilapidated Victorian streets that huddled around the shell of St Jude's church which was still hemmed in by corrugated iron barriers and scaffolding years after its tower had partially collapsed, almost taking Michael Thackeray and Laura Ackroyd with it. The church, like several of the streets of mainly boarded up houses, had been waiting years for the demolition men to finish the job. Halfway into the enclave the vans split up, two pulling up in Inkerman Street, where at least half the houses were boarded and derelict, and two making their way round to the alley that gave access to the backyards between the two rows of houses in adjacent streets.

DCI Michael Thackeray, in the passenger seat of one of the cars that had parked discreetly in Inkerman Street, listened as one by one the groups of officers reported that they were in position. Satisfied, he gave the order to enter number 52, a three-storey terraced house where all the windows were boarded and there was no external sign of human activity, but where comings and goings had been observed by his discreet observers over the last twenty four-hours.

The raid went smoothly and as planned. By the time Thackeray and Sergeant Mower picked their way across the overgrown strip of front garden to the door, now hanging half off its hinges, the uniformed officers had arrested several men who were detained, handcuffed and sullen, in the bleak front room of the house. Thackeray glanced at the prisoners, bitterly disappointed that none of them looked familiar. He raised an eyebrow at the uniformed sergeant who had led the assault.

'This the lot?'

'We haven't been upstairs yet, sir,' the officer said.

'Right, let's do it,' Thackeray ordered, and he and Mower followed half a dozen uniformed men, batons in hand, up the rickety staircase into the upper reaches of the house. The boarded up windows made the whole place dark and not all the lights worked. On the first landing there was a musty smell of dirt and bad drains, and possibly something worse, which seemed to be coming from a filthy bathroom where the door was ajar. The other doors leading off the landing were locked with heavy bolts on the outside of the doors.

Thackeray nodded.

'One at a time. Be careful,' he said, and the Sergeant unbolted the first of the bedroom doors. There was no light inside but from the dim illumination offered by the bare bulb on the landing Thackeray could just make out three girls cowering on the far side of the room across the three beds that had been crammed into the meagre space. The Sergeant handed him a powerful torch and he crossed towards them, illuminating pale faces, huge, terrified eyes, and skinny, barely pubescent bodies in skimpy tops and skirts. They were shivering, though whether from cold or fear was impossible to tell. A combination of both, he guessed.

'It's all right,' he said quietly, not able to tell whether they understood him or not. 'You're safe now. Do you understand me? We are the police. You're safe now.' Two of the girls sat down suddenly on a bed, as if their legs could no longer support them, and began to sob. The third stood rigid and still shaking against the wall as if waiting for her own execution.

Thackeray turned away abruptly and beckoned Mower and the uniformed sergeant out onto the landing where several uniformed officers were standing by, looking sick.

'Are there girls in all the rooms?' he asked, and the officers nodded, lost for words.

'There's a lass over here looks seriously poorly to me,' a burly constable said, gesturing towards the door on the other side of the landing, which he had just unbolted.

'Right, this is what we do,' Thackeray snapped. 'Get those

bastards downstairs off to the nick. We'll question them later. Then get some light in here, and send for social services, a doctor and an ambulance. These are children, most of them, and I'm not having them banged up in cells even for half an hour. They need proper care and medical attention and we'll sort out who they are and how they got here later.'

'Sir,' the Sergeant said, and stomped down the stairs as if relieved that someone knew what to do in a situation that was entirely foreign to him.

'Guv,' came an urgent voice from the landing above. 'Guv, I think you should see this.'

Thackeray and Mower exchanged a glance full of foreboding and climbed the final flight of stairs to the top of the house where a uniformed constable was leaning with his back to the wall outside a door that he had evidently just opened. He looked pale and sick and he waved a hand vaguely at the dark interior of the room.

'In there,' he said.

The stench and the swarming flies told Thackeray and Mower exactly what they would find in this final locked room. Taking a deep breath, Thackeray led the way. The room had two beds, one of them empty but the other occupied by a small crumpled shape underneath a duvet, a shape that, as Thackeray gingerly pulled back the bedclothes, revealed itself as the body of a young girl, naked and lying on her side, her eyes closed, her flesh waxen and showing the first signs of bloating. But even in its incipient decay it was possible to see that the girl's body was severely bruised, with contusions and abrasions on her back and shoulders and across one cheek. Thackeray pulled the duvet gently back up to cover her.

'Get Amos Atherton,' he said to Mower as he led the way out of the room and closed and bolted the door behind them. Mower nodded, finding it difficult to speak as the sickly smell of death filled their mouths and nostrils.

'Let's get out of here,' Thackeray said, as if reading his thoughts. 'I need some fresh air.' The two of them made their way downstairs and out of the front door where Thackeray lit a cigarette and pulled the smoke gratefully into his lungs while Mower got onto his mobile phone and set the wheels of another murder inquiry into motion. The four men who had been arrested were being loaded into one of the police vans and Thackeray beckoned the Sergeant back.

'Suspicion of murder,' he said flatly.

'I heard there was a body,' the Sergeant said. 'Jesus. What the hell's been going on in there?'

'I think hell just about sums it up,' Thackeray said. As he gazed bleakly away down the street where officers were beginning to thread blue and white tape across the road to isolate the crime scene, he was surprised to see two more officers heading in the direction of the house with, between them, an animated and struggling figure held firmly by the arms, his hands handcuffed behind his back.

'He tried to slip out the back,' one of the PCs said breathlessly. 'Gave us a run for it.'

'Did he?' Thackeray said, running a satisfied eye over the portly figure of Emanuel Asida, who suddenly seemed to subside in the officers' grasp, panting slightly from his exertions, as he recognised Thackeray. 'Well, I don't think he'll be running very far for a long time now, will you Mr Asida? Emanuel Asida, I'm arresting you on suspicion of murder...'

'What?' Asida screamed, beginning to struggle frantically again. 'I had nothing to do with murder. Nothing at all.'

'Caution him, Sergeant,' Thackeray said wearily, turning away in disgust. 'And take him down to the nick. We'll follow you. This looks like being a long, long day.'

Laura Ackroyd pulled back the curtain in her grandmother's front room and gazed through the gloom of a murky, damp evening towards the looming shape of Priestley House, behind its barricade of fences.

'Are you quite sure, Nan?' she said. 'You've only seen her picture in the paper.'

Joyce pursed her lips. 'Of course I'm sure,' she said. 'I'm not entirely senile yet. It was the girl who's run away, and if what you say is true, then Elena won't be far away either. This lass was carrying a bag of shopping and she went in through the fence there, where the gap is. I saw her as clearly as I can see you now.'

'What on earth are they doing still round here?' Laura asked incredulously. 'They must be crazy. I thought they'd be long gone by now.'

'Well, I can't answer that, but I think we should get them out of that filthy rabbit warren before they come to some harm. There's all sorts of young tearaways use that block at night. If Elena's frightened enough she might jump off the top. Even the police will terrify her. You know that. She's threatened it before.'

Laura gazed again at the flats, wishing that she could call Michael Thackeray and hand this problem over to him, but knowing that Joyce was right, Elena's panic could be triggered as much by the sight of police officers as by whoever else was trying to find her. She squared her shoulders.

'I'll go to the bottom and see if I can locate them,' she said. 'I expect they'll come down if they know it's only me.' She tried to sound optimistic to reassure her grandmother, though she knew she was clutching at straws. Jasmin Ibramovic might respond to her voice but she very much doubted that a terrified Elena would. She pulled her coat back on and went to the front door.

'Here,' Joyce said, pulling open a drawer in the hall-stand and handing her a torch. 'It's getting dark.'

'And if anything happens down here, call me on my mobile,' Laura said, switching her phone to vibrate so that no one else would hear it ring.

Once outside, Laura glanced cautiously up and down the road between her grandmother's house and the flats but could see no one about. Dusk was falling fast, and a light drizzle had slicked the road surface, turning the strip of grass on the other side to soggy mud.

She had not mentioned to her grandmother her own panic on the way up to The Heights as she became aware of a car close behind her that she was convinced was following her. Cautiously she had turned off the main road into a maze of small streets and become quite sure that her suspicions were right. Every turn she made was copied by a dark saloon with two people inside. Desperately anxious, she had stopped for a moment beside a streetlight and pulled out her mobile phone, making sure that whoever was behind her could see exactly what she was doing. The car seemed to hesitate for a moment and then overtook her and drove away quickly, but not before

Laura was able to see the registration plate. She had dialled Kevin Mower's number and was relieved to get straight through.

'I may be imagining it,' she had said. 'But I think I'm being followed and it's a bit scary.' She had given the Sergeant the number of the car she suspected.

'I'll check it out,' Mower had said, readily enough. 'What are you doing, Laura? Where are you going?'

'I'm on my way to my grandmother's,' Laura had answered. 'Don't worry. It's probably nothing.' But she knew as she cut the connection that Mower probably would not believe her and half hoped that he would pass on his concerns to Michael Thackeray.

She had not seen the suspect car again as she completed the journey to The Heights by a more devious route than normal, and there was no sign of it now as she stood outside Joyce's garden gate, wondering if she had the courage to venture into the looming block of flats on the other side of the road. She glanced down at the smart shoes she had put on that morning to go to police headquarters and shrugged. At least she had not chosen high heels, or her beautiful new red boots.

Slowly, deciding she had no choice but to try to find the runaway girls, she crossed the road and made her way along the protective fence until she came to the gap that her grandmother had described. She slid through the narrow space where one of the wooden sheets had become loose and stepped into the deeper darkness beyond, where the street lights did not penetrate, and through which she could only just about make out the entrance to the block across a muddy patch of ground. She shivered slightly. The flats on Wuthering, as The Heights was known locally, had always been regarded as slightly sinister, and few tears had been shed when the families had finally been moved out and redevelopment had been promised. But the scheme had progressed slowly and although three of the original four blocks had now been reduced to rubble, Priestley House remained, the last to be emptied of its occupants by the council, still standing defiantly four-square in the teeth of the worst wind, rain and the occasional fire could do to it.

She pushed at the front door and it swung open easily. To her left, the two lifts stood derelict, the doors forced open and no sign of the cars which should have occupied the echoing shafts. The ropes and pulleys swung eerily in the void, occasionally banging and slapping against the walls with an irregularity that made her jump. To her right the concrete stairs stretched upwards, every tread littered with the detritus of the illicit users of the empty building, discarded syringes and trash of impossibly indeterminate origin trampled into a damp and stinking mulch. She did not want to climb up those stairs. Her whole mind and body fought against the idea and she had to gulp down her nausea.

From somewhere above a door crashed shut and set her heart racing. If Elena and Jazzy were up there, she thought, she would have to find them before it became completely dark and the people of the night, who still terrorised the estate, came out and threatened them. Clutching her mobile phone in one hand and the torch in the other, she crossed the entrance hall and began to climb. The faint light from her torch cast shadows that moved as she took one slow step upwards after another, holding her breath as long as she could to avoid the stench. At the first landing she shone the beam along the outside walkway, where the doors of flats either lay shattered on the concrete floor or swung at crazy angles, occasionally creaking in the wind. She could see that most of the windows were smashed and here and there the concrete walls were blackened by smoke.

'Jazzy,' she called softly, not wanting to walk too far away from the stairs, her escape route if she needed one. She took a few tentative steps across the smashed glass which crunched under foot like pebbles on a beach, and then stopped, listening carefully for a moment, but could hear no response. Cautiously, she turned back to the stairs and went up the next flight, where she repeated the exercise.

Something Elena had said came back to her as she hesitated at the foot of the third flight. If she remembered correctly, the girl had said that she had found a safe haven on the top floor. As she turned back to the stairs this time she was startled by the sudden loud flutter of wings as a pair of birds flapped away upwards, driven in panic from their roosts by her approach. Heart thudding, she stopped for a moment, back to the wall, before she shrugged and pushed herself onward. At least if the birds were asleep, she thought, there was unlikely to be anyone else about.

After pausing on every landing and repeating her whispered call for the girls, she reached the top, feeling slightly more hopeful. The smell was less nauseating here, and the carpet of broken glass and litter less thick, but as the last of the daylight faded, the shadows were becoming more intense. Cautiously, she directed the beam of her torch along the landing, lighting up the same wrecked doors and windows as below, and the same the view of the derelict landscape surrounding Priestley, almost impossible to make out in detail now in the misty darkness beyond the reach of her feeble yellow light.

'Jazzy? Elena? Are you there?'

There was still no obvious response but she wondered if she had not heard the faintest movement further along the walkway. She hesitated, but only for a moment. She switched off the torch and, relying on the last vestige of daylight that was left, felt her way carefully along the passageway, glancing into each doorway as she passed. At the end she found a door that had been restored to an almost upright position and propped closed, though drunkenly.

'Jazzy?' she said, more loudly this time. 'It's Laura. Are you there?' Suddenly the door was pushed open, catching Laura off balance as it fell towards her and pushed her across the walkway hard against the retaining rail, which sagged alarmingly under her weight. Before she could regain her balance two figures rushed out of the flat and ran away from her, back towards the main staircase.

'Jazzy, Elena!' Laura cried out involuntarily as the two figures disappeared onto the top landing. 'It's me. Come back, please. Jazzy, please come back.'

But there was no response, and rubbing her elbow, which had taken a glancing blow from the falling door, she hurried after the fleeing pair. On the landing she hesitated, glancing down into the inky blackness below but, to her surprise, hearing nothing. They did not seem to be running down the stairs. But then she noticed the faintest hint of daylight on the floor to her left, just visible below another door, which she guessed led up to the roof. She felt for a handle, found it, and the door swung open. Above her, at the top of another flight of steps, she could see the night sky and she felt the force of the wind, which was blasting across the open roof. She felt sick with apprehension. Once, several years ago, she had seen a man fall off a roof like this. She did not want to witness the same thing again.

Forcing herself up the concrete steps she stepped out into the gusts of sleety rain, silently scanning the empty expanse of roof, broken only by the top of the lift shaft. She could see no one but she was absolutely sure that the two girls were there, no doubt hiding on the far side of the shaft. Cautiously, she made her way towards the structure.

'Jazzy,' she called as she got closer and thought her voice could be heard above the gusty wind. 'Elena. Please, it's me, Laura. I don't mean you any harm.' Then she saw them, not, as she had thought, behind the shaft, but crouching in the lee of the parapet on the side of the roof that overlooked the road. She changed direction and slowly walked towards the girls, but as she got closer, what she feared most suddenly happened. One of the figures jumped out of the shadows and climbed onto the parapet, where she stood for a moment, silhouetted against the faint light from the streetlights below and swaying slightly in the wind. Elena's friend Jazzy screamed and grabbed hold of her but the Albanian girl struggled as Laura ran towards them, her heart pounding, expecting Elena to lose her balance and disappear before she reached her. But she was quick enough to grab hold of the girl's emaciated body as she swayed between life and death and, between them, Laura and Jazzy managed to pull her down until she was sitting on the parapet with her legs safely on the inside.

'Elena,' Laura gasped. 'You mustn't, you mustn't! You're going to be all right.'

'Men down there,' Elena said, her voice shrill. 'Look, men down there.' Laura glanced down at the road and saw that the girl was right. A car that looked very like the one she had suspected of following her through the town earlier was now parked at the front of the flats and two figures could be seen making their way towards the gap in the fence. Her mouth went dry and she drew the two girls closer to her, so that they could not be seen from below, but Elena suddenly wriggled out of her grip and half climbed back across the parapet again.

'No,' Laura said. 'Please believe me, Elena. If we're quick we can get out of here before they find us. Come on, Elena. You said you did it yourself. We can do it too. If they come up the main stairs we'll go out the other way, down the emergency stairs. But you need to be quick.' The girl was sitting with her legs over the void now and Laura doubted that she could pull her back a second time if she was determined to launch herself over the edge.

'She doesn't understand,' Jazzy said dully. 'How can she understand you. She wants to die. She told me that over and over. She wants to die. I wanted her to come away from Bradfield but she wouldn't. I couldn't get her to go on the train with me...' Jasmin shuddered, evidently on the verge of collapse herself.

Laura tried to get a firmer grip around Elena's waist, feeling the tension in her thin frame as she flexed her arms ready to fling herself forward. But her own desperation and fury that the girl had been driven to this gave her extra strength.

'Help me,' she said to Jazzy through gritted teeth. 'For goodness sake, help me pull her back.' Almost reluctantly, it seemed, the other girl took hold of Elena's arms and between them they eased her back onto the floor. When they had got their breath back Laura hauled the weeping Albanian girl onto her feet and hung onto her arms grimly.

'We're going down now,' she said firmly. 'No argument. We're going down.' Very slowly the three of them, Elena supported on each side, made their way back down the first flight of stairs to the top landing, where they stood for a moment listening. Elena trembled between them but no longer offered any serious resistance, but she stiffened as they all saw a flicker of light far below and heard the sound of someone ascending the main stairs. Laura pulled the two girls onto the top walkway and they made their way to the far end where the second staircase led downwards. Not daring to use her torch, Laura led the way, feeling the sides of the stairwell with her hands and reaching for each tread tentatively with her feet. On the landings they could clearly hear noises from the other end of the building, but no one had apparently worked out that there was another exit. Breathlessly, they reached the ground floor, pushed open the door and ran across the muddy expanse of grass to the gap in the fencing.

To their amazement, as they struggled out of the darkness into the road, they were met by several burly policemen heading in the opposite direction. Behind them Laura saw parked police cars and vans and, amid the confusion, the welcome sight of Michael Thackeray and Kevin Mower at the kerbside deep in conversation with her grandmother. Seeing the three of them approach, the two men hurried in their direction.

'Look after the girls, Kevin,' Thackeray said, brusquely. Mower had watched Thackeray's growing anxiety, verging on panic, ever since he had discovered that the car number Laura had relayed to him on her way to The Heights was Stephen Stone's. His visible distress had intensified when Joyce Ackroyd had told him where Laura had gone to seek the runaway girls, and Mower could only sympathise with his boss's distraught expression now as Laura ignored him and addressed herself to Mower alone.

'Elena needs a doctor,' Laura said. 'Urgently, I think.'

'No problem. I'll take care of them,' Mower said, taking the two girls gently by the arm and leading them over to an ambulance that had just arrived, blue light flashing.

Thackeray stood speechless for a moment looking at Laura, while uniformed men streamed through the gap in the fence and into Priestley House. Laura turned to him slowly, and gave a small helpless shrug, her own face drained and pale as the shock kicked in.

'I think she would have jumped if I hadn't got there first.'

'Are you always going to live so dangerously?' Thackeray asked quietly, his voice hoarse.

'I knew she'd be spooked by anyone else,' Laura said, suddenly shaking and overcome with intense weariness. 'She tried to jump. Jazzy and I – we managed to stop her.'

Thackeray ran his hand lightly across Laura's cheek, as if to wipe away tears that she had not shed yet.

'You are impossible,' he said quietly. 'I thought you'd be killed. Stone is a bastard.'

'But...?' Laura whispered.

'But... I think you know. I can't live without you.' He

hugged her so close to his chest for a moment that she could barely breathe, then pulled away, glanced around at the frantic emergency scene around them and squared his shoulders.

'I've work to do here,' he said, with a sigh. 'It was Stone's car that followed you and I guess it's Stone who's looking for you in there now. When Kevin realised what was going on he pressed the panic button. If what we think Stone's been up to is true, he couldn't afford to let Elena escape alive. She's the only witness who can link him to the murder of Grace. Go home now, Laura, and get some rest. We'll talk later.'

In fact it was more than twenty-four hours before Laura saw Michael Thackeray again. He let himself into the flat around nine o'clock the following evening to find Laura curled up on the sofa listening to the local radio commentary on Bradfield United's FA Cup match against Chelsea. He dumped his coat on a chair and came round behind her, running his hands down her shoulders and breasts and kissing her awkwardly on the cheek.

'How are they doing?' he asked, nodding at the radio.

'Getting thrashed, five-nil,' she said with a smile. 'What did you expect? Come and sit down and tell me what's happened. You look exhausted.'

They had spoken several times on the phone since Laura had taken her grandmother home the previous evening and then driven home herself, leaving Thackeray and his search team to discover Stephen Stone and his sister Angelica on the top floor of Priestley House, kicking down any door that remained standing in furious frustration at their inability to find Elena. Ever since then, Thackeray had been supervising an apparently endless series of interrogations, which gradually unravelled some of the network of cruelty and exploitation and finally murder that had entrapped the trafficked girls.

'Have you finished?' Laura asked, turning the radio down on United's final humiliation as the sixth Chelsea goal was slammed home and the commentator slid into incoherent disappointment. Thackeray dropped onto the sofa beside her and closed his eyes, almost speechless with weariness.

'We've charged Stone with two counts of murder, Asida with one – we think he was the second man who gave chase when Grace and Elena ran away. He was certainly responsible for supplying Nigerian girls to various networks in this country. And we've charged the whole lot of them with trafficking every one of the girls we found. We needed four different interpreters before we could get any sense out of their stories – Albanian, Estonian, Moldovan and something else. I've almost lost track, to be honest.'

'Was Paolo Minelli involved?' Laura asked.

'I've found no evidence against him,' Thackeray said. 'He may have been turning a blind eye to what was going on, but no one has implicated him beyond that, in spite of his attachment to Angelica. He was probably paying Stone to supply the girls, but it will be hard to prove. He was certainly hoping to cash in on a transfer deal once United had had a good run. Angelica, on the other hand, was in it up to her neck. Several of the girls have said that the woman who came to the house was just as brutal as the men. Several have identified her beyond any doubt.'

'What will happen to the girls?' Laura asked.

'They'll go home, eventually. For the time being we've put most of them down as underage, so social services will take responsibility for them. We want as many of them to stay here to give evidence as possible. After that it's up to the Home Office.'

'And we all know they're not overflowing with the milk of human kindness,' Laura said. 'Girls like Elena will be outcasts if they're sent home. They'll probably be back in the next shipment to someone else's brothel.'

'Laura,' Thackeray said, putting an arm round her. 'You can't change the world single-handed.'

'I can try,' Laura said fiercely. 'You have to try, don't you?'

Thackeray thought for a moment of the long hours he had just spent piecing together a story of such depravity that it made him shudder, and he nodded slightly.

'I suppose you do,' he said. 'Don't misunderstand me, Laura. I'm very proud of what you did. You saved Elena's life, and probably Jasmin's as well. If Stone had caught up with them he'd undoubtedly have killed them.'

'Yes,' Laura said, quietly. 'I know.' The radio, which had been murmuring in the background, suddenly caught her attention again and she turned it up to hear the commentator compounding his own misery by speculating on the news that OK Okigbo would be seeking a transfer to another club.

'That will please his agent,' she said.

'And Paolo Minelli,' Thackeray said, to her surprise. 'My guess is that he'll do well out of any deal like that. He'll get – what do they call it – a bung?'

'Poor Jenna Heywood,' Laura said. 'It won't help her plans to rescue the club. She's hanging on by her fingernails already.

Still, she's a tough cookie. Maybe she'll find a way of saving them.'

'I'm not sure OK Okigbo would be much use to her anyway,' Thackeray said. 'He may well develop Aids, we'll certainly want him and his mates to give evidence in court, and we may still charge them all with having sex with underage girls. They must have known and I'm still going to try to prove it. I think his agent may find his value is seriously diminished by the time he comes to sell him on, and I suppose that's a rough sort of justice.'

'Has Jenna made a statement about what happened on the motorway?' Laura asked.

'She didn't need to. We have a witness on a bridge who saw the whole thing and had the sense to take the registration numbers of the cars involved. One of them belonged to Les Hardcastle. We've charged him with attempted murder and we're trying to trace the owner of the second car.'

'Another greedy man,' Laura said, thinking how her father would feel when he heard of his old friend and rival's downfall. Jack was not that much different, she thought, just slightly less ruthless in pursuit of profit.

'There is one bit of good news,' Thackeray said, pulling her closer to him. 'Val Ridley called Kevin Mower to tell him that she's decided not to give evidence at the inquiry.'

'Not at all?' Laura said quickly.

'Not at all. She wants no more to do with it, apparently. Which lets Jack Longley off the hook.'

'And me,' Laura said thankfully. She wanted no more investigations in that area.

She looked at Thackeray, whose eyes were almost closed.

'Can we start again?' she asked. He opened his eyes and smiled.

'You are pig-headed, impulsive and positively dangerous to know,' he said.

'And you are obstinate, depressive and a bit of a bastard.'

'We can't possibly inflict ourselves on anyone else then, can we?' he said.

And for the first time in many months their eyes met and they laughed.